"We have to

She hurried toward the sound of his voice, looking out the window.

"Why? What do you see?"

The pop of gunfire pierced the air, and she instinctively ducked her head, though the sounds came from below.

"The convoy is under attack." His voice was emotionless, almost businesslike in its lack of emotion.

"What?"

Zaire ran over to the window. Sure enough, two more SUVs were in the middle of the road, and four masked men were firing on the vehicles that had escorted her and Buck from the embassy.

"We have to go before they come up here." His voice was sharp as a whip.

Zaire spun to face him, fear clawing up her throat.

Buck took a chair from the kitchen and shoved it under the doorknob of the front door. "That should buy us some time," he said with grim determination.

Dear Reader,

I can't wait for you to meet Zaire and Buck!

Who would ever think a nerdy, multilingual interpreter and a tough-as-nails CIA black ops agent could fall in love? That's exactly what happens in the pages of this book.

They meet in one of the most beautiful cities in the world—Rome, Italy. Writing this setting reminded me of a trip I took years ago with my best friend. Just like the characters, we stopped at the Trevi Fountain and saw the Colosseum. Although, we spent much more time enjoying these landmarks than Zaire and Buck do. They're too busy running from assassins!

This story is more than the usual hair-raising adventure you've come to expect from me. You'll witness the characters' journey from initial attraction to deep, abiding love. It's incredibly satisfying to see two people fall for each other, especially when they both think they're wrong for one another.

Get ready for an adrenaline-fueled roller-coaster ride of adventure and romance. As you turn each page, I hope you'll be on the edge of your seat, cheering for Zaire and Buck as they race against time and danger.

Happy reading!

Delaney

HUNTED THROUGH ITALY

DELANEY DIAMOND

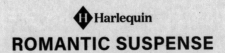

ROMANTIC SUSPENSE

Harlequin®
ROMANTIC SUSPENSE™

ISBN-13: 978-1-335-50284-1

Hunted Through Italy

Copyright © 2025 by Delaney Diamond

Recycling programs for this product may not exist in your area.

Harlequin Enterprises ULC
22 Adelaide St. West, 41st Floor
Toronto, Ontario M5H 4E3, Canada
www.Harlequin.com

Printed in Lithuania

MIX
Paper | Supporting responsible forestry
FSC® C021394

Delaney Diamond is the *USA TODAY* bestselling author of more than fifty contemporary romance and romantic suspense novels and dozens of romance short stories. She reads romance novels, mysteries, thrillers and a fair amount of nonfiction. When she's not busy reading or writing, she's in the kitchen trying out new recipes, dining at one of her favorite restaurants or traveling to an interesting locale. To get sneak peeks and notices of sale prices, and to find out about new releases, join her mailing list. And enjoy free stories on her website at delaneydiamond.com.

Books by Delaney Diamond

Harlequin Romantic Suspense

Hunted Through Italy

Visit the Author Profile page at Harlequin.com.

To all my readers, thank you for your continued support over the years. Because of you, I can do what I love.

Chapter 1

Zaire Nichols stared at her reflection in the bathroom mirror—the glasses, the pulled-back hair, the peach-colored top she'd picked out to lift her spirits.

The scary incident from the day before stormed her brain and broke through her consciousness like water bursting through a dam.

Maybe I shouldn't go to work today.

The more she thought about it, the more she liked the idea. If she didn't go to work, then she wouldn't have to worry whether the men who had chased her last night were lurking nearby, lying in wait.

She could only remember being that afraid one other time in her life—sixteen years ago, at the age of twelve. The memory was burned into her mind's eye, a cautionary tale that had influenced her life over the years.

What would those men have done if they'd caught her last night? She shuddered at the thought.

"I'm calling in," she muttered with finality.

She turned away from the mirror and stepped out of the small bathroom. She would call in and say she wasn't feeling well. *Or* she could tell the manager what had happened. Sighing, she stood in the hallway, indecisive. She needed to tell *someone* what had happened.

Was Josie here?

She hadn't seen her roommate since Sunday when she went out with friends. Zaire didn't know if she came home last night or not.

She went to Josie's bedroom door and knocked. "Josie?" she called out.

No answer.

She rapped lightly again as she pushed the door open. "Josie?"

Peering inside, she saw Josie's perfectly made empty bed, which meant she had stayed with her new man. Was she going to miss work today too? Maybe her roommate planned to go directly to work from the guy's house.

Knowing Josie, though, Zaire had her doubts. Her friend was probably enjoying her time. She was young and in Rome on someone else's dime. Zaire could take tips from her on living life to the fullest.

Unfortunately, she wouldn't be able to cover for Josie like she did yesterday. Not without knowing what she wanted her to say.

She sent a text to her roommate.

Where are you? Let me know if you need me to cover for you.

She could have added the word *again* but didn't. Her friend was enjoying herself, and she should be too. Except her mind was taken up with the events of yesterday.

The smart decision was to go to work and tell the manager what had happened.

In her bedroom, she applied tinted lip gloss in a neutral color. For some reason, the simple act of putting on lipstick always made her feel better. She slipped her cross-body bag across her torso and left the apartment.

Rome was a walkable city, and the distance to Worldwide Language Solutions, where she had been stationed for six weeks, wasn't a long trip and allowed her to get in a little exercise each day. Back in Atlanta, she would have been stuck in the car in traffic, so this was a nice change. She stopped at one of the bakeries en route and purchased two pastries—one for breakfast and one to eat later in the afternoon as a snack if she became hungry. She'd get a coffee in the break room at work.

Their office was located near the Ludovisi district, in a majestic building that exemplified Renaissance architecture, with lovely stonework and arched windows.

She walked into the atrium, where the soaring ceiling had been beautified with frescoes depicting scenes from Roman mythology. Some days she couldn't believe her good fortune, that she had been one of the few selected from the Atlanta location to help the company establish a presence in Italy before the offices were fully staffed.

Instead of taking the elevator, she climbed the stairs to the third floor, offering a smile and a *Buongiorno* to the people she encountered on their way downstairs.

The interior of Worldwide Language Solutions was modern, with cubicles and computers and glass-enclosed offices. Much different from the masterpiece of architecture that housed them.

"Hi, Zaire," one of her colleagues, Deidra, greeted her. She had also come from the States, but the New York office.

"Good morning," Zaire replied.

"Where's your roommate?"

The question reminded Zaire of why she kept her distance from Deidra. She was always in everybody's business.

"We haven't talked this morning."

"Why haven't you talked? Will she make it to work today?"

"You'll have to call and ask her yourself."

Her coworker harrumphed and then moved down the hall.

Zaire wished that Josie had called or at least texted so she knew what to tell people when they asked about her.

She went to the break room and poured herself a cup of coffee. Then she strolled to her cubicle, greeting the few co-workers she encountered on the way.

She spent most of her morning on reports. When it was almost lunchtime, she checked her messages. Still nothing from Josie. Okay, that was odd. Her roommate was usually really good about responding to messages. Where the heck was she?

"*Salut*, how are you this morning?" Quain, a French co-worker, stood by her desk.

"Fine. Trying to get all these reports completed. How about you?"

"Same. I'm meeting with some government officials to-night—a dinner thing where they need an interpreter." He rolled his eyes as if he dreaded the assignment.

Most of the staff pretended to dislike the formal events, but the truth was, it was kind of nice to get dressed up and rub elbows with government officials or captains of indus-try. The most interesting conversations weren't the ones you had to translate. They were the ones you overheard while in the client's company. Zaire had heard a really good stock tip while attending an event like that back in Atlanta months ago.

"Can I help you with something?" she asked.

"Do you have an extra red pen I can borrow?"

Quain came by to borrow office supplies often—supplies he could easily get from the supply closet.

She thought he used the requests as an excuse to talk to her because he might be interested, but he never did more than ask for supplies. She was too shy to make a move herself, worried about rejection.

She handed him a pen. "Don't forget where you got that."

"I definitely will not. Thanks."

She watched him walk away with his elegant stroll. One day, she'd have the courage to make the first move. That day was not today.

Story of my life, she thought.

By lunchtime, she still hadn't heard from Josie, so she sent another text.

Hey, Miss Party Animal I'm getting worried. Call me. Text me. Let me know you're alive.

Josie would probably roll her eyes when she saw that message. She thought Zaire worried too much. Despite having a love of travel, Zaire knew the world was a dangerous place. Which reminded her, she needed to tell someone about what she'd recorded yesterday at the client's location. She had avoided thinking about it but could no longer do that. What she had recorded was important, and she *had* to tell someone. Someone who'd know what to do.

She sent an email to her manager and let him know she wanted to talk to him about something important. That way, she couldn't back out of the conversation.

For now, it was time for lunch. She shut down her computer and exited the office. After taking the stairs to the first floor, she left the building and went to a favorite café she and Josie had discovered two streets over.

Crossing the street, she nodded at a group of nuns passing by. At the café, she found a table near the window and kept her order simple: a *panino con la porchetta* with cheese and a Chinotto, soda made from Sicilian oranges. She hadn't liked the bitter taste when she first drank it, but she'd grown accustomed to the flavor over time.

People-watching while she ate, a sense of nostalgia overtook her. Only six weeks left in the Eternal City, and she would miss it when she had to leave.

This was not her first trip to Italy, though it was her first time in Rome. Years ago, she and her family had spent two months in Florence, a time she remembered with fondness.

Since Zaire was a child, she had been traveling with her parents, and she always experienced a sense of loss whenever they left a country. Before she left Italy, there was a lot she wanted to see, not only in Rome but also other parts of the country.

She and Josie had discussed taking a few weekend trips to explore other towns, maybe renting a car for a drive in the countryside. They needed to prioritize getting out and doing more sightseeing, because before long, the time would be gone, and they'd have to return to Atlanta.

Zaire checked the time. "Whoops. I better get back to work." She left some euros on the table and rushed out of the restaurant.

She walked briskly down the street on the way to the office. At the corner, she waited for traffic to pass before she stepped off the curb. As she did, the glint of a moving object in her periphery caught her attention. A silver Audi, speeding toward her.

At first she was confused. Why was it moving so fast—faster than it should be on this street? Then she realized what was happening: he was going to hit her!

A surge of panic rushed through her veins, and she bolted to the other side of the street, barely escaping being run over as the driver swerved toward her and slammed into a parked car with the deafening crash of crunching metal.

Mouth falling open, Zaire stared at the carnage in disbelief. Had he actually tried to *hit* her? All around her, people chattered in Italian and pointed at the damaged vehicles.

Zaire stared at the man behind the wheel. She couldn't see his eyes behind dark sunglasses, but the firm set of his jaw indicated she was not out of danger yet.

Heart racing, she forced herself to move, hurrying into a walk-run. She had to get away from him.

She glanced over her shoulder, and her stomach dropped when the driver backed up. Then he gunned the engine and started after her.

The cold tentacles of fear closed around her heart. There was no misunderstanding about what was happening. He was coming for her.

Zaire broke into a run.

Chapter 2

At the sound of his cell phone going off, Atticus "Buck" Swanson turned over in bed with a groan of annoyance. The shrill noise had interrupted a particularly relaxing dream in which he'd been sunbathing on a beach in the Caribbean, a sign he was looking forward to his long overdue vacation in a few days.

Grabbing the phone, he squinted at the screen, which displayed the word *Unknown*. He swiped to answer.

"Hello?" His voice came out as a hoarse grumble.

"Buck, it's me, Benjamin. I need you to come downstairs right away. We need to talk."

The solemn, urgent sound of his commander's voice sloughed off the cobwebs of sleep, and Buck sat up, immediately alert.

"I'm on my way."

As a member of the CIA's special missions team, called the Omega Team, Buck was accustomed to urgent calls. The CIA recruited men and women from the special forces units of the various military branches and often called upon them on short notice to conduct targeted missions that included sabotage, kidnapping, hostage rescue and counterterrorism. The fact that Benjamin was waiting outside his home meant that something of dire importance was amiss.

He slipped out from under his sheets and went to the armchair in his dark bedroom, where he had tossed a pair of gray sweatpants earlier. He pulled them on, opened his dresser drawer, and found a faded blue T-shirt that he also tugged on. After he put on his sneakers, he combed his fingers through his blond hair and exited the bedroom.

He jogged down the staircase of the two-story town house in the suburbs of DC that had been his home for almost a decade. Exiting out the front door into the night, he did a quick assessment of the quiet neighborhood. A dark limousine idled beside the curb in front of his home. Because of the tinted windows, he couldn't see the interior but knew Benjamin waited inside for him. He opened the back door and slid onto the leather seat beside the older man, who wore his usual suit and tie, even at ten-thirty at night, which meant he'd come straight from the office.

Commander Benjamin Ray was a former Marine and almost six feet tall, with graying dark hair, a graying mustache and wrinkles lining his face that made him look every bit of his sixty-two years. Buck figured that running their special unit had probably accelerated the aging process.

He was a hellion in his day—but he'd had to be to arrive at this point, where he oversaw a team of black ops agents. His hands were dirty, and his brain held secrets that presidents weren't even privy to.

As soon as the door closed, Buck's superior turned to him. "I know you had plans to fly off for a vacation in a few days, but we need you. It's an emergency."

"When is it ever not an emergency?"

Benjamin's lips twisted into a semblance of a smile. He couldn't argue against what Buck had said. Heading up the Omega Team meant being ready at all times when called upon to complete a mission. For Benjamin and the men and women under his charge, that could be long hours with little to no sleep.

Most of them worked alone, but occasionally they worked with small teams for designated periods. Buck would soon learn if he was flying solo or with another member of the organization.

"You know Rick, Javelin Security's CEO," Benjamin said, with a nod toward the man seated across from him.

"Good to see you again," Buck said.

"Likewise. Wish it were under better circumstances." Dark-haired and wearing round spectacles, Rick spoke in a grim voice.

"I'll explain why he's here in a minute. We need you to fly to Rome." Benjamin handed over a dark blue folder.

Rome.

Hearing the destination was jarring. Buck had been there three times over the years. Twice for work and the last time for personal reasons. He hadn't been to the city in several years thanks to the bitter memories from his last visit, and he'd promised himself to avoid the place at all costs.

Firming his lips and pushing aside his personal prejudice, Buck flipped open the folder as Benjamin continued to speak.

"As you know, there have been two embassy bombings in the past eight months—Malaysia and Liberia. Each time, we were taken completely by surprise. There had been no rumblings of terrorist activity—and even more disturbing, we haven't been able to determine who committed these acts, because no one has laid claim to them. Embassy personnel around the world are on high alert and on edge as we investigate and try to find out who the hell is targeting us. We may have finally caught a break. Yesterday afternoon, a young woman by the name of Zaire Nichols walked into the

US embassy in Rome and claimed to not only have information about the last two bombings, she said another one will take place in six days."

"Where did she get this information?"

"She's an interpreter for a global interpretation-and-translation service called Worldwide Language Solutions, and she overheard a conversation at a client's site—an IT company called Zigna. She believes these men were visitors at Zigna. According to Ms. Nichols, they admitted to planting bombs at the embassies, and they have plans to plant another one in an unknown embassy somewhere else in the world. Ms. Nichols claims to have a recording capturing part of the conversation.

"The secretary of state wants her here yesterday," Benjamin continued, "but we need to keep this as quiet as possible. We've already had plenty of false alarms with people giving us bad information. Since we don't know if this woman is credible or simply a kook seeking attention, this is an off-the-books operation—per the secretary's request. She wants cold hard facts to take to the president."

"Understood," Buck said.

"Now, according to the embassy staff who interviewed her, Ms. Nichols appeared to be genuinely afraid for her safety when she entered the compound. After she captured the recording, she was chased from the building by the men. She claimed that she didn't know what to do, went to work the next day and was almost run over on her way back from lunch. She managed to escape her pursuers on foot."

"That's when she sought refuge at the embassy," Buck surmised.

"Correct."

Buck examined the photo of the woman included in the file. There was nothing particularly attention grabbing about her. Her hair was parted in the middle and pulled into a tight ponytail behind her head, exposing small ears adorned with simple gold-ball earrings. She wore no makeup on her russet brown skin except for on her lips, which were coated in a neutral brown lipstick that seemed more of an afterthought. He couldn't help but notice that her lips were full and lush, despite her unassuming appearance. Behind black-framed glasses, he saw evenly spaced deep brown eyes that hinted at a shy nature.

He liked bold, energetic, and exciting women, and she reminded him of the stereotypical quiet-librarian archetype. Yet he experienced an unexpected tug of attraction as he examined her features.

"Personnel from Javelin Security will meet you at the embassy and coordinate with you to get Ms. Nichols safely out of the country."

Rick spoke up then. "Our guys have been over there for a while working with the embassy and know the lay of the land. I seriously doubt anyone will try to hurt this woman again, but if they do, they'll have to go through my guys." His tone was grim, his resolve evident in the firm set of his jaw.

Embassies were guarded by the Marine Corps and local contractors in the host country, but Javelin Security was the State Department's go-to company to provide additional resources to the nation's embassies. Rick, the CEO and spokesperson, came from a military family and was also a former Marine, like Benjamin. His firm had become indispensable since the first attack by providing additional manpower to protect the men and women overseas.

Benjamin continued, "Miss Nichols claims to have moved the recorded file to an encrypted network for safekeeping. The secretary of state is adamant that we get her safely to the United States for a debriefing."

"On what network does she have the recording?" Buck asked.

"Embassy staff says she won't tell them. They've searched her and it's not on her person. She sees the recording as her insurance policy to ensure safe passage out of the country. Can't say I blame her. All she knows from the conversation she overheard is that the next bomb will go off in six days. We've already lost thirty-six hours since she overheard the conversation, so I need you to go to Rome immediately. I picked you because you've been there a couple of times and know the city. You won't have to stay long. Go to the embassy, pick her up, and bring her back here for a debriefing. Then you can proceed on your vacation. You have thirty minutes to pack a bag. We have a plane at the airfield ready to fly you to Rome nonstop. You should arrive there in the afternoon. Get her safely to the airport and onto that plane. When you arrive back here in DC, she'll give us access to the file."

"Understood." Buck closed the folder.

Benjamin started the timer on his watch and looked at Buck. "Thirty minutes."

Buck exited the vehicle and took long strides to the front door. After racing upstairs, he grabbed his go bag—which remained packed at all times with clothes, shoes, and personal hygiene products—from the top of the closet. He probably wouldn't need it but liked to be prepared for contingencies.

He tossed it onto the bench at the foot of the bed and went to the safe behind a painting on the wall. After he entered the code, he removed his passport, a stack of euros and a fully loaded Glock 34.

He stuffed the items from the safe into the side pockets of the bag and then made his bed. There was nothing worse than coming back to an unmade bed.

He then changed into a black shirt, black pants and black shoes. Hoisting the bag onto his shoulder, he did a final scan of the room and headed out.

When he opened the car door and sank onto the leather seat again, Benjamin's eyebrows lifted in surprise.

He stopped the timer. "That was less than ten minutes."

"You pay me to be ready at all times," Buck said with a grin.

"Are you going to be okay in Rome?" Benjamin asked.

Buck stiffened. His commander knew why he didn't like that city. "Of course," he said, voice peppered with a dash of annoyance. He wasn't some weakling. He'd go in, retrieve the asset and get out. Simple. Probably the easiest retrieval he'd had in years.

Benjamin nodded, clearly satisfied, and then his driver took off for the airfield.

Chapter 3

Zaire sat at a plain wooden table in the stark interrogation room of the US embassy in Rome—the same room she'd sat in for hours the day before when she arrived and pleaded for help. Across from her were two chairs, and behind them was a two-way mirror on the wall. At least, that's what she assumed it was since she was an avid watcher of cop shows.

Embassy personnel had taken all her possessions, including her phone, as if she were a criminal, but she understood their concern. She had arrived with a fantastic tale that sounded unbelievable even to her own ears. She'd claimed to have encountered men who had bombed two US embassies in recent months and had information about when the next bomb would explode. She'd be doubtful too. They probably thought she was either a liar or involved in the bombings.

She released a weary sigh. She'd managed to get only a few hours of sleep last night, which had been interrupted when she jerked awake, heart racing from a dream of being chased by a silver Audi with a faceless driver dressed in all black. She couldn't sleep again after that nightmare.

They had brought her in here to wait almost two hours ago, and she was getting restless. What were they doing? On the cop shows, they used a waiting technique to crack potential suspects. Well, they were wasting valuable time. She would not crack.

After being hit with a barrage of questions last night, she was proud that she'd held her ground and remained silent, steadfast in her decision to divulge only the information that was necessary. They'd have to waterboard her to get the location of the digital recording. That recording was her only leverage to ensure safe passage home. Once she told them where it was located, her life became worthless. She wouldn't be as important to them as she was now.

The door cracked open, and in walked the law enforcement officer from yesterday, Randolph Lane. Zaire straightened in the chair, and her eyes followed his movement across the floor.

With his imposing height and solemn face, he scared her a little. She suspected he would torture the information out of her if he could. To fight back the fear caused by her vivid imagination, she squeezed her hands together on her lap.

A female officer also entered the room: Heidi de Luca, a slender blonde whose face was equally stern and unfriendly. Zaire idly wondered if they'd been trained to appear so intimidating.

"Ms. Nichols," Randolph acknowledged her with a note of resignation as he dropped a manila folder on the table.

Zaire's hands tightened in her lap, but she froze her features in an emotionless mask.

"I know our accommodations are quite basic, but I hope you slept well?"

Basic was an understatement. They'd stuck her in a windowless room in the basement, the only furniture a simple twin bed cot and a small table with a bottle of water on top.

This morning, when a different embassy official came to

get her from the room, she'd been starving and gobbled the eggs, toast and orange juice they offered.

"I slept well, thank you." Her voice sounded low and raspy, so she cleared her throat.

The feet of one of the chairs scraped the tile floor as Randolph pulled it away from the table. He sat down, looked her directly in the eyes and smiled. Quite a surprise, but Zaire didn't react. Years of translating conversations had taught her the skill of keeping an impassive face. Her job was to translate, not to have a reaction to the message.

Heidi remained standing with her arms crossed over her white blouse and black jacket.

They were playing good cop / bad cop today instead of bad cop / bad cop. Well, they could switch things up all they wanted. She wasn't going to break.

"We have a bit of a problem," Randolph began slowly. "We need to go over what you told us yesterday, because we've spoken to your manager at Worldwide Language Solutions, and according to him, you were never scheduled to provide services for Zigna. In fact, that assignment went to…" He opened the manila file and then made eye contact with her again. "…your roommate, Josie Gonzalez. Would you like to tell us why you lied about working for Zigna?"

"I didn't lie."

"We spoke to your manager. You were not assigned to them—Josie was," Heidi said in a hard voice.

"Just because I wasn't assigned to them doesn't mean that I didn't work for Zigna. Josie…" Zaire paused. She hated to betray her friend's confidence.

"Yes?" Heidi prompted, resting her palms on the table and leaning toward Zaire.

"Josie didn't feel well and asked me to take her place."

Zaire lowered her gaze, hoping they hadn't guessed she

wasn't telling the whole truth. While it was true that she did go in Josie's place, the reason her coworker hadn't gone to the IT company that morning was because she'd stayed at her new Italian beau's apartment the night before and wanted to blow off her assignment to spend the day with him. She had called Zaire and begged her to go to the Zigna office in her place, to interpret conversations during a day-long meeting between their manager of operations in Rome and visiting French officials interested in contracting with the company.

Randolph leaned across the table, his gray eyes looking so surprisingly kind that she almost believed he wasn't trying to trick her into trusting him.

He spoke in a soothing voice. "Ms. Nichols, if you don't tell us the truth, we can't help you. We've already spoken to the people you met at the Zigna offices. They confirmed that they met with Josie Gonzalez, not Zaire Nichols."

"That's because I gave them her name. I didn't want her to get into trouble. It was my day off, and I was doing her a favor." She shifted her gaze between them both. "I know how this sounds, but what I'm telling you is the truth."

"All she had to do was call into work. Why would she get into trouble if she was sick?" Heidi asked, with skepticism thick in her voice.

Because Josie was out of sick days and couldn't afford to call in again without getting into serious trouble. Perhaps losing this assignment altogether and getting sent back to Atlanta.

Zaire hated lying, but she'd helped because…well, because Josie was living the type of life she longed for. One that was exciting and adventurous, and things like that never happened to her. She was boring old, dependable Zaire.

"If you really believe your life is in danger, you have to

tell us everything. Did you or did you not go to the Zigna offices two days ago to translate?" Randolph asked.

"I…" Zaire was confused. Why didn't they believe her?

Heidi slammed her open palm on the table, and Zaire jumped, her heart practically flying into her throat. The blonde leaned closer and fixed an antagonistic frown on her face.

"Did you or did you not? Answer the question!"

Randolph shot his partner a look. "Heidi…"

She straightened and glared at him, then jabbed a finger in Zaire's direction. "I'm tired of playing games with this woman."

Why was she so upset? Her fury was palpable.

Heidi continued, "We've had two embassy bombings in eight months, and she waltzes in here and expects us to believe she's privy to information that could stop the next one, but she won't tell us where this secret information is. I don't believe a word she's saying, and neither should you."

"I'm not lying," Zaire said in a low voice.

"You want attention—or something. Zigna is a reputable company. Why should we believe you somehow have evidence they're involved in the bombings when there's no record of you setting foot in their offices?"

"I never said they were involved in the bombings." Zaire took a deep breath and released it to calm her rapid heart rate. "If you don't believe I was there, call Josie and ask her yourself. She'll confirm that I went to Zigna in her place."

A look passed between the two officials, and Zaire's neck tingled with goose bumps.

She frowned. "Why did you look at each other like that?"

Heidi folded her arms over her chest and walked toward the mirror.

Randolph's expression morphed into one of deep concern.

"We won't be able to ask Josie any questions," he said, pulling something from the folder.

"Why not? Why—" Zaire gasped when she saw the photo he removed.

"We had someone go to your apartment this morning, and they found your roommate stabbed to death on the floor of the kitchen."

Zaire's hand flew to her mouth. "No…" she whispered, staring at Josie's bloodied body on the tile. Nausea bubbled in her stomach.

Heidi turned and glared at her from across the room. "Did you kill your roommate and then make up a cover story to give yourself an alibi?"

Zaire's mouth fell open in shock. She'd come there hoping to get help and hopefully safe passage back to the United States. Instead, they were accusing her of murder.

Chapter 4

"Right this way."

Nodding a greeting as he passed an embassy official, Buck followed Randolph Lane into a room off the hallway. He had arrived fifteen minutes ago and gone through security, fully expecting to be taken to Ms. Nichols.

Instead, Randolph introduced himself as one of the investigating agents. He explained that they had concerns about the veracity of the interpreter's claims, and she was being held for questioning. On the flight over, Buck read the full report and knew everything the government had collected about the bombings.

He stepped inside the empty room, his attention immediately taken by the two-way mirror that dominated one wall. Ms. Nichols sat on the other side of the mirror, facing them, wearing a peach-colored top and charcoal pants.

He frowned when he saw her bound wrists on the table. "Why is she in handcuffs?"

For some reason, seeing her handcuffed and alone in the stark room infuriated him. She was a striking woman. Not in a head-turning way, but by the quiet poise she depicted in her predicament. She stared at the mirrored wall as if she could see them, but he recognized anxiety in her wrinkled brow.

"As I mentioned before, we have doubts about her account of the events that took place. At first we thought she might have invented her knowledge about the bombings, but it's worse than that. We searched her and found nothing. No recording, like she said. Then we went by her apartment and didn't find it there either. We have IT going through her laptop as we speak. We did find a dead body, though," Randolph said in a grave voice.

Buck slid his gaze away from the woman to the man beside him. "Have you identified the victim?"

"Her roommate, Josie Gonzalez. According to the medical examiner, she's been dead since yesterday morning."

"And you think Ms. Nichols murdered her roommate and then clocked in to work like normal?"

"We don't know that for sure, but who else could have done it? There was no forced entry at their apartment, and Ms. Nichols went to the Zigna offices impersonating Josie Gonzalez."

"That doesn't mean she killed her," Buck said.

"We're not taking any chances."

They had no idea what they were doing. Time to pull rank. "Take off the cuffs."

"We haven't finished investigating."

"Take them off!" Buck snarled. "Better yet, give me the keys."

He didn't have time to waste. His job was to escort Ms. Nichols back to the States so she could be interviewed, before more lives were lost.

He extended his open palm, and Randolph reluctantly handed over the keys to the handcuffs.

"I'll take over from here, and any further questioning will be done by me. If I need your help, I'll let you know. If you have concerns about me taking over, you know who to call." He swiveled on his heel and marched through the door.

Looks could be deceiving, but Ms. Nichols didn't strike him as cold-blooded enough to kill her roommate and then go to work and make up a lie about the bombings. Even if she did, why would she then show up at the US embassy, which ensured she would be investigated and the body found? Unless she was simply killing for attention, she would want to keep the murder quiet for as long as possible.

When Buck entered the room where Zaire was being held, she glanced up, and alarm flickered across her face for a brief moment. Understandable. He had that effect on people. He was a big guy, at three inches over six feet and broad shouldered. Wearing all black made him more intimidating. She was probably also jumpy from being forced to sit and wait in handcuffs.

"Ms. Nichols, I'm Agent Buck Swanson. I'm here to escort you out of the country."

She frowned at him as if she didn't understand what he'd said. "*Who* are you?" she asked softly.

The dulcet tone of her voice made the hairs on the back of his neck stand up. This woman was affecting him in odd ways. He'd never experienced this type of reaction to a stranger before.

"Buck Swanson. I was asked to escort you back to the United States."

"Are you going to put me in jail?"

"No, ma'am." Jail time was not for him to decide. He was simply a transporter.

"I don't know how Josie ended up dead, but I swear I didn't kill her."

Buck heard the desperation in her voice. "We'll discuss that soon enough. May I?" He held up the keys.

"Yes, please," she said with profound relief.

He stepped closer and caught the whiff of some scent. It

was too delicate for perfume and only noticeable because he was now standing close to her. Whatever the fragrance, it pleased his nostrils, and his abs tightened in recognition of his ongoing attraction to a woman he should be eyeing with suspicion.

He inserted the key and unsnapped the cuffs. As Ms. Nichols rubbed her wrists, he noticed her hands—slender brown fingers, neatly polished nails trimmed low and rounded at the ends.

No ring.

Buck dragged one of the chairs around to her side of the table and sat down with his legs wide. Intimidation often backfired because people became scared, so his intention was to gain her trust and have her confide everything she knew.

"In a few minutes we're going to leave the embassy and go to your apartment to collect your belongings, and then we're flying to DC, where you'll be questioned by intelligence officials. Before we leave, I need to ask you a few questions myself, and I need you to answer me honestly."

"Ask me anything. I have no reason to lie."

Her voice wobbled, but she lifted her chin in a show of strength that earned his respect.

"Good. Let's begin." He took her hand and pressed two fingers to the inside of her wrist. Damn, her skin was soft.

She looked down at his fingers. "What are you doing?"

"I'm going to ask you a few questions, and I need to determine if you're being honest," Buck said in a calm voice.

She swallowed and shoved her glasses higher on her nose. "Okay."

"What is your name?" Baseline questions were necessary to establish her normal pulse rate.

"Um…er, Zaire Nichols."

Buck kept his eyes locked on hers. "Relax. Just answer honestly. May I call you Zaire?"

"Yes." She seemed about to smile but then thought better of it.

"Where were you born, Zaire?"

"Dallas, Texas."

"I spoke to Officer Lane, and he told me that Josie Gonzalez's body was found in your apartment. When was the last time you saw her?"

"I can't believe she's dead." The words came out in a soft, breathless voice, and her eyes filled with tears. She shook her head in disbelief and took a quivering breath. "The last time I saw her was Sunday night. She went out with friends—a couple of people from work."

Her pulse rate remained steady.

"Why didn't you go with them?" Buck asked, keeping his voice at an even level.

Zaire shrugged and wiped her eyes. "Their idea of fun isn't my idea of fun. They drink a lot, and I knew they'd be out late, and I had plans to go to the market early the next day since it was my day off. So I stayed home."

Buck watched her for a moment. Her breathing remained normal, and the beating under his fingers remained steady. "Sunday was three days ago, Zaire. Are you saying you haven't seen your roommate since then?"

"I haven't," she insisted with emphasis. She seemed to hesitate, then lowered her voice when she spoke next. "I didn't mention this to the other officers, but she ran into a guy she recently hooked up with and decided to spend the night at his place. She called on Monday morning and asked me to go to Zigna in her place, and that's what I did. It's the truth. Someone tried to run me over yesterday, and that must be the person who entered our apartment and killed her while I was at work. She's dead because of me." Her voice cracked, and she dropped her gaze to the clenched fist on her thigh.

"Why do you think that?"

"Because they must have been looking for me. I can't believe this is happening." She shook her head.

Buck hardened his heart against her distress. "Did you kill Josie Gonzalez?"

Her head snapped up. "No. I did not."

He felt the slight spike in her pulse rate, but it wasn't enough to indicate she was lying. Rather, she was probably agitated by the question.

"Did you overhear someone say that they will attack another US embassy in six days?"

She looked him directly in the eyes, unflinching. "Yes, I did."

"Will you cooperate in helping us find that person?"

"Yes, I will."

"Do you have a recording of the conversation you overheard?"

"Yes. Part of it."

She could be a pro at lying, but for now Buck was 80 percent certain she was telling the truth. At the very least, *she* believed what she said.

He released her arm and rested his hands on his thighs. His fingertips tingled from where he had touched her. What was wrong with him? One would think he'd never been with a woman before.

"If what you said is true, we don't have a lot of time. In a matter of days, another US embassy will be bombed. Do you know how many US embassies there are in the world?"

"One hundred and sixty-eight."

He stared, surprised that she knew the exact number. "That's right. That's a lot of embassies, Zaire. But with your help, maybe we can figure out which one will be targeted next—and by whom."

Chapter 5

The gravity of Buck's words chilled Zaire, but he was right. They didn't have much time, and they'd lost precious hours already.

In four days, another bomb would explode somewhere around the world, and lives would be lost. People who were mothers, fathers, sisters and brothers—all because terrorists wanted to make a point. Thinking about the death and destruction on the way made her physically ill. How could anyone think that causing suffering was the best way to persuade—or bully—others into accepting their point of view?

She eyed the man before her with interest. As escorts went, she could certainly do worse than Buck Swanson, whom she likened to an action hero. He was pretty, as in very handsome, but had a rugged edge courtesy of the stubble on his face, which was a couple of shades darker than the blond hair on his head.

He was also huge, easily several inches over six feet, with biceps the size of her thigh. His fingers were long and wide, and he could probably crush a boulder with his bare hands. His entire appearance—including the square jawline—was intimidating.

"How did you come to overhear the conversation at that company?" Buck asked.

Zaire took a deep breath, going back in time. "I wasn't supposed to go to Zigna. I was filling in for my roommate, Josie.
At the end of the day, I left the office, but I was halfway down
the block when I remembered that I had left my bag with my
lunch in the break room. I had eaten at a café across the street
because they had this dish I wanted to try—well, that's ir-
relevant. Because I ate lunch there, I didn't have my bag at
my desk. It was still in the fridge. I went back to get it, and
as I approached the break room, I heard two men talking."

Buck listened attentively, and Zaire had the impression
he was dissecting her words, looking for holes in her story.

"They were in the break room?" he asked.

She nodded. "I wouldn't have thought anything about it,
except they were talking in hushed tones, which made me
hesitate. I didn't want to intrude, but I also got the impression that they thought they were alone. Most of the staff had
gone for the day."

"Was that normal, to have clients in the building after the
close of business?"

"I don't know. I'd never been to Zigna before, but the men
weren't alone. There were people in the building, and probably what happened is, their meeting ended and they went
in there to get a snack from one of the machines and continued talking."

"Is it possible those men could have been Zigna employ-
ees?" Buck asked.

She mulled over the question for a moment and then shook
her head. "I don't think so. I had spent the day at Zigna and
didn't recognize any of the voices. It doesn't mean they didn't
work there, but I doubt it."

"So, as far as you know, these men were clients or visitors."

"Right."

He stared at the far wall in deep thought. "Which means we can probably figure out who they were by checking appointments for the day. Is there a main desk or a place people have to check in when they visit?"

"Now that you mention it, yes! When I arrived, I had to sign in. All visitors have to do that, and you receive a visitor sticker."

"Good to know. Were they speaking English?"

"Yes. One man sounded American, but the other was Italian."

Buck studied her in the silence for a moment, and she resisted the urge to squirm.

"How many languages do you speak?" he finally asked.

"Five. English, Italian, Spanish, French and Portuguese."

His eyebrows lifted higher. "That's impressive."

Her cheeks warmed. She was accustomed to people being impressed by her language skills, but his admiration was particularly satisfying. "Not really. There are similarities between the languages that make them easy to learn."

"All I speak is English, so I'm impressed." A line carved into his brow. "Where's the recording?"

"In a safe place." She braced for his disapproval.

He arched an eyebrow. "You're going to have to share that information at some point."

"I'll do that when I'm back in the United States. Not before. I know how this works. You won't need me once you have the recording."

"You think we'll leave you out to dry."

"Right now, you have to keep me alive to get the recording. If you get it, you won't protect me the same way." She was certain of it.

"That's not the way this works, Zaire. We want to keep you alive, regardless."

"And I want to stay alive, and the best way to make sure of that is, I know where the recording is and you don't."

Suddenly, she had a terrible thought. What if they tortured her? Her gaze dropped to his hands again—boulder-crushing hands. A slap or punch from him would do major damage. Or if he curled his long fingers around her neck, he could darn near crush her larynx.

"Do you understand that refusing to share the evidence you claim you have could cause people to be suspicious of you? We don't know if you really have a recording."

"You'll have to trust me, like I have to trust you."

His eyes narrowed slightly. "Fine. We'll play it your way."

She assumed the words *for now* were about to follow, but they didn't. She breathed easier, the tension seeping out of her tight muscles.

"Right now, we need to get out of here," Buck continued in a brisk voice, getting to his feet.

Zaire gazed up at him. "That's it? We're done?"

"Yes. Where is your purse, phone—whatever you came here with?"

"Someone on the embassy staff has my stuff. They took everything from me yesterday when I arrived." Zaire stood, the top of her head coming only to his shoulder. Wow, he was tall.

"Randolph can probably get your things for you, and then we'll leave." He faced the mirror, and without saying a word, it was clear that he'd silently instructed the agent to do just that.

As she'd suspected, it was a two-way mirror.

The tightness she'd carried in her chest since arriving at the embassy dissolved. The past couple of days had been dreadful, filling her with fear about her future and making her wonder whether she'd live to see her family again. She'd need to call her parents. If she didn't talk to them every couple of days, they worried. Never mind that she was a twenty-eight-year-old woman with her own place.

And she'd be going home soon. *Yes!*

"Will we stop at my job? I should probably tell them that I'm leaving the country."

"You can call them, but we won't be stopping by there. We're going straight from your apartment to the airport, where a plane is waiting for us. We have a direct flight to DC."

"That's too bad. I was thinking I should clear out my desk and let them know what's going on."

He looked at her as if she was nuts. "No one will know what's going on, and clearing out your desk should be the least of your concerns."

"Right. Of course. I hate to leave people in the lurch, that's all."

Zaire adjusted her glasses and looked around their stark surroundings. Restless, she sat on the table. Buck continued to stand in the middle of the room, back straight, clasping the wrist of one hand in front of him.

He seemed relaxed but alert at the same time. If someone burst in there, she didn't doubt he'd tackle them to the ground and incapacitate them.

Zaire cleared her throat. "It's crazy, but three days ago I was thinking about what I wanted to buy at the market to cook for dinner and making plans to visit other parts of Italy. Then yesterday… Well, I can't believe how my life has changed so suddenly. I feel like I'm living inside a spy movie." She laughed nervously.

"I'm sure it's a lot to take in, but we'll get you back safely."

"Thanks."

They fell into silence again, but she hated silence. Her

mind raced with too much information, and she often felt the need to fill the void with conversation.

"Did you know that embassies have been around for centuries?"

"No, I didn't know that."

"The very first embassy was established right here in Italy, in the fourteenth century. The concept of diplomacy has been around forever, of course, but the first permanent embassy was established in Northern Italy. Milan, to be exact."

"That's good to know." His voice held no emotion.

"Do you know where the largest embassy is? In Iraq, in Baghdad's fortified Green Zone. It's almost the size of Vatican City, which I'm sure you know is the smallest country in the world."

He didn't respond. Maybe he did know. He was some kind of government official, after all. Or maybe he didn't. Or he simply didn't care.

Shut up, Zaire.

The poor guy probably wanted to get on the plane and get back home to his wife. No, she didn't see a ring on his finger. Girlfriend, then. No way a hunk like him was single.

The door opened and Randolph entered, looking very displeased, but he had her possessions. He handed her bag, laptop, and phone to Buck, who held on to the laptop and handed the other items over to her. She felt a lot better now that she had them in hand.

She slipped on her cross-body bag, tucked her phone inside and followed the men out of the room. She had a million questions, but now was not the time to ask. She wanted to get out of the embassy, pack her bags and get on that plane Buck had promised was waiting for them.

Everything would be okay now. She was certain that no one could hurt her with him by her side.

Chapter 6

Randolph escorted them to the first floor, where Buck collected a mean-looking black gun he had checked before coming to see Zaire.

Randolph stopped short of walking them outside. "I hope you know what you're doing," he said to Buck, as if she wasn't standing right there.

"I do. We'll be fine from here." Buck extended his hand and shook Randolph's.

Zaire didn't bother extending her hand. By the dismissive expression on the embassy agent's face, she figured he didn't want anything more to do with her. He clearly didn't think she should be leaving at all while the investigation into the death of her roommate was ongoing, but Buck must have greater authority than he did. Randolph couldn't keep her there—no matter what he and Heidi thought.

Zaire followed Buck to a waiting black sedan, where he deposited her laptop in the trunk, next to a bag she assumed belonged to him. He opened the passenger door, and she slid onto the leather seat and watched him walk around the front of the car.

Yeah, he was definitely intimidating, with his straight-backed military posture and striking blue eyes, which seemed to constantly be searching the area for threats. She was definitely in good hands. Whoever those men were that had chased her, they'd have to go through Buck first to get to her.

He settled behind the wheel.

"Randolph doesn't like me very much, does he?"

"No, he doesn't," Buck admitted.

She appreciated candor, but she wished he'd lied.

"We have two escort vehicles from Javelin Security. That SUV and the one in the back. They're contracted with the government to provide additional security. If what you're saying is the truth, we want to be very careful."

I am *telling the truth,* Zaire wanted to scream, but she didn't.

She hadn't paid attention to the other vehicles until he mentioned them. Standing beside the SUV in front was a man with dark hair, dressed in black tactical gear. He had probably been in the military too. The SUV pulled off, and Buck started the sedan and followed them out of the gate.

"How long have you been doing this—escorting people or…whatever *this* is?" Zaire asked, gesturing with her hands between the two of them.

"I don't usually do this. My assignments tend to be more… covert."

"Oh really? What part of the government are you a member of?"

He slid a glance at her. She couldn't tell whether he was annoyed and wanted her to shut up or was simply trying to figure out how to answer. "I'm part of a special unit in the CIA, and I've been on the team for six years."

"Does your team have a name?"

This time he looked at her and didn't answer.

"Let me guess—if you told me, you'd have to kill me."

Zaire thought she saw the corner of his mouth lift slightly higher, as if he was amused. Well, at least the man had a sense of humor. For that split second, when his features had softened, he'd appeared even more handsome. She hadn't thought that was possible.

"Not quite. We're the Omega Team," he answered.

"Do you like your job?" She hoped she wasn't being annoying, but she was curious about him and the work he did, and talking kept her mind off the scary notion that someone wanted her dead. She was always curious about other people's lives, anyway, since hers was so…unexciting.

"Yes, I do."

"What did you do before you became a member of the Omega Team?"

"I was a Navy SEAL. What about you? Do you like your job?"

While Buck spoke, she noticed his eyes. He wasn't only paying attention to the road ahead. He also watched pedestrians and parked cars. It was interesting to observe him.

"I do. I learn a lot because I meet all kinds of people from different backgrounds and cultures. The hours can sometimes be long, though. This is the first time I've been stationed overseas. My company needed several people to fill a hole in the staff here while they expanded, and I jumped at the chance. Normally, I'm local or work remotely with clients."

Her work was also mentally stimulating because she couldn't zone out. She had to constantly remain alert and pay attention to context and the inflection of the speakers' voices to properly convey the words to the listener. She was proud of the work she did, helping people understand each other across cultures and nationalities.

They pulled onto the street where she lived. One of the men in the SUV ahead of them exited the vehicle with a large automatic weapon in his hand, while the driver remained in the parked car.

The man, almost as big as Buck, went inside the building. He came out a few seconds later and signaled to Buck.

"Let's go."

Zaire followed him out of the car. They waited for a truck to pass by before they walked swiftly across the street.

On the fourth-floor landing, Buck tore off the poliçe tape across the door and tossed it to the floor. Zaire removed her keys from her purse, but Buck took them from her. Their fingers brushed for a split second, sending a rabble of butterflies swooping through her insides. What a silly reaction to have to a complete stranger!

Buck opened the door and raised his hand, silently telling her to wait while he entered. She watched him walk into the apartment on surprisingly light feet, quieter than a mouse. He went down the hall, opening doors, checking inside, then coming out seconds later. Once he'd entered all the rooms, he returned to the front door.

"Pack your bags. I'll wait out here."

Walking gingerly into the apartment, Zaire cast a glance toward the small kitchen. A red stain covered several tiles, and her blood ran cold. Her roommate had been murdered there. Bile bubbled up in her stomach, and she had the sudden urge to throw up.

Buck stepped in front of her line of sight. "Don't look at that. Get your things. Pack. Now."

Zaire nodded, but tears filled her eyes. Poor Josie. They had become close—eating breakfast at the small table in the kitchen, huddling on the couch while watching Italian sitcoms, exploring the city on their days off…

Had the embassy notified their workplace? Did her parents know? She and Josie had met for the first time on this assignment, so she didn't know her family personally. All she knew was that they had the same birthplace. They both were from Dallas, Texas.

Zaire scurried into her small bedroom and grabbed her rolling suitcase from the top shelf of the closet. After taking items from the dresser drawer, she stuffed in her clothes, unconcerned about packing them neatly since she just wanted to get the heck out of there. She also suspected that Buck was timing her and at some point he'd come back there and tell her she was out of time and they had to go.

In the one bathroom she and Josie shared, she scraped her toothbrush and toiletries into a smaller bag and spun around in a circle.

Have I forgotten anything? she thought.

It looked like she had all her belongings. If she didn't... well, she'd buy new ones.

Right as she stepped into the hallway, the boom of an explosion shattered the peaceful day. The entire building rocked, and the walls trembled around her. Zaire dropped her toiletry bag and placed a steadying hand on the wall.

"What was that?" she called out to Buck.

"We have to get out of here."

She hurried toward the sound of his voice and saw him looking out the window.

"Why? What do you see?"

The pop of gunfire pierced the air, and she instinctively ducked her head, though the sounds came from below.

"The convoy is under attack." His voice was emotionless, almost businesslike.

"What?"

Zaire ran over to the window. Sure enough, two more SUVs were in the middle of the road, and four masked men were firing on the first vehicle that had escorted her and

Buck from the embassy. Only charred remains of the second one existed.

"We have to go before they come up here." His voice was sharp as a whip.

Zaire swung around to face him, fear clawing up her throat.

Buck took a chair from the kitchen and shoved it under the doorknob of the front door. "That should buy us some time," he said with grim determination.

He marched toward the bedroom, and Zaire hurried after him. She watched as he yanked the sheets off the bed. His movements were fast and efficient, as if he had preplanned the steps long before today, but that simply meant he was always prepared.

"What are you doing? What's happening?" she asked.

"Creating our way out since we can't leave through the front."

Zaire didn't understand until he shoved the window open and peered down at the street below.

"Oh, hell no, you're not suggesting that we...?" She gulped, her words fading like wind-blown mist when he turned to her with a fierce expression.

"That's exactly what I'm suggesting. It's the only way out of here."

"That's a forty-foot drop."

"If you jumped from the windowsill to the ground, yes. But we'll have a bedsheet rope, and the drop to the ground will only be a few feet."

Zaire watched in horror as he tied the corners of the sheets, the throw at the end of the bed and the pillow cases together. Then he tested the knots one by one with a firm yank.

She gazed down at the street below, and her stomach became queasy. They were four floors up—and she wasn't a mountain climber, for heaven's sake! She was the least athletic person she knew.

"Buck, I don't think I can do this," she whispered.

"Of course you can. You don't have a choice. Look at me." He stood in front of her, staring into her eyes. "I'm going first, and you'll climb down after me. Grip the rope like this, and slowly ease yourself lower by walking backwards down the side of the building. Whatever you do, do *not* look down."

Staring at him in shock, Zaire had her doubts that she could do what he'd suggested. Her head throbbed. She couldn't believe it. This wasn't happening.

"Watch me, okay? Do what I do."

Right, easy peasy. Zaire wanted to laugh out loud. Instead, she nodded vigorously, though her heart was about to jump into her throat.

"What about my clothes, and my—"

"You can't take anything with you. We need to leave. *Now.*"

Buck tied the corner of the bedsheet to the iron radiator near the window and gave it a test tug. The sheet held firm, so he tossed the makeshift rope out the window. He hoisted himself over the windowsill and placed his feet on the ledge on the side of the building.

He and Zaire made temporary eye contact before he started lowering himself toward the ground.

Chapter 7

Once on the ground, Buck looked right and then left. Then he turned his face up to the window and signaled for Zaire to follow him.

She took a deep breath and expelled it through her mouth. "You got this, Zaire," she told herself in a soft voice.

What a lie. She did not, in fact, have this. She was terrified. What if the sheets tore on her way down? Granted, a man larger than her had just, seconds before, used them to climb down the side of the building—but what if he'd weakened the fibers of the linens? Speaking of *weak*, was she strong enough to lower herself to the ground without falling?

A loud crash at the front of the apartment made her head snap up. Oh no! The assailants were trying to break into the apartment. She couldn't waste any more time.

Zaire shut the bedroom door and locked it. She didn't doubt they could easily break in, but locking the door created a temporary barrier that might buy her a few seconds if the masked men forced their way into the apartment.

She hurried to the window, legs shaking as she swung one foot over the sill, then the other. Feet dangling, she clutched the window, the edge pressing into her forearms with the bite of a dulled blade. With labored breathing, she slowly lowered her feet onto the narrow ledge between the third and fourth floors, wincing as she scraped the underside of her arms along the way.

"Don't look down, don't look down…" she said in a shaky voice, repeating Buck's warning.

Her fingers curled around the sheet, and she pressed her toes into the side of the building. Now the hard part. The part where she needed to put on her big-girl panties and lower herself toward Buck.

"Good job," he called up in a loud whisper.

She didn't feel like she was doing a good job, yet she had no choice but to continue going. With jagged breaths, Zaire began her descent, movements careful, placing one foot behind the other and one hand behind the other. Her muscles strained and she wished she could move faster, but she was afraid to lose her footing.

A loud crash echoed in the apartment, filling her ears with the sound of splintering wood and sending her heartbeat into overdrive. Her eyes flew to the window.

They must be inside the apartment!

"You're doing great," Buck coached from below.

Muscles quivering and her heartbeat increasing rapidly, Zaire moved faster in reverse. Then the unthinkable happened: she lost her footing and her feet slid off the side of the building.

Terror slammed into her, and she swung her legs higher to brace them against the building again, but she overcorrected and tilted back too far.

No!

She wrestled with the bedsheets, causing her body to swing to the right and spin in an almost-upside-down position. Dizzy and unable to hold herself upright, she felt her hands slide off the makeshift rope, and she fell backward.

A soft cry of fear escaped her throat as she plummeted

toward the ground. She reached wildly for the rope yet encountered nothing but empty space. Panic pummeled her as a rush of air swept over her skin.

She was going to break her back, or her neck, or—

"Gotcha."

She landed in Buck's firm arms.

Holy crap. He'd caught her. He really was an action hero.

She stared at him in disbelief, temporarily mesmerized by the up-close view of his sharp blue eyes. Their mouths were so close together, his breath brushed her parted lips. If they moved a fraction of an inch, she'd taste him. She had a sudden urge to kiss his broad, unreasonably sensual-looking lips. Now her heart raced for a completely different reason than before.

Another crash came to them from above. The bedroom! They had to be inside now.

Buck's gaze shot upward. He dropped her unceremoniously to her feet and, in one fluid motion, pulled his gun from his back waistband and fired at the window above.

Zaire ducked, covering her head as broken glass rained down to their feet. A stray fragment clipped her arm, and a thin line of blood appeared on her brown skin.

"Run!" Buck said in a harsh voice.

He extended a hand, and she took it, placing all her trust in him.

Maybe he saw the residual fear in her eyes, because he added, "I won't let anything happen to you."

That was all the reassurance she needed. She believed him, and those words calmed the last bit of her jitters. They took off at a fast clip down the cobblestone street.

The gunshots at the front of the building had stopped— a bad sign that the masked men had killed all their escorts. There were no more shots, yet the street was far from quiet.

Multiple car alarms screeched continuously, and the smell of gunpowder permeated the air.

Hand in hand, they dashed toward the back of the building. Buck's long legs stretched farther than hers, eating up the distance and forcing Zaire to keep up.

She heard the men yelling at them from four stories above and made the mistake of looking back. One of the masked men pointed a menacingly large gun right at them. Then the loud pop of automatic rifle fire cut through the air, and Zaire screamed.

Buck dragged her around the corner of a building, out of the line of fire. With his hand fastened like a vise around her fingers, he pulled her along as they ran for their lives, their feet pounding on the pavement. She knew she was slowing him down, so she pumped her legs twice as fast as his long-legged strides.

They passed a woman walking two dogs, staring at them with her mouth open.

Then an SUV came careening around the corner with a screech of tires. Two men in front coming right at them.

Zaire and Buck skidded to a halt and made a U-turn, racing in the opposite direction. More shots rang out. A stray bullet busted the side mirror of a parked car, and glass spewed in the air. Zaire screamed, ducking and covering her face to avoid getting hit by the fragments.

All of a sudden, Buck turned and swung toward their pursuers.

"Keep going!" he barked at her.

Standing in the middle of the street, he fired off two rounds that shattered the windshield on the driver's side. The SUV veered to the left and slammed into a parked car to the jarring sound of crunching metal.

He continued shooting while Zaire took off, arms and

legs pumping fast to get away. Why couldn't she be more athletic? She was winded and her feet hurt. These were not the shoes to be running in.

Within seconds of having that thought, she skidded on a smooth stone. Arms flailing, she lost her balance and fell to the ground on her hip bone. Pain shot up her side, and she whimpered. But she couldn't stop. She had to keep moving.

She scrambled on her hands and knees and pushed herself up. She barely had time to recover before a firm hand grabbed her by the upper arm and yanked her fully upright.

"I can't. I *can't*," she panted, tears filling her eyes. She was tired and bruised. Her palms stung, her feet hurt and her ears rang from the sounds of gunshots aimed at *her*.

Buck got in her face. "Do you want to die?" he growled.

Zaire shrank back and shook her head. "No."

"Then let's go. This way."

He pulled her between two buildings. Buck didn't seem particularly concerned about her ability to keep up, so she had no choice but to do so.

They burst onto another street—much busier than the side street—one filled with pedestrians and traffic going by at a slumberous pace.

Buck swiveled his head right and then left.

Panting hard, Zaire took the pause to try to catch her breath. If she ever got out of this mess alive, she was going to hit the gym every day to build up her endurance because she was downright pathetic. Buck wasn't even winded. He might as well have been on a leisurely stroll, while she was running a 100 meter dash.

He turned suddenly as if he'd heard something, and his eyes narrowed. He fired off two more shots.

They sounded like firecrackers going off inside her ears, and Zaire grimaced at the loud sound. Onlookers screamed and scattered. One woman lifted her daughter into her arms and took off running. Several other people ran away in fear.

Two of the masked men—probably the same ones from the apartment—ran for cover.

Then Zaire heard the unmistakable click of an empty gun cartridge. Buck was out of bullets.

But he appeared unfazed. He tossed the weapon and focused on a man across the street who was getting off a sleek black motorcycle.

"Come on," he said in a grim tone.

Not waiting for a break in the traffic, he bolted across the street. Car tires shrieked in protest. The driver of a Mercedes jammed the heel of his hand against the horn. The driver of a gray Fiat slammed on the brakes within inches of Buck's legs and looked at him as if he were crazy, belatedly banging the horn.

Buck ignored all that and approached the motorcycle rider. "I need your bike."

The man looked at them in confusion. *"Che?"*

"I need your bike," Buck repeated, louder and slower, as if that would make a difference.

Zaire shook out of her stupor. She was an interpreter. Time to communicate the message.

"I'm sorry, but we need to take your motorcycle," she told the man in Italian.

His eyes widened. "No!" he exclaimed, then burst into a stream of Italian that included some very colorful words.

Buck shoved him out of the way, and the man stumbled backward.

As Buck flung his long leg over the body of the bike, the man yelled at them, gesticulating with sweeping hand movements.

"We don't have time to talk. Get on," Buck told Zaire.

"*Mi dispiace*," she apologized to the stranger.

She climbed on behind Buck and hugged his waist. She had never ridden on a motorcycle before. So many firsts today, and none of them good. First time getting shot at. First time climbing down the side of a building using bedsheets as a rope. Now she was about to take a ride on a bike—a *stolen* bike.

She leaned against Buck's firm back.

For all his loud exclamations, the Italian didn't try to stop them. Not that she blamed him. What fool would try to stop this big man dressed in all black from doing whatever he wanted?

Buck started the bike and took off, merging into traffic as the two men came rushing out from between the buildings.

Zaire kept her eyes trained on them. One man lifted his gun to aim, but his partner knocked the muzzle lower. He said something to the shorter man, and they ran back in the direction they'd come from.

Zaire closed her eyes, relieved that she was safe. For now.

She prayed this nightmare would soon be over.

Chapter 8

Buck knew better than to believe their nightmare was over. Those men had murdered the Javelin guards in the middle of the street. They were not going to give up that easily.

Sure enough, the squeal of tires caught his attention when a black SUV raced out of a side street and pulled in behind them.

He cursed in his head.

"Hang on," he yelled over his shoulder, though Zaire was clinging pretty tightly to him already.

Revving the engine, he accelerated the powerful machine and checked the fuel gauge. The last thing he wanted was to run out of gas while pursued by men who wanted to murder them. Satisfied with what he saw, he started mapping out a plan of escape in his head based on his knowledge of Rome.

Right now, there wasn't much traffic—a blessing and a curse. Very few cars obstructed his view as he roared down the street, but that meant the driver of the SUV was able to keep track of them.

Buck weaved between the cars and slipped past a bus, racing by ancient ruins and modern buildings. He zipped through a traffic light as it turned red and took a sharp right. Pedestrians crossing the street hopped out of the way, one man shaking a raised fist and shouting at them.

With a quick glance in the side-view mirror, Buck saw that the SUV continued full speed behind them, the masked assailants hot on their heels. His pulse raced as he scanned the street ahead and looked for other ways to escape.

He accidentally knocked off a van's side mirror and almost ran over a dog that darted out from behind a parked car. Continuing to drive like a bat out of hell, he zoomed past a woman on a bicycle.

With another glance in the side mirror, he saw one of the men leaning out the passenger window and aiming his AR-15 at them.

No way. The guy was nuts. There were innocent pedestrians everywhere.

Buck leaned into the curve and put distance between them and the men, darting past pedestrians to drive up on the sidewalk. He leaned on the horn, and people screamed, parting like the Red Sea to avoid getting hit. He bounced off the sidewalk and back into traffic, maneuvering the bike at a dangerously high speed.

Eyes focused up ahead, he remembered walking along this street on a previous trip and recognized the potential opportunity to escape. There was a flight of outdoor steps around the bend. He and his girlfriend at the time had strolled down them and taken photos on one of their walking tours of the city.

Buck checked the location of the SUV in the side mirror. "Hang on!" he called back to Zaire.

She let out a low squeal right as he veered toward the steps with a sharp turn.

He started down the stairs, leaning back and guarding the brakes to keep from tipping forward.

The bike rattled and shook as they continued downward, each step jarring beneath the tires. Keeping a firm grip on the handlebars, Buck controlled the descent, his muscles bunching tightly with every bump along the way.

Zaire pressed closer to him, her soft breasts resting on his back, her thighs clenched around his. Under other circumstances, the way she held him would be a massive turn-on. But he remained focused and kept the motorcycle balanced.

Two women who were walking up scrambled out of the way, but Buck barely registered them. He leaned on the horn, and the Romans scattered, gawking as the motorcycle bounced down the incline with muscle-jarring force.

When they reached street level, a female driver in a Mercedes came out from the left and skidded to a stop with a screech of tires. A man on a motorcycle behind her slammed into her rear bumper.

Horns honked as dozens of eyes followed their progress, but Buck ignored them all, determined to put as much distance between them and the men hunting them as possible.

When the ancient Colosseum came into view, a surge of excitement rushed through him. The popular tourist attraction would be the perfect place to lose their pursuers for good. He slowed the bike as he maneuvered through the crowded area, dodging traffic and tourists along the way.

Buck stopped in front of the Colosseum, and he and Zaire dismounted the bike. She looked at him with a question in her eyes.

"Give me your phone," he said, opening his palm.

She looked at him through her glasses with confusion. "My phone?"

"Yes. We have to get rid of it. I think they're tracking you through your phone."

"But—but my life is on my phone."

"Your life is here." He jabbed a finger at her chest without touching. "The phone is replaceable. You're not."

She frowned, but his words got through to her. After a moment's hesitation, she reached into her bag and handed over the phone.

"I hope I have everything properly backed up so I can retrieve my photos and data when I buy a new one."

Buck didn't comment. That was her problem, not his. His job was to keep her alive, and getting rid of this phone was one of the steps toward making sure he accomplished his goal.

"Is the recording on here?" he asked.

"No."

"Stay here."

He ran inside the Colosseum and made a beeline for the public restrooms. He dropped the phone inside the trash and then returned to where he had left Zaire. She looked relieved when he returned.

"This way," he muttered.

He grabbed her hand, intending to pretend they were a couple on vacation like everyone else. But the moment they touched, a current ran through him as if he'd curled his fingers around exposed wire. Compared to his, her hand was small and her skin soft. Delicate. He flinched and gritted his teeth, forcing himself to ignore the unexpected surge of electricity that ignited every nerve in his body, creating a sensation that was both exhilarating and terrifying in its intensity.

He guided her toward a bunch of tourists lined up in single file to get on a long red-and-white bus marked *European Tours*.

Following Buck's lead, Zaire stepped in line behind a man with two cameras around his neck. When it was their turn, they climbed onto the bus and settled in a seat near the middle.

After everyone had entered the vehicle, a woman with platinum blond hair let her gaze sweep the interior of the bus. "Is that everyone?" she asked in a nasal British accent.

A murmur of *yes*es and a wave of head nods passed through the group. Buck joined in.

The guide's eyes settled on him and Zaire, and he smiled. She smiled back, then frowned a little, as if questioning how he happened to be on her bus.

Knowing human nature, Buck maintained eye contact. Averting his eyes was more likely to draw her attention. Better to pretend and act with confidence, as if he and Zaire had been on the tour all along. She was less likely to challenge him that way.

Sure enough, her gaze finally left them. "Next stop, the Trevi Fountain," she announced before taking her seat at the front.

Buck relaxed and looked out the window for a sign of their pursuers. He caught a glimpse of them standing in the middle of a flurry of tourist activity. They were on foot and no longer wore masks or carried their weapons, but he recognized them immediately from the black outfits, boots and their upright, square-shouldered stance—indicative of their military background.

"Is that them?" Zaire whispered.

"Yeah." His eyes narrowed as he watched the men.

One had dark hair and a puckered scar on the side of his neck. The other was a few inches shorter and bald. The bald one's eyes darted to and fro, while the taller one looked down at an electronic device in his hand. He pointed, and they took off.

Buck watched them jog toward the entrance of the Colosseum—probably tracking Zaire's phone, as he'd suspected.

·

They'd be in for a surprise when they found the device in the restroom's trash.

He committed their faces to memory. Just in case he had the displeasure of running into them again.

Chapter 9

They were alive. A little banged up, but alive.

Zaire trembled beside Buck on the seat, still clearly scared after the chase through the streets of Rome.

To calm her nerves, he took her hand again and experienced the same shock as before.

Zaire looked at him with a mixture of fear and hope, searching his eyes for reassurance.

"It's okay. You're safe," he said quietly.

A grateful smile touched her lips, and the tension visibly melted from her shoulders as she relaxed. He held her hand for a few more minutes until he was certain she had calmed enough for him to let go.

He couldn't imagine what she was thinking, but right now was not the time to discuss what had happened. He was still processing the ambush himself.

Who were those men? Whoever they were, they were good. They'd killed the Javelin Security escorts and tried to kill him and Zaire, which meant they had to have been connected to the men Zaire had overheard at Zigna.

Their firepower came as no surprise. Anyone capable of attacking an embassy and killing innocent staff had to have some serious connections to acquire the explosives necessary to do that without setting off any international alarms beforehand.

Buck stroked his fingers over his stubble. He hated that they'd had to leave behind Zaire's belongings, and his bag with his passport and clothes had been in the car at her apartment. Their situation had gone south fast. He needed to talk to Benjamin, stat, and get word to the pilot regarding their flight out.

Job one: find a phone.

The European Tours bus pulled to a stop at the Trevi Fountain, and the passengers disembarked. He and Zaire followed.

As Buck descended the bus, the soothing sound of splashing water hit his ears, but so did the buzz of chatter from the horde of tourists milling around. For the most part, they were gleeful and energetic as they posed for photos in front of the iconic landmark, a stunning monument at eighty-five feet high and one hundred and sixty-one feet wide. Its impressive appearance explained why it had been included in so many movies over the years.

Buck shot a glance at the sculptures carved from travertine stone, the same material used for the Colosseum. The images depicted the Greek god Oceanus flanked by seahorses and mermen. He recalled another time when he'd visited, filled with hope and anticipation as he took photos with the woman he'd thought he would marry.

Gritting his teeth, he switched off the memories and led Zaire away from the monument as the guide launched into a history of the fountain.

"Where are we going?" she asked, falling into step beside him.

"I need to find a phone to get in touch with my commander in DC and get word to the pilot about what happened."

What he didn't tell her was that he had bought them some time with his evasive tactics but they were pretty much on their own since this trip was off the books. There was no telling what the pilot had been told. He might have instructions to leave if they didn't show up on time. It was imperative that Buck get a message to him right away.

"'What happened' is that someone tried to kill us. They want me dead because of what I know. You believe me now, don't you?" Her wide brown eyes stared up at him through her glasses.

"Yes, I believe you. There's no doubt someone is after you, and they're professionals. They're not going to stop until they find you, which means we have to be extra careful. Our way out of the country might already be compromised."

Her brow puckered with worry, and a stab of guilt hit him in the chest. He didn't want to scare her any more than she already was, but he needed to be honest and realistic.

Buck spotted a Telecom Italia Mobile store in a salmon-colored brick building. TIM had a wide network across the country and would be a good place to purchase a phone. He removed his wallet from his pocket to see how much money he had.

Satisfied, he stuck it back in his pocket and turned to Zaire. "In there."

There was only one other person inside the shop—a German, from the way he spoke English. He was purchasing a SIM card for his phone.

They stepped in line behind him and waited until he completed the purchase transaction. Then Buck walked up to the counter.

"*Buongiorno*," he said in greeting to the clerk, a slight man with a narrow nose and thin lips.

"*Buongiorno*," the man repeated with a smile.

"I need a prepaid phone with call and text," Buck explained.

"Ah, yes, I have the perfect plan for you," the man said in accented English. "It includes two hundred minutes in the month." He held up two fingers.

"I don't need that many minutes," Buck said, thinking about the limited cash he carried. Since he didn't know what would happen in the next twenty-four hours, he needed to conserve as much of it as possible. "Do you have a different plan—with, say, a hundred minutes?"

"Yes, we can do one hundred minutes."

"The plan includes texting?" Buck asked, taking out his wallet.

"Yes." The clerk nodded vigorously.

"How much?"

The man gave him the price, and Buck handed over the euros.

After he finished purchasing the phone, he and Zaire exited the building, and his eyes swept the area for a spot where he could make a private call. They had to remain vigilant since they didn't know where the men were that had chased them or how many there were. Now that they'd seen him with Zaire, they would be looking for them as a couple.

He walked down a less occupied side street.

"How soon do you think we'll be able to get out of here?" Zaire asked, sounding anxious. She wrapped her arms around her waist.

"Ideally, in a couple of hours. Worst case, tomorrow."

"A couple of hours would be great," she said, looking around her, clearly uneasy.

Buck dialed Benjamin's number. Thankfully, his commander picked up right away.

"It's me," he said.

"Where the hell are you? I just got word that the escort was attacked and you and Ms. Nichols are missing. I thought this would be an easy pickup."

"It's definitely not that. Zaire is with me now," Buck said.

When he mentioned her name, Zaire turned her attention to him.

"We're both fine," Buck added, "but I wanted to know if you could get word to the pilot that we intend to get to the airport as soon as possible. If we can get there within the hour, will he be able to fly us out right away?"

"That's not going to happen, Buck. The pilot is dead."

Buck's heart dropped like a pebble off a ninety-foot cliff. "Shit," he whispered.

Zaire stared at him, her eyes silently asking for an explanation.

He started pacing. "What the hell is going on?"

"This thing might be bigger than we thought. We're working with Rick to locate the culprits. He's furious and determined because he lost four men today."

"Commander, I saw these guys in action. They're good. They're relentless, they're not going to stop. If today is any indication, they don't care about making a scene. What now?"

"Now that I know you're alive, we need to make arrangements to get you and Ms. Nichols out of the country before they find you. I spoke to the secretary, and she expressed to me the amount of pressure she's under for the loss of life in the field. We need something concrete, and with this being an election year…"

He didn't have to finish the sentence. They needed results, or the opposition party would use the failure to find and punish the terrorists as a cudgel in the lead-up to the election.

Buck hated the politicization of human life. "I understand," he said.

"Lay low for an hour or two and give me time to make other arrangements—but I'm in a tough spot. I don't have the usual resources available to me."

"I know."

Benjamin sighed. "Can I reach you back at this number?"

"Yes. It's a burner."

"Good. I'll be in touch. And Buck? Keep her alive."

"I'll do my best." He hung up the phone.

"What did he say?" Zaire asked.

He hesitated, unsure how she'd take the news. "He needs an hour or two to work on an exit for us."

"Why can't we just go to the airport and meet the pilot now?"

"The pilot is dead, Zaire," Buck said in an even voice.

Her eyes widened, and one hand flew to her mouth. "No. Someone else died because of me?"

"Not because of *you*," Buck corrected in a firm voice. "Because these people are determined to stop you from sharing what you know. They're monsters and don't care who they have to kill to achieve their goals. Remember, they blew up two embassies."

She nodded and looked nauseous. "So what do we do? Just wait?"

"Pretty much. Commander Ray is working on getting us out of Italy."

She nodded again but appeared glum. A lot was happening, and none of it was good.

She rubbed her hands up and down her arms as if she was cold. "I don't want to die, Buck."

"You're not going to die," he said.

"A lot of people have died already. Josie. The pilot. Our escorts," she whispered.

Buck reminded himself that she was a civilian. He, however, was a former Navy SEAL and current black ops agent who'd killed more men than he had fingers and toes, and lived through some pretty hair-raising experiences. He'd trained for this life and could handle the ugliness that came along with that decision. It was different for her.

Of course she was scared. Of course she felt overwhelmed.

"I was sent here to escort you back to the States, and that's what I intend to do. I know it's a lot to take in, but we're safe now, and in a short while, we'll be in the air and on our way to DC. Believe me, I want to get out of Rome as much as you do—maybe more. Let's head over to the McDonald's and wait there for the call back, out of the public eye."

She forced a smile to her lips and walked beside him.

Chapter 10

McDonald's Roma Fontana di Trevi was the first McDonald's in Italy and was a well-known tourist attraction. Crowded and filled with customers, the two-story restaurant contained a separate gelato bar and served coffee and pastries that aligned with Italian tastes. The beautiful interior included common Roman design elements, such as marble walls and frescoes.

Zaire followed Buck to a booth in the back.

"I need to use the restroom," she announced. She didn't wait for a reply, making a beeline for the ladies' room.

Checking the stalls, she made sure she was alone and then braced her hands on the sink. She stared at her reflection and took deep, even breaths to keep from hyperventilating.

Memories of the first time she and Josie had visited this part of Rome came back with a vengeance. They had been in the city for a week, most of their time spent in orientation. Since they hadn't known anyone at first, as roommates they immediately became close and took advantage of their first free weekend.

Josie had suggested they visit the Trevi Fountain to toss coins in the water for good luck. One coin ensured a return trip to Rome, two coins led to romance and three coins meant marriage was in the future. When they had arrived, Josie tossed in two coins. At first Zaire had refused to participate because she thought the whole idea of tossing in coins and making a wish was cute but ridiculous.

Nonetheless, as they'd walked away in the direction of the Spanish Steps, she had a sudden urge to participate. Without a word to Josie, she had rushed back to the fountain and squeezed her way through a group of tourists. She'd removed three coins from her purse and tossed them into the water. A silly, impulsive act that Josie never saw.

She had caught up to her friend, and they took photos on the Spanish Steps and then entered the McDonald's, amazed by the beauty of the interior. They'd ordered chicken sandwiches and croissants for dessert and climbed the stairs to the second floor. Idling over their meals, they'd discussed how lucky they were to be chosen for the special assignment in Rome.

If only she had known then what she knew now, she would have made different decisions. Josie would be alive, and she wouldn't be on the run for her life.

"You've been through bad situations before. You can handle this. You're strong."

Zaire touched the keloid scar on her shoulder, a reminder of her strength and will to survive.

Finally, her breathing returned to normal and her heart rate decreased. She closed her eyes, took a deep breath and breathed out slowly through her mouth. When she was fully calm, she stared at her reflection.

Three giggling teenagers burst into the room, and she took their entrance as her signal to move on. She left the bathroom and went back to the table, sliding onto the seat across from Buck, who kept a watchful eye toward the front.

"Are you okay?" he asked.

"I've been better," she admitted, rolling her shoulders to release the last vestiges of tension.

"We'll be out of here soon enough."

She studied his handsome face. "Do you really believe that, or are you saying that to make me feel better?"

"I really believe that. I know this is a tough situation for you to be in, but right now we're safe, and pretty soon we'll have a flight out of the country. The sooner we get back to the States, the sooner the right people can listen to that recording and figure out when the next embassy bombing will take place. Unless...you want to share that information with me right now."

"Why would I do that?" Zaire asked.

"What if something happens to you? Then we won't have any information to track down the perpetrators."

"You don't sound very confident in your ability to keep me alive," she said.

His eyes narrowed. "I'm good at my job, but anything can happen."

"I choose to trust in your abilities." She shot him a tight smile.

"Or you could give me the recording."

Zaire bristled. "No."

Buck's jaw clenched. He was *not* happy. He was probably used to being in charge and having people ask *how high* when he said *jump.*

"Why not?"

"I want safe passage into the United States. I've watched enough thrillers to know that once I give up my leverage, I become expendable." She was no fool.

"You watch too much TV." He leaned back in the booth, resting a corded forearm on the table.

"Maybe so, but I'm not taking any chances. You'll know

where the recording is when I arrive safely on US soil," Zaire said with finality, hoping to put an end to the conversation.

"Or I could beat it out of you."

She stiffened. Was he serious?

A faint smile touched his lips, and her tight muscles relaxed.

"That's not funny."

"You're right. It's not. You've been through a lot today." He didn't exactly sound contrite.

"I have. Normally, my life is pretty quiet. This is probably a typical day for you," she mumbled.

"Not exactly." His eyes flicked to a point over her shoulder.

"What? Did you see something?" Zaire twisted her head around.

"No, just paying attention to the people passing in and out, that's all." His attention returned to her.

"I'm going to get something to drink. Do you think it would be safe for me to do that?" Her nerves were frazzled, but she was also thirsty.

"Should be fine."

"Do you want anything?"

"No. Use cash. We don't know the extent of these people's network. If you use your credit card, they might be able to find you."

"Right."

She slid out from the booth and went into one of the lines. Casting a quick glance at the guy next to her, she smiled briefly. He smiled back.

She knew it was her imagination, but all of a sudden, everyone looked suspicious. The man and woman with their three kids; the elderly couple; the girl standing alone, gazing at the menu. Any of them could be a killer or a snitch for killers.

What had she gotten herself into? If she hadn't overheard that conversation, she wouldn't be in this mess.

At the counter, she ordered a Coke and water. When she returned to the table, she handed Buck the water as a peace offering, hoping to eliminate the tension that had arisen during their conversation.

"I know you said you didn't want anything, but I figured you might want water at least."

"Thank you."

"You're welcome." She shoved the straw into her Coke and took a sip.

Buck unscrewed the cap from the water. "What's the real reason why you didn't go out with your roommate and your coworkers?" he asked.

The question took Zaire by surprise, and at first she wasn't sure how to reply. She was nothing like Josie. In the short time they'd known each other, she envied her friend's joie de vivre and the way she made friends everywhere they went. Meanwhile, Zaire stood on the sidelines, observing, trying to be invisible while also hoping to be spoken to so she wouldn't have to initiate communication.

She adjusted her glasses. "I told you why. The partying lifestyle isn't for me. I'm not that kind of person," she said, hoping that would be the end of the conversation.

Buck fixed her with a soul-searching stare as he tapped his forefinger on the table. "What kind of person are you?"

She decided to be honest and didn't care if he judged her. "The kind who likes quiet evenings at home, curled up with a good book or watching a crime show on TV, like *Buried in the Backyard*."

His eyebrows drew together. "There's a show called *Buried in the Backyard*?"

Zaire nodded.

"There are so many people being buried in backyards that they created a show about it?"

She almost laughed at his disbelief. "Yes. Surprising, I know. People do terrible things, but it makes for interesting television."

"Apparently it's more interesting than drinking and partying with friends."

She didn't reply, and to her dismay, he continued with the questions.

"Did Josie go out a lot without you?" Keeping his eyes trained on her, Buck took a swig of water.

Zaire shrugged. "I guess. She was the outgoing type."

"Okay, there are people who don't like partying, and you're one of them. I understand that. But you don't expect me to believe you only like to stay home and watch crime shows."

"What's wrong with that?" Zaire demanded.

"You're too young to be staying home all the time. You haven't found an Italian boyfriend while you're here?"

"No," Zaire muttered, her cheeks growing hot.

"You haven't found anyone to interest you?"

"What's with all the questions?" she snapped.

He arched an eyebrow as if surprised by her reaction, but he wasn't a stupid man. In fact, she suspected he was quite intelligent, so he had to know his barrage of questions skirted the line of prying.

"I'm killing time, making conversation," he said.

"If that's what we're doing, then will you answer one of my questions? A question for a question."

He mulled over her suggestion, eyes slightly narrowed

again in that way he had a habit of doing, as if he was suspicious of her motives.

"That's fair," he said slowly. "As long as what you ask isn't classified."

She didn't think he'd agree to her suggestion, but she was glad he did. She wanted to learn more about Buck. If she had to tell a little about herself in exchange, she'd do that.

"Back to my question, have you met anyone that interested you?" Buck asked.

Zaire shifted on the chair. "There was one guy that I was interested in. He works at Worldwide with me, but he's kinda shy, so…" She shrugged.

"Two shy people will never work. Someone has to make the first move."

"I'm not shy. I'm quiet. That's not the same thing." Why did she sound so defensive?

"So did you make the first move?"

"That's two questions. My turn to ask a question. What do you like to do in your spare time, when you're not doing CIA business?"

Buck lifted the water to his lips and took a sip. "I enjoy picnics in the park."

"No you don't," Zaire said with a laugh.

"I do. A day in the park, tossing a Frisbee or lounging around doing nothing is a pleasure. Finding time to relax is very important to me because of the work I do."

It was Zaire's turn to narrow her eyes. "Interesting. I assumed you'd be involved in extreme sports."

"Not to relax, but I do enjoy the occasional skydiving and cave-diving trip."

"I knew it! I'm good at reading people."

"Good for you," he drawled, which sounded suspiciously

like he was teasing her. "Back to my last question. Did you make a move on your shy coworker?"

"No, I didn't. There was no point. He might be shy, but he goes out with other people at work. I've heard him talk about his nights out with them. I'm sure I'd be too boring and quiet for him." She hoped she didn't sound as pathetic as she thought she did.

Buck's gaze became thoughtful for a moment. "There are men out there looking for the quiet type."

"I'm pretty sure most men would pass on the quiet type."

"You'd be surprised," Buck murmured.

So far Zaire hadn't seen anything to the contrary, but it was nice to fantasize about a man finding her alluring and interesting.

Especially a man like Buck.

Chapter 11

The sudden ringing of his phone pulled Buck's attention away. He looked at the screen and saw an unknown number, which suggested Benjamin was calling. He was surprised. He'd expected they'd have to wait at least another hour before he heard back from his commander.

"Is that your contact?" Zaire asked.

"Yes." Buck answered the call. "Hello?"

"Buck, it's me, Benjamin. I wish I had better news. I wanted to get you out of the country right away, but you'll have to wait at least twenty-four hours before another plane can arrive in Italy. We don't have any transportation available in Europe at the moment."

Dammit.

He looked across the table at Zaire, who watched him closely, anxiousness brimming in her eyes as she waited for an update.

"That's the best we could do," Benjamin said, sounding defeated.

"If that's the best you can do, I'll make it work."

"We don't have the extraction point yet, but it won't be the main airport in Rome. I don't want to take a chance that these people—whoever they are—find out and ambush you before you get there or while you're there."

"Any idea who did this?"

"Nothing yet. Still working on it. By the way, it's possible that I can have you out of there sooner, so keep your phone nearby."

"Done." Buck hung up.

"You don't have good news, do you?" Zaire asked.

"He can't get us out for twenty-four hours. He's going to try—"

"What?" she said, sounding distressed.

"He's going to try to get us out sooner, Zaire."

"Why can't he do it now?"

Time to tell her the truth. "Because my trip here isn't sanctioned by the government."

"What does that mean?"

"Before you, other people contacted the State Department claiming they had information on the bombings that have taken place. Flakes. Every lead has been investigated and proven false."

Realization dawned in her dark brown eyes. "You guys thought I was the same—a flake. A false lead. Someone making up a story about the information that I had."

He let silence be his answer.

"That means we're basically on our own, right? Because you don't have the usual resources available to you."

"Yes and no. Look, we're in Italy, not the mountains of a third-world country where neither of us speaks the language. We have access to a phone and some cash. We'll be okay."

"Unless they find us." Zaire sat back, shoulders slumped.

"They won't, and if they do, I'll kill them—just like I did earlier."

He let his words sink in.

"If that's the best he can do, I guess we have to wait," she said.

Her voice was soft and made him want to hug her and provide comfort and confirm she had nothing to worry about.

"One thing we can do to make it harder for them to find us is change our clothes. They'll be looking for us in these outfits. We can go to one of the souvenir stores nearby and try to look more like tourists. There was one a couple doors down from the TIM store."

Zaire perked up, as if having something to do gave her energy. "Okay."

There were plenty of stores in the area selling tourist souvenirs like T-shirts, baseball caps and miniature versions of Rome's landmarks on key chains. They left McDonald's and walked in the direction of the TIM store to the one Buck had mentioned.

He went immediately to the T-shirt rack with a sign that advertised major discounts.

"These are inexpensive." He held up a white T-shirt with three of Rome's major landmarks on the front—the Colosseum, the Trevi Fountain and Saint Peter's Basilica. "What do you think? For you?" he asked Zaire.

She wrinkled her nose. "I guess it's okay."

"Do you want something else?" He flipped through the rack and found another shirt. "How about this?"

It had *I* ♥ *Roma* on the front.

"The first one you chose is fine," she insisted.

"That's for you, and I'll take *I* ♥ *Roma*."

Humor touched her lips. "You'll need a bigger size."

"No kidding." He handed her the first T-shirt and then thumbed through the rest of the sizes, looking for one that would fit him.

"Found one," Buck said, folding a powder blue T-shirt over one arm. His gaze swept the room. "We need caps. Let's go over there," he said, pointing with his chin.

Zaire followed behind him.

"Which one?" He took a blue cap off the stand and examined the Italian flag on the front.

"I like that one," Zaire replied.

"We'll get matching caps." He removed another one from the display and handed it to her. "All right, last thing—sunglasses. Can you wear them?"

"I can, but then I won't be able to see much."

He frowned. "Never mind, then. This should be enough to change our appearance, but we need to get you another pair of shoes. We don't want you to fall a second time."

Zaire frowned. "Do you think we'll be in that type of situation again?"

Buck shrugged and took off across the store. "You never know," he said over his shoulder.

"'You never know'?" Zaire hissed, falling into step beside him.

"That's what I said." He stopped in front of a stand with tennis shoes covered in Italian landmarks and words like *Ciao* and *Bella*. "How about these? We just need to find your size."

"I thought we just needed a place to lay low for a bit before we were flown out," she whispered, continuing the conversation.

He met her gaze. "I like to be prepared for all contingencies. I doubt anything will happen, but we should always be careful."

"I can't wait until this is over and I'm back at home," she muttered.

Buck sympathized with her. She was an ordinary citizen who had tried to do the right thing and was now caught up in a dangerous situation—one where she could lose her life.

So far, nothing she'd said had differed from what he'd

seen in the top secret file or what Randolph at the embassy had told him about her. If she was lying, she was good at it. But he didn't believe she was lying.

He believed what she'd said about Josie too. He couldn't think of a single reason why she would want to kill her roommate—unless Zaire was jealous of her, but she didn't give off that impression. When she spoke about Josie, admiration filled her voice, not envy or dislike. She clearly wanted to be more like her friend.

"The shoes," he said pointedly.

"I'd like to keep my shoes." Her shoulders squared.

"Why?"

"Because I do."

Buck stared at her and watched her throat move as she swallowed. Using two strides, he closed the space between them and backed her up against the wall. "You're getting another pair of shoes. That's nonnegotiable."

She glared at him. "Yes, sir."

If she thought being a smart aleck would bother him, she had another think coming.

A salesperson helped them get her correct size, and then they walked up to the register and got in line behind two other customers.

"Buck, look," Zaire whispered.

The news was on a TV behind the counter. He couldn't hear what the newscaster was saying, but the video on the screen displayed the chaotic scene in front of Zaire's apartment. The street looked like a war zone—broken glass and metal shards littering the ground, a crowd of onlookers behind police tape holding up phones to record the damage for their personal video collection.

One SUV was riddled with bullet holes, with the driver's-side door hanging open. Most of its windows were shattered, and smoke rose from both vehicles, adding to the grim picture of carnage.

The surrounding buildings and cars, including the sedan Buck had driven, also bore the scars of the attack—broken windows, bullet holes, flat tires.

The camera panned over to the lifeless body of one of the guards covered by a white sheet, with a black boot visible. A brief sweep of the camera's lens also showed the blurred images of one member of the convoy lying across the front of the sedan and others laid out in the street.

"What does the ticker say at the bottom?" Buck asked.

Zaire swallowed. "'Live update: Violent attack in central Rome leaves multiple casualties. Authorities searching for suspects.'"

When they reached the counter, Buck took the items from her hand and laid them next to his. He pulled out some euros and paid, noting his dwindling cash. Luckily, they wouldn't be in the country much longer.

They left the shop in silence.

"We'll change in the McDonald's, and then we need to take a trip."

"Where?" Zaire asked.

"To Zigna. You said visitors have to sign in, right?"

"Yes."

"Then we need to find out who signed in the day you overheard the conversation."

Chapter 12

Feeling very much like a tourist now that she had on her souvenir shirt and baseball cap with the Italian flag on front, Zaire watched the Zigna building from the shadows in an alley across the street.

During the day, the area was busy, but tonight it was quiet, with only the occasional car passing by. The first floor was filled with light, and she clearly saw that no one was manning the front desk where visitors stopped during normal business hours.

Most of the windows on the second floor—where staff offices were located—were dark. Light shone from two of them, and she saw one person she recognized working at his desk. Paul. Otherwise, she didn't see any activity evident in the building.

Zaire shifted her focus to across the street, where Buck perfectly blended into the darkness. He had started out on this side with her, his gaze scouring one corner to the next, checking for movement in the windows and doorways of other buildings.

From her position, he was barely visible. In fact, she wouldn't have noticed him had she not seen him go over there to view the street from another angle, to make sure no one was watching the building, lying in wait for them.

The very thought made her queasy. Knowing that some-one—or more than one someone—could be hiding and wait-ing for the chance to pounce. What made this whole situation crazy was that she didn't know much. The men she'd over-heard hadn't revealed where the next bombing would take place, and she hadn't seen their faces. She certainly couldn't pick them out in a lineup. They were both white, one dark hair, and she thought one of them might have been bald, like the guy who chased them to the Colosseum. That was the best she could do if pressed.

Buck jogged over, looking sexy as all get-out. So sexy, she had to lick her dry lips. Two women at the souvenir store couldn't keep their eyes off him. Not that she could blame them. He had stood out among the other patrons. Tall and good-looking, with rugged sexiness.

Did he have any idea how women regularly turned and looked at him, or had he become oblivious to the attention over the years? She'd noticed women checking him out at the McDonald's, too, but he seemed unaware, as if they were invisible.

But it was a waste of time, being attracted to him, partic-ularly in their predicament. In less than twenty-four hours, they would go their separate ways and never see each other again.

Despite the dangerous and chaotic experience of the day, the thought of never seeing him again filled her with mo-mentary sadness.

Get a grip, Zaire, she scolded herself.

"I guess you didn't see anything?" she asked.

Buck shook his head. He had pulled the bill of the cap low on his forehead, creating a shadow over his eyes.

"Should we go in now?" she asked.

"Let's do it."

They crossed the street side by side and Zaire entered before him.

"The visitors' log was right here," she said, pointing at the clean surface of the reception desk.

She hadn't considered that the log would be put up at night.

"It must be here somewhere. Probably in one of the drawers." Buck walked around to the other side of the desk.

Her eyes darted to the front of the building, where the wall of glass offered a view of the street and anyone approaching from outside.

Buck pulled at the middle drawer.

Locked.

He then yanked open the smaller drawer to the left.

Nothing but pens, paper and the usual office supplies.

He opened the second drawer.

More office supplies.

The last one—empty.

Buck pulled on the wide middle drawer again. "How much do you want to bet it's in here?"

"It's locked, though," Zaire said, feeling defeated. The answer to all the questions was probably right there, but they couldn't access it.

"Not for long. I need something to jimmy the lock open." His eyes cast about for an object to do just that.

"You want us to break in?" Zaire asked in an uneasy whisper.

"You have a better idea?" He arched a blond eyebrow at her.

She didn't, but she also didn't like the idea of breaking into the desk.

Buck opened the top-left drawer again and rummaged under the supplies.

"This should work." He held up a letter opener and sounded as if he was talking more to himself than her.

Zaire cast another quick glance at the wall of windows, hoping no one would come along right then and catch them. She didn't know what explanation she'd give for what they were doing.

Buck inserted the letter opener between the top of the desk and the drawer. Using the heel of his hand like a hammer, he gave the end of the handle two hard taps. Then he grabbed the drawer and pulled. It popped open, and inside was the leather-bound guest book.

Zaire had never been so happy to see a book before in her life, and she was an avid reader. She didn't realize how anxious she'd been until right then. She grinned with relief as Buck placed it on the desk. They'd finally have some answers.

"We need to go back to Monday," Buck said, flipping open the book.

Zaire peeked at the book upside down.

"What are you doing?" a male voice asked.

Buck looked up and Zaire spun around.

"Paul, I didn't know you were here," Zaire lied, clutching her chest.

"I'm working late."

Originally from the UK, Paul wore his hair in a classic rounded Afro, and tonight his attire consisted of a button-down shirt and tie.

His gaze flicked to Buck, then the book, then back to Zaire. "So…what's going on?" he said slowly, suspicion filling his dark eyes.

"We're looking for something," Buck answered, sounding antagonistic and acting as if he didn't want to be bothered.

"What are you looking for?"

Zaire responded this time. "We need to find out the names of every person who visited your office on Monday."

He frowned. "Does this have anything to do with Josie being murdered?"

Buck rose to his feet. "What do you know about that?"

"Nothing," Paul answered quickly, stepping back as he stared up at the larger man. "Except, well, what they told us, which included that…the police are looking for *you*. Quite a surprise, because I thought *you* were Josie."

His eyes landed on Zaire, and her throat tightened.

"Your name is Zaire," he said.

"Yes."

"Why did you tell us you were Josie?" Paul asked.

"I was filling in for her," Zaire explained carefully. "Who said the police are looking for me?"

"Harry and Margo," Paul answered.

Harry and Margo were the managing directors of the office.

"I didn't kill Josie. She was my friend," Zaire said.

"Good heavens, I never suggested any such thing! I only met you the other day, but I don't think you're capable of murder, Zaire—but do you know what happened to her or why?"

She relaxed and shook her head. "I was at the US embassy earlier today. I didn't even know she was dead until one of the officials told me. We—Buck and I—went to my apartment to get my things for a trip back to the States, and I saw the blood in the kitchen. It was awful." She shivered.

"You're going back to the States?" Paul asked, a surprising amount of alarm in his voice.

Zaire nodded. Was Paul interested in her? She hadn't picked up on it when she subbed for Josie.

Buck cleared his throat, and she fully understood the signal. He didn't want her to share too much with Paul. He probably didn't trust Paul, though he hardly seemed the type to be involved with assassins. But looks could be deceiving...

"There's a lot going on that I can't explain. I can't tell you much more except that I need to see who came to Zigna on Monday," she said.

Paul took another look at Buck, who kept an impassive expression on his face. Then, as if he'd come to a private decision, Paul nodded his head. "Go ahead."

Buck flipped to Monday's log and dragged his finger down each line. He stopped near the bottom of the page, and Zaire gasped.

Two of the lines had been blacked out so the visitor names and company could not be read, but the column for *New Client* had check marks.

"That must be them," she said.

She saw where she had signed in and read the names of the other visitors—two women and three other men from three separate companies.

"Why would someone black out the visitor names?" Paul asked, his brow creasing in confusion.

"Because they don't want a record of their visit," Buck replied.

"Now we'll never know who came here," Zaire said, feeling defeated. She thought for sure they'd get answers.

Paul held up a finger. "Not necessarily. It's possible Nico would remember. It wouldn't hurt to ask him."

"Nico is the front desk greeter," Zaire explained for Buck's benefit. "If he doesn't remember, maybe Margo or Harry would, you think? One of them probably met with the guests if their company is a new client."

"Harry wasn't here on Monday, and yesterday Margo left town. Family emergency. An email HR sent out said she'd be back in a few days," Paul explained. "Nico should be here tomorrow, though, and I can inquire about the visitors then, see if he remembers. How can I reach you when I find out?"

Buck interjected. "We don't have a phone at the moment. Give us your number, and we'll get in touch with you first thing in the morning."

Paul wrote his number on a piece of paper and handed it to Zaire. "I can't believe you're going back to America. I thought about contacting Worldwide Language Solutions to find you and see if you'd like to grab a coffee some time," he said a little shyly.

Zaire blushed. She hadn't paid much attention to Paul when she worked there, but apparently he'd noticed her. "Thank you. That would be nice, if I were staying. I, um, I appreciate your help, Paul."

"Any time. Where are you going now?"

Zaire glanced at Buck. "We don't know yet."

"Take care of yourself." He looked like he was about to say more but then seemed to think better of it, pressing his lips together.

"We need to go," Buck said, a hard note in his voice.

Zaire finger-waved at Paul and followed Buck out of the building and into the street.

"How well do you know good ole Paul?" Buck asked.

There was an odd note to his voice that Zaire didn't recognize.

"Not well. He was friendly and helpful the day I worked at Zigna. He's lived in Rome longer than me and Josie, and he recommended a couple of lesser known restaurants that he suggested I visit. If I were staying in the country, he'd be a good source of information."

Pain arched through her when she realized she'd spoken about Josie as if she were still alive. Her friend was dead. She still couldn't believe it.

"He wants to be more than a source of information." Buck cast a sidelong glance at her.

"I don't know anything about that. *I* only see *him* as a potential friend," Zaire said.

They walked in silence for a minute. "What do you think about the names being blocked out? Could someone at Zigna be involved?"

"Possibly, but maybe the men you overheard did it after you got away. It was easy enough to break into the desk. They probably did the same thing we did, found the lines with their company name and scratched them out."

"We have to figure out who these people are. Not only because of the embassy but because we need justice for Josie."

"Don't worry, we'll find them soon enough. They can't hide forever."

"Where are we going?" Zaire asked.

"Someplace where we can rest for the night."

"Where is that?"

"Testaccio."

Chapter 13

The CIA operated safe houses so agents in the field could have inconspicuous locations to conduct agency operations. Some were special facilities with interrogation rooms and advanced technological equipment. Others were basic, more or less a stopover that contained the essentials for anyone who needed them. The property in Testaccio was the latter, and Buck hoped it was available.

Testaccio was a working-class neighborhood in the city's historic center that offered a slice of authentic Roman life, known for its old slaughterhouse—now an art museum—and chic restaurants serving traditional Italian dishes.

Buck took advantage of Rome's walkability and set out for the district on foot, making sure to keep a slower pace than he normally would so Zaire could keep up. She didn't say much as they walked, simply followed his lead. The stress of the past couple of days had probably started to weigh on her.

He had to admit to being impressed by her tenacity thus far. Other than the moment when she'd fallen and seemed about to give up, she'd been a trouper during this entire ordeal.

The vibrant culture of Testaccio could be seen in the colorful street art and the sounds of revelry spilling from the bars and restaurants. They passed by an older man playing an accordion on the corner, the melodic sounds serenading the tourists and locals as they strolled the cobblestone streets.

Zaire and Buck made their way between two buildings that opened up into a small plaza and stood in front of a modest fountain with water dribbling from an urn held by a cherub. Three teenagers loitered nearby, their boisterous conversation punctuated by laughter and the clack of skateboards on the stone surface of the ground.

"Which one is it?" Zaire asked.

"Second from the left."

Most of the apartments had their lights on, and of the ones that didn't, the windows were open to allow in natural air-conditioning. The one he pointed out was dark and unusually still, with a closed window and a plant box hanging from the sill with plants dried up and dead from neglect.

Buck's eyes swept the area before he started toward the front door of the building and climbed the dark stairs to the third-floor apartment. When he pulled out the letter opener, Zaire's eyebrows shifted higher.

"I didn't know you took that."

"Figured we might need it. Keep an eye out," he said, though he wouldn't need long.

He crouched in front of the doorknob and shimmied the metal wedge between the frame and the door. With a quick shove at the same time he turned the knob, the lock popped. Pushing his way inside, he listened for movement. He didn't think anyone was there, but he couldn't be too careful. As he wasn't in Rome on official business and hadn't been granted use of the apartment, he could be interrupting the work of other agents in the field.

"Hello?" he called out.

Hearing nothing, he ushered Zaire inside with him.

He'd already guessed the safe house hadn't been in use

for months, but the musty staleness of the air confirmed it. He turned on the light and walked deeper into the room. Dust covered wooden surfaces, and a sofa and chairs were arranged in a horseshoe around a wall-mounted television. He went down the hall and checked the other rooms. The place wasn't very big—containing one bedroom with a full-size bed, a bathroom, and a smaller bedroom set up like an office with a desk and lamp.

He returned to the living room in time to see Zaire remove her bag and place it on the arm of the sofa.

Buck crossed the floor to the window looking out onto the square below. The boys continued to play with their skateboards. Across the way, an old man sat outside a café, drinking coffee with a small dog on a leash at his feet.

He cracked the window to let in fresh air. "This should do for the night. There's only one bed, so I'll sleep out here."

Zaire eyed the sofa. "That's not big enough. I can sleep out here and you take the bed."

He shook his head. "Not gonna happen."

"But you're bigger than I am. That's going to be uncomfortable."

"It's nothing compared to some of the places I've slept in the past."

She fell silent, a frown creasing her brow.

"It's not a problem," he assured her.

"Well, if you're sure…"

"I'm sure. We should take advantage of the opportunity to freshen up and get some sleep. If my commander calls with details about an earlier flight, we need to be ready to go."

She nodded. "It'll be nice to take a shower."

"Then take one. I plan to."

"Okay," she said, sounding as though she was warming up to the idea.

"Check the closet in the bedroom. There might be clothes in there you can sleep in."

"Okay. I won't be long."

She left the room, and Buck sank onto the sofa.

He squeezed the cushions to test them. Firm and comfy enough for a good night's sleep. He should be fine here, though his legs would be hanging off the edge.

Hunched forward, elbows on his knees, he reviewed the day's events in his head. These terrorists had found him and Zaire at her apartment and murdered their escorts. They'd murdered the pilot. They'd chased them through the streets of Rome. They'd deleted proof of their visit to Zigna. Whoever they were, they were thorough and well-connected.

He stared at the far wall, eyes locking on the cheap knock-off of Van Gogh's *Sunflowers* hanging in a frame.

Could there have been a leak at the embassy?

Randolph had not been happy about him taking Zaire, as he considered her a suspect in her roommate's murder. Not finding the recording on her person didn't help. But Buck couldn't see the guy leaking the information to terrorists. There was also the other official Zaire had mentioned— Heidi, whom he hadn't met. Could she have leaked their information?

Buck shook his head. None of it made sense, but that didn't mean it wasn't possible. They could be on the terrorists' payroll. Or there could have been someone else at the embassy who had leaked the information. They could have planted a tracker on Zaire's phone so that when he and she left—

His thoughts screeched to a halt at the sound of running water. Zaire was in the shower.

Naked.

Soapsuds and water running down her body.

Buck shook his head and shoved to his feet. She was absolutely not his type and asked too many questions.

So why did his body temperature suddenly increase by fifty degrees? And why did he have an almost violent response to the attention she'd received from good ole Paul? He'd been ready to choke him out where he stood.

"I can't believe you're going back to America."

Buck blew out a puff of frustrated air.

His attraction to Zaire was a problem for two reasons. One, he'd sworn off women for the foreseeable future. They were a complication he didn't need. Two, he never, *ever* got involved with women while on a mission. It created challenges that could affect decision-making—a major problem when making a split-second choice could mean the difference between life and death.

He opened the window wider and let in more of the night's cool air. Music floated in from somewhere nearby. He heard laughter and the occasional clink of glasses as diners enjoyed late-night drinks at one of the trattorias, the enticing aroma of garlic and rosemary making his mouth water.

Was there any food in this place?

He checked the refrigerator and found an unopened bottle of red wine, moldy cheese and questionable-looking salami. The cabinets contained a couple bags of dried linguine and canned vegetables, including chickpeas and tomatoes. He checked the expiration dates. None of them had expired, so they were an option for a simple dinner. He placed the items on the counter.

The shower stopped.

He waited, tense, ears cocked for the sound of movement.

Moments later, the door opened, and the pounding of his heart beat as loud as a bass drum. He had to get rid of the inappropriate thoughts about Zaire. She was under his care.

He walked down the short, dim hall and was about to go through the open bathroom door when the bedroom door suddenly opened.

"Oh!" Zaire froze and her eyes widened with surprise.

Buck froze too. And he stared.

The pale yellow towel highlighted the richness of her dark brown skin, which carried a dewy sheen from her shower. His gaze drifted down the length of her body, and his dick hardened at the thought that she was completely and utterly naked under the towel.

He didn't need this. They were in the middle of a danger-ous situation, and he was supposed to protect her.

"I found food in the cabinets," he said, hardly recogniz-ing the strangled sound of his voice.

"That's good." Zaire cleared her throat before continuing. "I was feeling kind of hungry, especially after we passed a couple of restaurants where I could smell the food. This area is known for its restaurants. I never got the chance to visit before, but it was on my list of places to check out before I return to the States. Did you know there's a non-Catholic cemetery in this neighborhood and English Romantic poets John Keats and Percy Bysshe Shelley are buried there?"

He almost laughed. "No, I—"

"*Testaccio* means *Monte Testaccio* or *mount of shards*. That's because of the hill made of broken terra-cotta ves-sels used to transport olive oil. They estimate that there are millions of fragments that make up the mound, which is one hundred and fifteen feet tall."

He stared at her. She stared at him. Now that they were in a safe location and didn't have fear and worry to distract them, an odd energy had emerged between them.

Zaire bit the corner of her lip.

"Thank you for that information," Buck said in a thick voice.

"I need to get my clothes from in there." She pointed at the bathroom. Without waiting for him to respond, she ducked into the bathroom, came out seconds later and didn't give him another look before she quickly shut the door to the bedroom.

As if she knew another kind of danger had entered her life.

Chapter 14

They ate dinner at a small table in the corner of the living room. The food was very basic: chickpeas in a tomato sauce served over a bed of linguine.

There were no fresh herbs to flavor the dish, but Buck had stirred in some wine and they'd lucked out and found dried basil on a shelf in the cabinet, recently expired—but it still had some flavor.

The combination of wine and the herb helped, but as meals went, it was high on the list of one of the most tasteless dinners Zaire had ever had the displeasure of eating. By the end, however, she had a full belly and at least wouldn't have to go to bed hungry.

They washed the dishes and cleaned the kitchen. After drinking two glasses of wine, Zaire had a slight buzz and hoped it would help her have a restful sleep.

"What time should we call Paul in the morning?" she asked, watching Buck make his bed with blankets and a pillow.

She still felt guilty about him sleeping out here on a sofa that was obviously too short for his long body.

"What time does their office open?"

"Nine."

"A little after nine, then. Hopefully, he'll talk to Nico right away." He placed the pillow at the end of the sofa so he was facing the door as he lay down.

Zaire watched him, wanting to ask a question about a comment he'd made earlier in the day.

"Was there something else?" Buck asked.

"Actually, there is. Why don't you like Rome? You said you probably wanted to get out of here even more than I do. It's a beautiful city with a rich history and great food. What's not to like?"

Sitting on the sofa, he tugged off one of his shoes. "Why are you so nosy?"

"I'm not being nosy. I'm curious."

"You ask too many questions."

"You've asked plenty yourself—and by the way, there's no such thing as asking too many questions. That's something rude people say to shut up people they don't want to answer because they're either hiding something or don't know the answer to a question." She folded her arms over her chest.

He removed his other shoe. "You should go to bed."

"You're really not going to tell me?"

"You're a stranger."

"I'm hardly a stranger, at least at this point. Besides, it's obvious you need to talk. I can see it in your eyes."

He rose to his full height, tension tightening his body into a rigid mass of muscle. "Even if I needed to talk, why would I talk to you? Why do you think I'd want to divulge my secrets to you? *Go to bed.*"

His tone aggravated her. It was fine if he didn't want to talk, but he didn't have to be so rude.

"I know exactly what you're doing, but do you know what you're doing? Running and hiding from your problems. The big bad action hero is afraid of his *feelings*. You're not so brave after all, are you?"

Zaire didn't know why she was taunting him.

Buck's eyes narrowed. "What did you say?"

"You heard me." She tilted her chin higher.

"You have a smart mouth."

"Thank you."

He stared at her in disbelief. "That wasn't a compliment."

"I know. I said that to annoy you."

He let out a humorless laugh. "You're good at annoying people. Maybe that's the real reason you don't hang out with anyone. Because deep down you know you're annoying as hell with all your random facts. Nobody wants to hear about the use of toilet paper in ancient Greece!"

"Toilet paper was not available in ancient Greece. The first documented use of toilet paper was in China, sixth century AD," Zaire muttered.

"That's what I'm talking about," he said, jabbing a finger at her. "Useless information."

His words hit at the heart of her insecurities. Boring old Zaire who shares useless facts with people. Why would anyone want to spend time with her?

She squared her shoulders. "Point made. But for the record, I was trying to be nice because I thought you might need someone to talk to. You barely said a word during dinner."

"Because I was thinking about our situation. We have to figure out how to get to whatever location we're flying out of tomorrow, and we don't have any form of transportation and very little money. I don't know what's going on inside your head, but that's what's going on inside mine."

"Understood, Buck. Just know that it's not good to bottle up your feelings. It causes stress, and stress can cause serious harm to your physical and mental health. I won't quote you any statistics, because I'm sure you don't want to hear anymore useless information. Good night."

Zaire was almost out of the room when Buck's voice halted her.

"I got hurt."

She paused. Had she heard him correctly? As she turned, her gaze connected with his. "Hurt?"

"Not physically," he said, his voice sounding tight and dropping an octave. He spoke in such a low voice that she wasn't sure she'd heard him correctly.

What he said sounded odd to her ears, and she realized she'd made an assumption in her head about what was bothering him. The pain the big bad action hero was experiencing had to have been caused by his work—right? Maybe not.

"Do you want to hear this or not?" Buck asked, clearly mistaking her silence for disinterest.

"I want to hear it!" Zaire sat in an armchair.

"I can't believe I'm doing this," he muttered, dropping into the chair across from her.

She didn't say a word because she didn't want him to change his mind. Silence filled the room, dragging on for a long time before he finally spoke.

"Three years ago I had a bad experience in Rome and promised myself I'd never return. I planned an engagement trip for me and my girlfriend at the time."

"Interesting. I don't see you as the romantic type."

"I'm not. But it was something I was willing to do for her. We had been together for about a year and a half, and she had mentioned on more than one occasion that she wanted to visit Italy. So I planned an elaborate two-week vacation for us. Since I'd been here for work before, I knew my way around. We had a great time, and I assumed we were on the same page. Two days before we were supposed to return to DC, I asked her to marry me."

"Wow." That sounded romantic, but Zaire could tell his proposal hadn't gone well.

"Yeah," Buck said in a deadpan voice, obvious tension in his body.

"It didn't go well, did it?" Zaire asked in a gentle voice.

"Not at all. She turned me down, said that she couldn't be with someone who had killed people."

Her mouth fell open. "You're kidding. It's not like you're a serial killer."

A faint smile lifted the corners of his lips. "Didn't matter. Her stance surprised me because she worked in Homeland Security, so she was very much aware of my...skill set before we became serious. Matter of fact, I saw her career as a plus because I didn't think a woman in a different field of work could understand what I did."

"Why did she stay with you if she couldn't tolerate what you did?"

"That's the question I never received an answer to."

Zaire fell silent for a moment. "She was a fool. You're a handsome, sexy guy. Your personality needs a little work, but you seem like a decent human being—except for when you were a jerk a few minutes ago."

"Wow, never had someone insult me quite so eloquently," Buck said sarcastically.

"Sorry, I shouldn't have done that. You opened up, and I—"

"You're fine. I *was* a jerk." He leaned back, his gaze traveling over her in an assessing way, as if seeing her for the first time. "You don't have much of a filter, do you?"

Zaire shifted in the chair. "I have one, but sometimes I forget to use it. Something else people don't like about me."

"Something else?"

"As you pointed out, reciting facts doesn't exactly make me the life of the party."

"You'd be great in those trivia games they always play at bars."

"If I got invited to any."

Silence once again filled the room, during which Zaire refused to look at him and kept her eyes focused on the colorful pattern in the sofa's upholstery. Man, she sounded pathetic.

"I don't want you to think I have no friends. I do have friends, but I admit to rubbing some people the wrong way." She tugged at a loose thread on the chair's armrest. "Sunday night I didn't get invited to go out with my coworkers. People either like me or they don't, and one of the people Josie was going out with from the office was a girl who doesn't like me, and I wasn't about to push myself on them. Josie offered to cancel and said she and I could go out together instead, but I wouldn't let her. I told her I'd promised to call my parents and afterward was going to curl up with a new book."

"Which wasn't true?"

"It was, sorta. I did end up calling my parents and found a new book to read. So the evening wasn't totally bad."

"How do you know the other girl didn't like you?"

"She called me Jeopardy—you know, like the game show—behind my back. And not in a good way."

Buck laughed.

"Really? You're laughing at me?" Zaire glared at him.

"My turn to apologize, but you do know a lot." He smiled.

"I read a lot. I've always had an inquisitive mind and like to share what I learn." Zaire shrugged.

"That's a good thing—but it *can* be annoying at times."

"Gee, thanks."

He chuckled again, and she liked the sound. Liked even

more that she was the reason for him making it, though it was at her expense.

"I was going to say, if you let me finish—that yes, your chatter can be annoying at times, but knowledge is a good trait to have. One of these days all that information might come in handy."

"Like in a trivia game?"

"Hey, you never know."

They smiled at each other. Genuinely, for the first time since they'd met.

"I meant what I said, Buck. It's her loss. There's someone out there for each of us, and your fiancée not accepting your proposal cleared the way for the right woman to come along."

In the silence, his gaze scrolled over her, more slowly this time. Heat scraped her skin, a reminder that not only was she attracted to this man, but they were also alone together in the apartment.

"You really believe that?" he asked, his voice sounding low again.

"Of course I do. You just haven't found your person yet. But she's out there."

"What about you, Zaire?" He held her gaze, his blue eyes probing, making her heart flutter.

She cleared her throat. "Me? Oh, there's someone out there for an oddball like me too."

He smiled. "I don't think you're so odd. A bit chatty, but not odd."

Her pulse skipped. She was too excited by his backhanded compliment.

She stood abruptly, needing to get away from him and her percolating attraction. "Thanks, I think. Have a good night, Buck."

The smile hadn't left his lips. "You, too, Zaire."

Chapter 15

Zaire stripped down to her T-shirt and removed her bra, then folded it and her jeans and placed them atop the bureau in the room.

She climbed into bed and lay on her back, staring up at the ceiling, and reflected. It had been a long, arduous day where a lot had happened. Josie was dead, and she was on the run from assassins.

How was this her life? She had wanted more excitement, but sheesh—this was way more dangerous and outrageous than she had wanted or expected.

Should she give Buck the recording from Zigna? Almost immediately, she decided the answer was no. Not yet, anyway. When she was safely back on US soil, she'd hand it over to the government and let them figure out the details. She had to stay positive that she'd have that opportunity.

Turning onto her side, she fought the rise of fear that threatened to consume her in the dark. She didn't want anyone else to die. *She* didn't want to die. She wanted to see her parents again, and her friends back in Atlanta.

"God, please let everything work out," she whispered. She yawned and closed her eyes, letting sleep pull her under.

It seemed like only seconds later that someone was calling her name, as if from a distance.

"Zaire, wake up. Zaire."

The voice was familiar. Male. He was shaking her shoulder.

She opened her eyes and saw Buck in the ambient light. Blinking, she tried to focus. He stood next to the full-size bed, shirtless and wearing only boxers. Hair covered his chest and arrowed down below the waistband of his underwear. Shadows filled the carved lines of his six-pack, and his biceps appeared larger without the covering of a shirt.

Her stomach did a complete somersault.

"You were crying and talking in your sleep. I could hear you in the living room," he said.

"I was?"

"Yes. You kept saying, 'I'm sorry.'"

Zaire sat up and wiped sleep from her eyes, surprised to find her cheeks wet.

"Are you going to be all right?" Buck asked with deep concern in his voice.

"I..."

Her voice quivered and her lower lip trembled. She didn't know where the emotion was coming from, but she suddenly had the urgent need to cry—to expel pent-up emotion that had banked inside her over the past few days.

"I don't know," she whispered, her voice shaking.

Then she covered her face and burst into tears.

"Hey..." Buck climbed onto the bed and pulled her against his warm chest.

He rolled onto his back, his arms a comforting cocoon of muscle that promised to keep her safe from harm. Each breath she took was filled with the clean scent of him, and as the seconds ticked by, she calmed against the steady rise and fall of his chest.

"It's going to be okay." Buck's voice was low, warm and reassuring.

Zaire clung to him and buried her face in his neck. He continued talking to her, whispering soothing words to put her mind at ease.

"I'm sorry. I'm such a bumbling mess," Zaire apologized.

"No need to apologize, and you're not a mess. Your reaction is normal. I'm surprised you didn't crack sooner. I was wondering when it would happen."

Zaire wiped away the tears from her eyes and looked at him in the dark. "You expected this?"

"You've been through a lot. Chased by two men, almost run over, shot at… This isn't normal. Anyone would fall apart, but you've held it together all this time. You're tougher than you think."

Since he had taken the second pillow out to the living room, they shared a single pillow, their faces close together in the darkness—close enough to kiss.

"What were you dreaming about?" Buck asked.

For a moment, she couldn't remember—dreams were funny like that. But then the video in her mind slowly came back.

"My funeral," she answered in a tight voice. "Then Josie's. The dream was strange. One minute I was looking at myself in the casket, the next minute I was looking at Josie."

Buck brushed a stray strand of hair from her forehead. "You're not going to die," he said.

"You can't guarantee that."

"No, but I can guarantee that I'll do my best to keep you safe, and I can tell you I've never lost anyone I was assigned to protect."

"Never?"

"Not one."

"That does make me feel better," Zaire said quietly.

They lay there in silence for a moment, her fingers spread across his chest, the soft hairs tickling her palms. His arm was thrown over her waist, and she suddenly became very aware that all she was wearing was a T-shirt and panties. They were both half-naked, and because of his size, Buck took up most of the bed.

She shifted, and her leg came into contact with his—muscular, hard and sprinkled with hair like his chest. The contrast to the smoothness of her legs stirred arousal in her loins. Buck was so very male, and they were lying here in bed together in the middle of the night. Was it any surprise that her nipples ached for the touch of his hands and the inside of her thighs longed for the slide of his hair-roughened leg?

"Tell me about your life in Atlanta," Buck said, in an obvious attempt to distract her.

He was trying to comfort her—but little did he know, she wanted him to roll her onto her back and climb on top of her.

"There's not much to tell. My life is pretty quiet. I go to work and go home most nights."

"What do you do on the weekends?"

"Spend time with my family—my parents, mostly. My mother and I like to go to yard sales and flea markets to find deals. When I go out with friends, it's usually to the movies or out to dinner—nothing exciting."

"Tell me about your family," he said.

He sounded genuinely interested, which made sharing easy.

"I'm an only child, and my parents are *very* protective, even at my big age. If they knew what I was going through here, they would be *sick*."

"Protective how?" Buck asked.

She let out a heavy breath. "I didn't get to do much growing up because they were always worried about me getting hurt or something bad happening to me. As long as I was with them, though, they didn't worry. One cool thing about my parents, they love to travel, and we travel together all the time. It started when I was a child, taking extended trips overseas. They believe we should immerse ourselves in a culture, so we'd always spend months at a time in one location. That's how I developed a love for languages."

"What are some of your favorite things about those trips with your parents?"

Zaire thought for a moment. "I love sightseeing and learning the history of the places we visit. And, oh my goodness, the food."

"You said that with enthusiasm," Buck said with a hint of playfulness.

"I'm pretty adventurous when it comes to eating."

"Are you?" He sounded surprised.

Zaire nodded. "Oh yeah, I'll try just about anything once."

He frowned, skepticism evident in his eyes, even in the dim interior of the room. "What's the most interesting thing you've eaten in your travels?"

"Hmm… I'd have to say puffer fish in Japan."

"Isn't that the fish that can kill you if you don't cook it properly?"

"That's the one."

He stared at her in disbelief, and she giggled, enjoying his shock.

"It has to be prepared by highly trained chefs because puffer fish—or fugu, as it's called in Japan—contains lethal amounts of toxins that can kill you if it's not properly cleaned."

"And you *ate* that?" Buck asked, sounding alarmed.

She giggled again. "Yes, I did."

"Your parents aren't as protective as you think if they allowed you to eat that."

"I was traveling with them, remember? It was a family affair. They had puffer fish too. We just considered it part of the adventure."

"Or maybe you all have a death wish."

"Says the man who dodges bullets for a living."

"Touché. What else have you eaten that was exotic?"

Zaire pondered the question. "In Scotland, I had haggis, the national dish."

"What's that?"

"It's a pudding made from a sheep's liver, heart and lungs."

He stared at her. "Tell me you're kidding."

"I'm not kidding."

Buck shook his head, laughter in his eyes. "I was right."

"About what?"

"That you're tougher than you think, and you're going to be just fine."

The compliment warmed her insides, and because he said it, she wanted to be exactly what he said—tough. Fine. She could handle whatever came at them, as long as he was by her side.

"Thank you, Buck."

"For what?"

"For saving me today. For…everything."

If not for his bravery—risking his own life to protect hers—she'd be dead.

"You don't have to thank me—but you're welcome."

She smiled at him and closed her eyes.

He stroked her hair and kissed her forehead. She wished he'd kiss her lips, but that was almost as good.

Sighing, she snuggled closer, feeling safe and content.

Chapter 16

The following morning, Zaire awoke to a slightly disorienting feeling. Her eyes fluttered open and focused on the strange room.

She bolted upright.

Where am I?

Then she remembered that she was in a barely used CIA safe house with Buck Swanson, the man charged with taking her safely back to the United States. The very sexy man who had held her while she cried last night, overcome with grief and exhaustion. Being in his strong arms, she had felt safe and secure, and he had shown a gentleness that she appreciated.

She lay back down, and her nose picked up a pleasing scent. She turned her face into the pillow and breathed in the oatmeal-scented soap she and Buck had used last night. Underneath that she also caught the earthy tang of his skin.

Her body came alive, her nipples aching and a dull throb emerging between her thighs.

With a groan, she rolled into a sitting position. She couldn't allow herself to be distracted by sexual desire. She hadn't been with a man in over a year, and her last encounter had been mediocre at best.

"Buck wouldn't be mediocre," she muttered to herself.

He'd know where to put it and how to work it, and probably make her beg for more.

Zaire dressed in her clothes from the day before and applied lip gloss before going into the living room. Buck was already out there, and for at least the hundredth time, she thought about what a sexy man he was and wondered how his fiancée could have walked away from him.

"Sleep okay?" he asked, rising from the sofa.

"Yes, thank you." She stood awkwardly, unsure how last night had affected their relationship.

"Good. I thought we could get breakfast before we call Paul."

So they were going to act like last night hadn't happened? Okay, she could do that.

"Sounds good. I'm starving."

Buck insisted they wear their caps, and with Zaire's black bag and their casual clothes, they should easily blend in with the tourists.

They chose to eat at a small restaurant not too far from the apartment. Ever vigilant, they didn't sit outside on the sidewalk but stayed inside at the back. Relieved to have decent food to eat, Zaire opted for a typical Roman breakfast of *cornetto*, a pastry shaped like a croissant, stuffed with cream and accompanied by an espresso.

Buck ordered two *ciambella*, fried dough similar to a doughnut and covered in sugar crystals, and *maritozzo*, a bread-like pastry cut open lengthwise and filled with whipped cream. He also had an espresso.

While they ate, he explained that he hadn't received any messages from Benjamin, and because of the time difference, he'd refrained from reaching out about the status of their transportation out of the country.

"We have to be patient," he told Zaire, which wasn't easy. She was ready to leave Rome and didn't want to have to keep hiding and looking over her shoulder.

As they finished their meal, Buck checked the time. "It's ten after nine. Paul should have talked to Nico by now. We should call him."

He didn't wait for her to respond. He stood, and she quickly drained the last of her espresso and hurried after him.

She used to be annoyed at his take-charge attitude, but not anymore. Their conversation and his gentleness with her had allowed her to see another side of Buck, and she had a better understanding of him. He was disciplined and focused, which were good qualities, considering their predicament. He was caring, too, concerned about her well-being. The last thing she needed was someone who was easily distracted and disorderly. In a life-and-death situation, he was exactly the kind of person needed to lead the way.

Back in the apartment, they sat next to each other on the sofa. Sitting so close meant being very aware of Buck's large, muscular body beside hers. She willed herself not to pay attention to his bulging triceps and the thickness of his thighs, but she'd have to be blind not to notice, especially after last night when his bare skin touched hers.

She called Paul and put him on speakerphone.

"Hi, Paul! This is Zaire," she said, greeting him with a lot more exuberance than she felt. Her insides were tense as she wondered what news he had uncovered for them.

"Zaire, hi," Paul said in a subdued voice.

"Did you get a chance to talk to Nico?" she asked.

"No, I didn't," he replied.

Buck's brow puckered. "Why didn't you talk to him?" he asked.

Paul sighed heavily. "Because this morning we found out that Nico is dead."

Zaire's mouth fell open, and she turned to Buck, whose frown deepened.

"What?" she said in a shocked whisper.

"He committed suicide. His wife found him hanging from the ceiling."

The hand Zaire was holding the phone with began to shake. The bodies were piling up.

"The news took all of us by surprise," Paul continued. "I'm sorry, but I can't tell you who could have come to the company on Monday. The only person who can answer that question at the moment is Margo, and she won't return for at least another day. At this rate, I wouldn't be surprised if we receive a message that she died too. Oh, shoot, what am I saying? I'm sorry, I should *not* have said that." Paul sighed again.

Zaire was worried he could be right. These terrorists were efficient at eliminating threats and covering their tracks.

"I know this is a lot to take in, Paul. Thank you for trying to help," she said.

"Not a problem at all. Look, I don't understand everything that's going on, but apparently whatever it is—it's not good. Should I be worried?"

"You have nothing to worry about," Buck interjected.

Paul let out a breath of relief. "That's good to hear, considering two people have died in the past couple of days. Zaire, please be careful. We don't want to lose you too."

Buck stiffened, and Zaire looked at him curiously.

"Thanks, Paul. I will."

"Please keep in touch?" he added, sounding unsure.

"I will. Take care." She hung up.

"He definitely likes you," Buck said.

Zaire hadn't expected him to say that. "I don't think so," she said, feeling self-conscious.

"You're blind if you can't see it," he said in a terse voice.

Why did he sound as if he was angry because Paul was allegedly interested?

"Whatever Paul may or may not feel for me doesn't matter. I'm not interested in him, so…" She shrugged.

Buck pushed to his feet. "I can't believe we hit another dead end."

His abrupt change of topic gave Zaire whiplash, but she kept up.

"Who are these people?" she asked.

He faced her. "I have a hunch, but they're better than I expected. I think they could be related to an anarchist extremist group called the Hammer of Justice."

"Anarchists?"

Zaire knew a little about anarchists, knew that they believed society was better off without government, laws or any other type of authority. The extremists among them used violence to try to orchestrate change.

"I was thinking about it this morning, and for the most part it makes sense. What type of people bomb an embassy, and what message are they trying to relay? No one has claimed responsibility for the attacks in the past year, but here's why I think the Hammer could be responsible. We've had anarchists attack embassies before. In 2007, a group called the Revolutionary Struggle fired an RPG at the US embassy in Athens. In 2018, another set of extremists used guns to attack the US embassy in Ankara, Turkey.

"The Hammer has been on our radar for the past few years, gaining in strength and increasing their numbers by recruiting young people through social media and encrypted chat applications. They're particularly anti-American, believing that the United States has too much power and influence on the rest of the world. Two years ago there was some chatter about them hitting one of our embassies, but nothing came of it—or so we thought. I think they simply went underground and planned every detail until the first strike eight months ago."

Zaire let the words sink in, wondering if she truly could have stumbled upon two of their members at Zigna. "If this group is the one attacking the embassies, what can we do to stop them?"

Gripping the back of his neck, Buck paced the carpeted floor. "It's not easy. They're scattered around Europe and the United States mostly, with members sworn to a code of silence that makes it difficult to infiltrate their ranks and know when and where they'll strike next. Your recording might help."

He stopped moving. "These attacks would have taken years to plan and collect the equipment they needed to carry out the bombings. To be honest, I'm impressed. They have very advanced technology, which is probably how they were able to track you by phone. If I'm right and the culprit is the Hammer of Justice, they're more sophisticated than we knew."

"If they're pulling in younger people, it makes sense that they'd use technology not only to recruit but to carry out their plans," Zaire opined.

"Exactly. Now we have to figure out their motive. Could they have been trying to tell us something in the embassies they chose to attack?"

Zaire pondered the question. Malaysia. Liberia. Was there a common thread? She couldn't think of one.

"Is it possible that striking in those countries was completely random? Because I can't think of anything that ties them together," she said.

"Neither can I," Buck admitted. "Our relationship with Liberia is positive, and so is our relationship with Malaysia."

"Is it possible the second bombing was a copycat?"

"I thought about that, but no. The bombings were done differently. In Liberia, a remote-controlled truck with explosives was driven through the gate. In Malaysia, the explosive device was taken into the building in pieces, assembled and then detonated remotely."

The phone rang, and Zaire glanced down at the screen. *Unknown* popped up.

"I think this is your contact," she said, extending the phone to Buck.

He took it. "Benjamin?"

Zaire watched him as he listened to his commander. A faint smile touched his lips, and he gave her the thumbs-up.

She suddenly felt as if the weight of the world had shifted off her shoulders. Good news. Finally.

"You get us that flight, and we'll make it to the airfield," Buck said with confidence.

He paused and listened.

"Zaire and I were just going over the possibilities, but I don't have any concrete ideas. Just a hunch." He then launched into an explanation about the log book and Nico's alleged suicide.

As Benjamin talked, Buck nodded his head. "I agree, the sooner we figure out the connection between the embassies, the better. There's a connection there that we're missing, that would tell us where the next attack will take place." He paused and locked eyes with Zaire. "Don't worry, getting her safely back to the States is my number one priority."

After several more seconds, he hung up.

"Benjamin has arranged for us to fly out earlier from Trentobene Airfield, an abandoned World War II airfield two hours south of here. He'll have a plane ready and wait-ing for us at one o'clock." He checked the time. "That means we have less than an hour to find a car and hit the road."

Zaire stood immediately, anxious to leave their troubles behind. "I'm ready when you are."

Chapter 17

They left the apartment within minutes of the phone call.

The neighborhood was even busier than when they'd had breakfast, with people crowding around the various stalls at the market. Locals bought from the fishmongers, butchers, and vendors selling fruits and vegetables.

The Hammer of Justice was a large group and could have members all over Rome searching for him and Zaire, so Buck gave a visual sweep of the area, conscious that they were out in the open.

He checked the time.

"We should get food for the road." He pulled out his wallet and examined the cash he had left. He was running low, down to thirty euros and some change. "I have enough to buy sandwiches at one of the stands." He inclined his head to one nearby.

They fell into the line, and he continued assessing their surroundings for threats.

"You're making me nervous. Is something wrong?" Zaire asked.

"Being cautious, that's all. We can't be too careful."

She nodded, eyes scanning the area as well.

With the cap and her jaw set in a firm line, she almost looked capable of tackling anyone who stepped in her way.

She seemed stronger today. Having a good cry had probably helped.

Their talk had helped him. All along he'd been bitter about Lana, but maybe he had been looking at her rejection the wrong way. Maybe she had done him a favor and cleared the way for the right woman to come along, as Zaire had suggested.

He'd forced his last trip with her to the farthest regions of his mind, but now he allowed himself to reflect on that period. How he'd lowered himself to one knee and proposed to the woman he thought he'd spend the rest of his life with, but then she'd told him succinctly and clearly that she couldn't marry him. That she loved him but didn't envision spending her life with someone who had killed people.

That was the first time he'd learned she had an issue with his chosen career path. He'd never forget the embarrassment of gazing up at her and seeing the pity in her eyes. She never gave him the option to leave behind the job he loved. Her answer had simply been *No*.

Lana had chosen to stay in Rome, though she'd complained about the high prices, the heat and the crowds at the tourist hotspots. Humiliated and brokenhearted, he had taken an early flight back to the States, no longer interested in sightseeing tours and dining on delicious pasta dishes.

If he had to do it all over again, he'd much rather come to Rome with someone interested in exploring all the city had to offer. Someone like… Zaire.

Standing in front of him with her blue Italy cap and her ponytail falling between her shoulder blades, he had to admit she'd be the perfect companion. Not one time had he heard her complain about her stay in Rome. She wouldn't mind touring the city and exploring the popular sites as well as the lesser-known areas. She'd revel in it, in fact, because it would mean learning something new.

His gaze slid idly over her charcoal pants and the way they hugged her round derriere. He'd enjoyed holding her last night, her body soft and warm and fitting perfectly against his. His own body had betrayed him, signaling he wanted to do much more than hold her, but common sense had prevailed. Thankfully. He couldn't afford to get distracted when their lives were on the line.

They stepped up to the counter and perused the menu, written in Italian and English. Buck ordered a beef sandwich and then Zaire ordered one filled with veal and artichokes.

He looked at her. "Veal? You know that's a baby cow."

"Yes, I do, thanks." She smiled at the man who took the order.

"Unbelievable," Buck muttered.

"What's unbelievable?" Zaire asked.

"I can't believe how adventurous you are about food."

"Veal is hardly adventurous. Lots of people eat it—but I can't believe how safe you play when it comes to food," Zaire remarked.

Buck shrugged. "I like what I like."

"Yes, the same thing every day. You know, I figured in your line of work you must have had times when you had to eat worms and bugs for protein or risk starving to death."

He chuckled. "Nothing like that has happened yet, thank goodness. If it came to that, I'd do what I have to do, but I wouldn't like it."

The man behind the counter wrapped the sandwiches in white paper and handed them across the counter.

"*Grazie*," they both said.

After paying, they went into a small store, where they bought bottled water and Zaire bought a bag of chips.

Back on the street, she asked, "Where to now?"

"We need to find a car, and I know exactly where we can get one," Buck answered.

He led the way through the crowd to the outskirts of the market, a part of the district that was less crowded.

They stood on the street while Buck took a look at the various vehicles available.

"You're going to steal a car, aren't you?" Zaire asked.

"Do you have a better idea for how we can get a car to meet our flight? And don't you dare say, 'Rent one with a credit card.'"

"I know better than that," Zaire said dryly.

He smiled at her sarcastic response.

"What about that one?" She nodded at a green Fiat.

"Too conspicuous. We need something that won't draw a lot of attention and is easy to overlook even if the owner calls in the theft. We also need an older-model vehicle."

"Because it's easier to hot-wire. New models have the chip in the key fob, which you won't be able to bypass."

Buck shot a look of admiration at her, and she smiled, shrugging one shoulder.

"I know a little something."

He chuckled. "All right, Miss Know-It-All, so which one do you think?" He'd already spotted the vehicle he wanted to take but was curious to see if she'd pick the same car.

"That one. The black Fiat Panda." Zaire let her eyes signal the direction she wanted him to look.

"Good job. That's our ride out of here. Let's hope they have at least two hours' worth of gas in that baby."

Buck handed Zaire his food and jogged across the street to the passenger side of the Fiat. After a quick visual sweep of the street to make sure no one would see him, he removed a wire hanger from his back waistband. He had taken it from the closet at the safe house in anticipation of stealing a car.

He kept his head low so the bill of the cap hid most of his face. Moving quickly, he inserted the trusty letter opener between the door and the frame of the car at the top, using brute strength to pull back the car door as far as possible and wedge the tool in between the space. Then he stretched the wire hanger into one long piece and inserted it between the gap until it hit the power window button. He pushed the window down and then reached in and unlocked the door.

Buck climbed onto the driver's seat. As he did, an older gentleman walked by Zaire with his dog on a leash and nodded at her. She smiled at the man and, after he'd walked past, made eye contact with Buck.

She didn't look scared or worried, which was a good thing.

Buck used the letter opener like a screwdriver and removed the plastic cover that hid the wires below the steering wheel. When he located the frayed ends, he wound them together, using his T-shirt as a barrier to protect his skin from the charge.

The engine roared to life, and he smiled with satisfaction. Checking the gas gauge, he saw it was at the three-quarter mark. Excellent. Luck was on their side.

Buck shifted into Drive and made a U-turn in the street, pulling up beside Zaire. Grinning, she hopped onto the passenger seat.

"I need to learn how to do that," she said, closing the door.

"You should never have a need to break into a car and hot-wire it."

"I might. What if I lost my keys?"

He glanced at her and felt a tug of emotion in his chest. She was definitely in better spirits, her brown eyes alight with excitement. No doubt, knowing they'd soon be in the air helped her mood.

Contrary to his initial assessment of her, she was beautiful—inside and out. He had the sudden urge again to kiss her—to wind his hand around her ponytail and pull her against him, crushing her lips beneath his until she moaned and trembled. Those glasses would be fogged up by the time he was through with her.

Buck pushed aside those thoughts and returned to the present. "If you lose your keys, call a locksmith."

He drove casually down the street and away from the market, careful to maintain a normal speed so as not to draw attention. As they neared a corner, he saw two men wearing jeans and dark shirts on the sidewalk.

They caught his attention because they didn't fit in. They didn't look like they lived in the neighborhood, weren't dressed in the usual tourist attire, and their faces were stern and harsh in appearance.

One of the men cast a cursory look at the car and then did a double take when he saw Buck. He elbowed the man beside him. The second man reacted quickly and reached toward his back waistband. Buck knew what that meant.

He swerved right at them.

Zaire gasped. "What are you—"

"Get down!"

He grabbed her neck and forced her head toward her knees while driving the Fiat Panda at the men. They dove out of the way, and he swung the vehicle hard to the left, knocking over a public trash can as he bounced off the sidewalk.

Hitting the accelerator, he drove into traffic, honking the horn to warn other vehicles to get out of the way. In the rearview mirror, he saw the men running after them, but they were too late.

"You can sit up now," he said to Zaire.

Slowly, she sat up and swallowed, the humor and excitement gone from her eyes and replaced with fear.

It didn't matter that he'd managed to escape without the men firing a single shot.

The morning had been ruined.

Chapter 18

Almost forty-five minutes ago, they'd left the bustling streets of Rome behind, and ever since then Zaire had been quiet, obviously shaken by the sight of the two men.

"Are you all right?" Buck asked, keeping his attention on the road.

"Getting there." From the corner of his eye, he saw her check the side mirror.

"We're not being followed," he assured her.

"How do you know?"

"I know," he said in a firm voice. He removed his cap and propped it on top of the dashboard. Running his fingers through his hair, he loosened the flattened strands.

She glanced at him and then looked away, refocusing her gaze through the windshield.

A while back, they'd passed a small town with pastel-colored houses. Buck had never explored this part of Italy before, but the drive so far was picturesque. The rural landscape was filled with flowers and cypress trees.

"Look at that," he said, pointing.

Atop the hillside ahead on the right was a crumbling castle.

"Oh," Zaire said, a bit more upbeat. "The Italian countryside probably has just as much interesting history as the city of Rome."

Buck nodded in agreement.

"How do you think they found us?" Zaire asked.

She didn't have to elaborate for him to know who she was asking about.

Buck checked the rearview mirror, something he had been doing every few miles to make sure they weren't being followed. "They didn't find us. They were looking for us, and we stumbled onto each other. They've probably been searching since yesterday." A frown creased her forehead, and he made an attempt to distract her. "Mind opening the chips? I could munch on something right now."

She reached for the bright yellow bag of San Carlo chips on the floor. She popped it open and extended it to him.

Buck took a few. "Are these good?"

"Of course. At least, *I* think they're good. Tell me what you think."

He chewed on the crispy snack and nodded. "I guess you're not wrong."

She dipped her hand into the bag. "I've become somewhat of a connoisseur of Italian snacks, and these are some of the better ones."

"How long were you supposed to stay in Rome?" Buck eased past a vehicle containing five adults who looked like sardines squeezed into the compact car.

"The assignment was for three months. This is kind of embarrassing, but it's the first time I've been overseas on my own. I've only ever traveled abroad with my parents."

Surprised, Buck glanced at her. "You're twenty-eight, right?" He recalled her age from the file Benjamin had given him.

"Yes, almost thirty. That's lame, isn't it?"

"It's not lame. Your parents love you."

"Yeah. I'm their miracle baby. They had accepted that

they'd never be able to have kids and then, poof—I showed up when my mother was forty-two. She sometimes calls me 'My Gift.'"

"Did you tell me what your parents do for a living?" Buck reached into the chips bag again. They really were good.

"I don't think so. They're both professors. My father is an English lit professor at Morehouse, and my mom teaches history at Emory University."

Buck chuckled.

She swung her head in his direction. "What's so funny?"

"You're not going to believe this, but we have a little something in common. Our parents have similar careers. Both of my parents teach English. My father teaches in high school and my mother teaches in middle school."

"No way."

"I'm serious." He smiled at the surprised expression on her face.

"I never figured you to be the son of English teachers."

Buck arched an eyebrow. "And why not?"

"Don't get offended," Zaire said with a laugh. "I guess I assumed you come from a long line of athletes or something. *Intelligent* athletes."

"I like the way you cleaned that up."

An adorable smile touched her lips, and she continued munching on the chips.

"Do you have siblings?" Zaire asked.

Buck shook his head. "Just me, though I grew up with three cousins in a town outside Austin, Texas."

Zaire sat up and stared at him with wide eyes. "You're from Texas too? We moved to Atlanta my sophomore year in high school. I absolutely hated it, but Emory offered my dad a position. Much better pay, blah, blah, blah. Basically, it was an opportunity he couldn't pass up. He's now the chair of the department. At the time, I begged my parents to let me stay in Dallas with my aunt. She said she'd take care of me—that way I could finish my last two years at the same high school and graduate with my friends. But they said no."

She sounded so sad.

"That sucks," Buck said.

"Yeah. That overprotective thing again," she muttered. Sighing, she gazed out the window at the passing scenery.

He had the impression there was more to the story than her mother and father simply being helicopter parents. Before he could probe her past, she asked, "So, you said you're from a town outside of Austin? Which one?"

"One you've probably never heard of. Ever heard of Dripping Springs?"

Her brow furrowed. "I don't think so."

Buck accelerated past a slow-moving truck. "We're known as 'the Gateway to Hill Country.' It's a great place to grow up, especially if you like the outdoors. My three cousins and I—all boys—were always hunting and fishing and hiking, mostly with my uncle, my father's brother. Neither of my parents are the outdoorsy type."

"Something tells me you were always getting into trouble," Zaire said, a teasing note to her voice.

"Four boys? Hell yeah."

They both laughed.

"One time, my cousin Bo stole his father's truck, and the four of us rode into Austin to go to a concert we were told we couldn't attend. When we got back home that night, our parents were livid, but man, we had a great time. It was worth being grounded for a month."

"That's nuts!" Zaire said.

"Looking back, yeah, it was. I'd probably have a heart attack dealing with kids like us. I don't know how our parents did it." He had great memories.

"Sounds like you had a lot of fun," Zaire said, her voice wistful. "I didn't have the opportunity to get into trouble. I usually went straight from school to home. When I hung out with friends, they came to my house, and I rarely went to theirs. The best times of my life were when I traveled with my parents. I learned a lot about different cultures and ate a lot of cool food."

"Yeah, you told me. I'm not an adventurous eater."

"No kidding," Zaire said sarcastically.

"Was that necessary?"

"Sorry," she said, fighting a smile.

"My ex, Lana, used to make fun of my limited diet."

"The almost fiancée?"

"Yes, her." Usually he had a hard time talking about her, but oddly he wasn't experiencing the anger that usually surged through him. "She used to question how I could be so adventurous in other parts of my life and have no problem eating the same breakfast every morning."

"You eat the same breakfast every morning?" Zaire asked, sounding appalled.

Buck nodded. "Two eggs over easy, four strips of bacon, a bowl of oatmeal and two pieces of buttered toast."

"Do you really eat that every morning, or are you pulling my leg?"

"That's what I eat every day, except when I'm on a mission."

"How do you not get tired?"

Buck laughed. "Consistency is ingrained in me, and I like the way those things taste. Since I like the way they taste, it's easy to pick up the same food at the store and make the same meal every morning. I don't have to think about what to buy or cook. Makes life easier."

"I guess," Zaire said, sounding doubtful. She ate a few more chips.

She let out a cute little giggle all of a sudden.

"What's so funny?"

"I was thinking about Josie. Gosh, she was crazy, and so much fun. She had a silly streak too. She used to call everything good *cake*. She'd say stuff like, 'We had a good time, the night was cake.' Or 'Sex with him was cake.' She was silly like that." Her voice thickened, and she looked out the window.

"I'm sorry you lost your friend, Zaire."

She sighed. "Me too."

"We're gonna get these guys."

She looked at him, her eyes glassy with tears. "I hope so," she said, her voice husky with emotion.

The ride continued on a more upbeat note when Zaire mentioned she was looking forward to eating a big plate of ribs at her favorite restaurant once they returned stateside. Their lighthearted conversation didn't end until they left the highway and drove onto a dirt road toward the airfield. They entered a clearing surrounded by trees and covered in grass and dirt. Buck drove slowly, the car bouncing over the rugged ground. The runway was barely visible, but there was a definite patch of cracked tarmac where a plane could land, albeit very carefully.

Zaire sat up straight. "We're a little early," she said.

"Yeah." Buck slowed the vehicle to a stop. Nothing looked out of place or untoward. Just a stretch of land surrounded by woods and shrubbery. Yet tension rested on his shoulders—an instinctual warning. A warning he never ignored.

"Is there something wrong?" Zaire whispered.

He didn't answer, becoming perfectly still. "Nothing I can put my finger on, but this doesn't feel right."

"What do you mean?" she asked in a low voice.

"The energy of this place is off. I can't explain it."

"Maybe we're in the wrong spot?" Zaire suggested.

He double-checked the GPS on the phone. "No, this is the right place."

Buck continued to survey the landscape, and Zaire followed suit. Then he noticed a glint of light in the shrubs ahead and stiffened. His instincts had been correct.

"We're not alone."

Chapter 19

"Across the way, a little to the right. I saw a flash. We should be the only ones out here until the plane lands."

Buck slammed the car into Reverse, and the pop of gunshots followed.

A black Jeep roared through the brush toward them. It was huge, with large tires and a grille guard attached to the front.

"Hang on," Buck said through gritted teeth. He made a sharp U-turn, kicking up dust and pebbles in the wake of the spinning vehicle.

Zaire grabbed the handle above the window, her heart stampeding through her chest.

Another vehicle, a black SUV, rushed toward them. They were getting boxed in!

Zaire whimpered, and Buck muttered a series of four-letter words. He slammed on the brakes, and the Panda slid to a stop.

Zaire tried not to give in to panic, but fear had her in a choke hold. How many were there? For all they knew, they were surrounded on all sides by their pursuers.

Buck swung a hard right. The vehicle jostled and bounced over the uneven terrain as he sped toward the woods surrounding the field.

Gunshots peppered the air and smashed out the rear window. Zaire screamed. Ducked. Horrified the assassins might actually kill them. How had they found her and Buck? She was supposed to be going home.

She knew the moment two of the tires were blown out. The back of the car sank to the earth.

"We're not going to make it," Buck said in a grim voice.

Zaire stared at him in dismay. If he believed that—if he'd lost hope—then they truly had no chance of escape.

"Give us the girl," a voice commanded through a megaphone.

A loud boom, and then smoke hissed from under the hood. The car sputtered and slowed to a crawl before stopping altogether.

Buck unhooked his seat belt and looked her in the eyes. "They're going to take you, but they won't kill you. They need you."

"Huh? What?"

"Be strong. I won't let anything happen to you." He shoved open the door and shot toward the woods.

"Buck!" Zaire screamed.

More gunshots as he zigzagged toward the trees and disappeared from view.

Two of the men hopped down from the Jeep and approached on foot. Zaire unhooked her seat belt and scrambled across the middle console. She bumped her knee on the gear shift but ignored the pain.

Get out. She had to get out.

She fell through the open driver's-side door, and her palms hit the ground. She was half in, half out of the vehicle. A third man rushed around the side of the car and pointed a gun at her.

Zaire whimpered and dropped her head. Buck was wrong. They were going to kill her.

But she didn't die.

Instead, firm fingers wrapped around her upper arm and dragged her the rest of the way out of the Fiat. The man yanked her upright and shoved her against the body of the car. Dark, angry eyes locked with hers, and she recognized him as one of the men outside the Colosseum the day before. The one with the scar on his neck.

"You've caused a lot of trouble, lady."

That voice!

Shock punched through her. He was one of the men she'd overheard talking about the embassy bombing. "You were at Zinga."

A wicked smile slid across his mouth. "That's right. We meet again."

His fingers tightened around her arm, and she winced. Securing his weapon in a holster on his hip, he looked at the other men.

"Go get him. Kill him!" he shouted.

As the men raced after Buck, Zaire tried to reason with the one holding her captive. She shoved her glasses higher on the bridge of her nose. "Please, I don't know anything. Whatever you think I know, you're wrong."

"That's not for me to decide, sweetheart. Someone higher up wants to know what you heard and who you told."

"Nothing! I didn't hear anything."

"Then why did you run, hmm?"

Her mouth opened, but she couldn't think of a lie fast enough.

The man chuckled. "Exactly. Come along."

He dragged her behind him toward the SUV, but she dug in her heels and twisted her arm to escape.

"Stop fighting me! Open the door," he growled to the bald-headed man standing nearby.

The bald guy did as he was told, and her captor shoved her forward, but Zaire dug in her heels again. "No! No!"

Never let them take you to the next location. Never let them take you to the next location.

The familiar words came back like a mantra.

She struggled. She twisted. She turned.

She did everything she possibly could to keep from being dragged into the SUV. She fought so much, her cap fell off and her hair came undone, becoming a tangled mess and falling across her cheeks.

Within inches of the vehicle, she swung one leg up and pushed against the side of the SUV. The move took her captor by surprise, and he staggered backward, but he didn't let her go.

"No!" she screamed again. Her voice was hoarse, as if she'd been screaming for hours.

The bald man laughed. "She is a feisty little thing, isn't she?" He spoke English with an Italian accent.

"If he didn't want her alive, I'd slit her throat right here." He temporarily let Zaire go and hit her with a backhanded blow to the cheek.

The stinging slap jerked her head to the left. He'd hit her so hard that he knocked off her glasses. Pain spliced her skin. Disoriented, head spinning, she staggered and fell to her knees in the grass.

"There's more where that came from if you don't act right, sweetheart."

Tears stung Zaire's eyes, and she bit the inside of her lip to keep from crying out loud, feeling helpless and alone. She reached for her glasses, but the brunet crushed them under the heel of his boot. The crunch of the glass and frame only added to her trauma.

The bald-headed man chuckled.

"Tape, Luca."

Zaire looked up, and the brunet was holding out his hand.

Luca, the bald man, handed him a roll of duct tape. Seeing that spurred Zaire into action. She shot to her feet, but Luca grabbed her crossbody bag, yanked her backward and locked her arms to her body.

"No! Please, no!" Zaire cried out, wiggling and kicking her feet.

"Saying no isn't going to change a thing," the brunet said. He covered her mouth with tape.

Her cries were nothing but muted whimpers now.

"Much better," he said.

He lifted her feet. She kicked, but he was stronger. He wrapped her calves in duct tape and dropped her feet to the grass.

Zaire wiggled like a worm, but her movements were all in vain. He taped her hands together in front of her body and then presented a mean-looking knife, holding it in front of her face.

She flinched, closing her eyes, but all he did was cut the bag off her body and toss it to the floor of the SUV. When he finished, Luca easily shoved her onto the back seat.

The brunet climbed in beside her. "Comfy? No? Don't worry. It'll all be over soon. We just need to know what you heard."

He spoke in a pleasant voice, as if he wasn't in the midst of kidnapping another person.

Zaire searched the vehicle for a way to escape but saw none. How could she escape, anyway, with her legs taped together? She couldn't walk, much less run.

After some time, the men who'd pursued Buck in the woods returned, looking dejected.

The one in front shook his head with regret. "Sorry, Cain. We couldn't catch him," he said, speaking to the brunet.

"What do you mean, you couldn't catch him?"

"He disappeared," another man added.

"Does it matter?" Luca asked Cain. "We do not need him. We have secured the girl."

"Payne is going to be pissed. He wanted us to tie up all loose ends—and *he's* a loose end. Don't forget, he killed members of our team."

"But we do not need to waste more time on him now that we have what we want. We can leave him out here. He'll never find us."

The men waited for Cain's response. He was clearly the leader, at least out here. Based on what he'd just said, they reported to someone else who wanted Zaire alive.

"All right. We can leave now," Cain said, sounding reluctant.

The four men marched toward the Jeep a distance away, and Luca climbed in behind the wheel of the SUV.

"Relax and enjoy the ride," Cain said to Zaire, securing a seat belt around her.

Luca started the vehicle and drove toward the highway. She assumed the Jeep was following but didn't check. She kept her eyes straight ahead.

What were they going to do to her? The dull throb in her cheek reminded her of what they were capable of. A slap was nothing. They might do much worse when she arrived at the final destination. They might torture her.

Zaire started shaking, and a tear streamed down her face despite her efforts to stop it. This wasn't supposed to happen. She took a deep breath and sniffled to stifle her despair.

Buck had left her.

I won't let anything happen to you.

That's what he had promised. Twice.

But he had lied.

Chapter 20

Buck clung to the bottom of the Jeep as it cruised down the highway. He had looped his belt behind his hips and attached it to the underside. He braced his foot against one of the components and gripped the axis to keep his upper body from scraping the ground.

The Jeep's large tires afforded greater ground clearance than a car, but the back of his shirt was dirty from the vehicle bouncing over the uneven ground at the airfield. He'd have some bruises for sure, but it would all be worth it.

He had taken a big risk leaving Zaire, and the sound of her cracked voice crying out his name would haunt him for many nights to come. She might have thought they wanted to kill her, but he realized when one of the assailants spoke through the megaphone that they wanted her alive to find out what she knew and what she had shared.

Unfortunately, he'd had to leave her to have any chance of saving her. They were outnumbered, and each one of those men had a gun. All he had was a letter opener. Only Superman could have stopped them, and he was no bulletproof hero.

After seeing that he and Zaire were outmanned and outgunned, Buck had quickly devised his plan. While the men had tramped after him through the brush, he did the opposite of what they expected. He'd circled around behind them and crept out from the trees, low on his belly, to the Jeep.

It had taken every bit of willpower not to charge the one who was obviously the leader when he'd struck Zaire to the ground, but he couldn't help her if he was dead. He took advantage of their distraction with her to slip beneath the Jeep. He would deal with that piece of shit later and make him pay for hurting her.

The roadway passed beneath him quickly, and he continued to hold on. He didn't know how far away their lair was, but no matter how far, he'd hang on. He'd been through tough situations before and had persevered. His SEAL training had already kicked in. He was in the zone, his mind focused and centered, his conditioned body ready to endure the rigorous journey ahead.

After almost two hours, the Jeep slowed as they turned off the highway onto a dirt track. Dust kicked up in a cloud around Buck, and he shifted to holding on with one hand and protecting his nose and mouth with the other. Eyes narrowed, he kept them open enough to see as much of his surroundings as possible from his vantage point.

The driver continued at a much slower pace for about half a mile, and then Buck heard the scrape of a metal gate as it opened. They eased through and then came to a stop.

The men from both the SUV and the Jeep descended from the vehicles, talking and joking. They sounded like Americans, but he also detected an Italian accent from one of them.

"Bring the girl," one of the men said. Probably the leader.

He heard scuffling sounds, and then the voices receded.

Buck waited another minute in case one of the men forgot something and came right back outside. Then he unhooked the belt and lowered himself onto the dirt.

Slowly, he slid sideways, then froze. An external camera was mounted on the outside of the building, but fortunately the black lens was pointed at an angle that wouldn't capture him.

He slid over to the other side, gravel biting into his back. No camera there, but the building itself looked like a large warehouse with a steel door leading to the inside. There were no windows on this side of the building, though there was a small square window in the middle of the door.

Buck scooted from under the Jeep and looped his belt back through his jeans, staying low, eyes surveying the area. There were two other SUVs, another Jeep and several sedans parked on the property, which was completely surrounded by wire fencing. From his vantage point, he couldn't see houses or other buildings nearby, which made sense. Whatever they were up to out here, they would not want to risk anyone finding out.

And what were they up to? Were these really members of the Hammer of Justice? From what he knew of them, this entire setup didn't seem likely to be theirs. They'd executed Zaire's kidnapping with military precision. It was possible the group had military members in their ranks, but he had his doubts. And how had they known the location of their flight out? He had his thoughts, but for now, he needed to figure out how to get her out of here.

Buck checked the back door of the Jeep, and it popped open. He crawled inside the vehicle and did a quick search but found no weapons. He did, however, notice the driver had left the keys in the ignition. He made a mental note of that information since it might be useful later. He found the same situation in the SUV—keys in the ignition and no weapons.

Which meant he'd have to rescue Zaire with his bare hands and only the element of surprise.

Buck stayed low and hurried over to the building, where he eased open the steel door. Peeking inside, he saw an empty hallway with white walls and a cement floor. After a quick check over his shoulder, he went in and walked on light feet toward the sound of male voices coming from a room up ahead.

Back flat against the wall, he leaned to the left and peered inside the room. Two men watched a soccer game while eating sandwiches. The setup seemed like some kind of break room, with a table and comfy chairs. The men sat in front of the television with their backs to the door.

Buck slipped past the opening and turned down the hall, pulling up short when he saw a man up ahead. The guy stood with his shoulder against the wall as he checked his phone.

Buck walked up behind him, as quiet as a cat, and grabbed his head and twisted. The movement was quick. The phone clattered to the tile, but the man never had a chance to make a sound. Bones cracked in his neck, and his heavy body slumped against Buck's chest. He lowered the dead man carefully to the floor, dragged him into an empty room, and tossed the phone inside with him.

Taking the man's weapon from his holster, Buck checked the clip. A fully loaded magazine. Perfect. He hoisted the man's pants leg and found a KA-BAR knife. Now he had a gun *and* a knife. Much better. Though using a gun was a last resort.

The knife was a quieter way to kill that wouldn't alert the enemy to his presence. He lodged the gun into his back waistband and slipped out of the room.

Traveling through the building, he kept his eyes peeled for more cameras and listened for approaching men. Each time he came to a door, he eased it open and checked inside for any sign of Zaire.

Finally, he came to an open area and saw stairs leading

up to a second story. He climbed them at a slow pace, careful not to make any noise. At the top, Buck came to a sudden stop when he encountered the bald man. He was the one who had laughed when Zaire was knocked to the ground and helped the leader haul her into the SUV.

Baldy looked at him in shock, and before he could react, Buck swung the knife at him. He dodged the blow, and Buck followed up with a left hook to the face.

The bald man clutched his nose but quickly recovered with a side kick. Buck caught his foot and yanked him off his feet. He fell with a thud.

"You—"

Buck dropped onto his chest and slammed a hand over his mouth. He jabbed the knife between the man's ribs, pulled it out and jabbed again. The bald man's body convulsed, and the gurgling sound of death rattled in his throat as life left him. Buck straddled his chest until the light in his eyes was extinguished.

Two down. Who knew how many more to go.

He hopped to his feet and went to the first door on his right. He peered through the window. Empty. He did the same two more times, either peering through the window or cracking the door open. One room was an office filled with computers. Another was used for storage. His frustration grew when he saw no sign of Zaire.

Where was she?

When he cracked the third door, he got his answer. She was sitting inside a room, facing a man at a desk. The man was busy reading a porno magazine, feet propped on the desktop.

Zaire sat with her mouth taped and her body tied to a metal chair with rope. With her head bent, her loose hair covered her face. No glasses because the leader had slapped them off back at the airfield. The memory of her falling to the ground caused his heart to seize with emotion and an overwhelming primal protectiveness, the urge stronger than he had ever felt before.

His grip on the knife tightened in anger as he entered the room.

Zaire looked up. He didn't know if she heard him or simply sensed his presence. Her eyes widened to the size of bottle caps.

Buck lifted a finger to his lips as he crept across the floor.

Her captor's phone rang, and Buck stopped moving.

"Hello?"

Pause.

"What!" he said in a sharp, alarmed voice. His feet dropped to the floor. "I'll be right there." He hopped up from the chair, and as he turned, Buck pounced, swinging the KA-BAR knife.

The man's hand shot up and blocked the hit, but the sharp blade sliced his forearm. Blood trickled from the cut to the floor.

Buck shoved him into the wall, and the man shot a fist into Buck's stomach, knocking the wind from him.

Then the guy hauled out his gun, but Buck slammed his wrist against the wall, and the weapon clattered to the floor.

He swung the knife at the man's throat in a downward arc, but the man caught the blow. They engaged in a battle of strength. Both grunting, both gritting their teeth, the man's eyes on the blade edging ever closer to his face.

Buck took advantage and head-butted him. The man was temporarily stunned, and Buck shoved the knife into his neck. He yanked it out and pushed the man to the ground. Then he took the precautionary measure of slicing his carotid.

Blood dripping from the blade, he straightened and looked at Zaire.

Chapter 21

*B*uck!

When Zaire first saw him, she thought she was hallucinating. Was Buck really standing in the room with her?

Yes. Yes, it was him. He hadn't abandoned her after all. The entire time, she had been thinking that she just wanted to get out of this place alive. If by some miracle she managed to do that, she'd change her ways. She'd go out drinking with friends, even if someone in the group didn't want her there. She'd stop being so shy and afraid.

Deep down, though, she hadn't believed she'd make it out of there alive. But now Buck was here.

When he stood up and faced her, a whimper escaped her throat. His souvenir shirt was torn and dirty, but he looked tall and strong. He looked dangerous.

Tears of relief and gratitude filled her eyes as he marched over.

"I need to rip this off. Quick is better, okay?"

Zaire nodded.

Buck tore off the duct tape, and she winced when it yanked the hairs on her skin.

"Other than the obvious, are you okay?" he asked, stepping behind her. He cut the ropes.

Free for the first time in hours, relief filled every crevice of her body.

"Much better now," Zaire replied.

Ignoring the soreness in her arms, she jumped up from the chair and flung her arms around Buck's neck. "I'm so glad to see you. I thought you left me. I didn't…"

Overcome with emotion, she lost her voice and rested her forehead to his chest.

He was absolutely filthy. He smelled musty and was covered in dust and blood splatter, but she didn't care. She held tight to him and melted when his arms wrapped around her.

His hands threaded through her hair. Holding a handful, he tilted back her head. "We have to get out of here, okay?"

Zaire nodded. She knew that but had temporarily lost her ability to think clearly while wrapped in his arms.

His eyebrows drew together as he touched her bruised cheek with the back of his hand. "I'm sorry you went through that, but I had to get out of there so I'd have a chance to save you."

"I understand that now, but at the time…"

"I know."

His gaze dropped to her mouth, and he kissed her. It was brief but impactful. His facial hair brushed her cheeks and sent a tiny thrill through her. His lips were firm but tender, and she wanted much more. The kiss lasted no more than two seconds, but the unexpectedness of it caused a delicious shock to her system.

What did it mean? Was it just a kiss of affection to calm her nerves, or was there more?

"We need to move quickly. I have a feeling that phone call alerted our friend here that they found one or more of his dead team members."

Buck was all business again, and her cloudy brain struggled to keep up.

He picked up the weapon that had fallen from the dead man's hand. "Have you ever used a gun before?"

Zaire shook her head. "No."

"Consider this your crash course." He pointed as he spoke. "This is a Beretta, and I'm sure you know this is the trigger and you pull it to fire the gun. Push this lever here with your thumb to unlock the safety. Make sure it's off before you pull the trigger. Hopefully, you won't need to use the gun at all, but if you do, grip it in both hands to help with your aim."

"Got it."

"One more thing—always point your firearm at the ground. Never at a person unless you're ready to shoot. Kill or be killed, understand?"

Zaire nodded vigorously. She understood, but could she really kill someone?

Once upon a time, she would have answered no, but right now, if someone threatened her life or Buck's, she was pretty certain she would end their life without thinking twice.

"Stay close. You got this." Buck cracked the door open and made sure the hallway was clear.

They both slipped out and moved quickly through the corridor. For a big man, Buck was surprisingly light on his feet, moving with the agility of a big jungle cat.

Suddenly, the steel door only one foot ahead swung open, and he stopped abruptly. His arm swept back to push her against the wall behind him.

Neither of them moved. They didn't make a sound.

Two men exited, but Zaire and Buck remained undetected behind the door.

"Luca, where the hell are you? Answer me! He's not answering," one of the men yelled into the phone in his hand. Both of them disappeared down the hall with brisk steps.

"This way," Buck whispered.

He and Zaire went in a different direction. When Zaire had arrived at the warehouse, Cain had cut the tape around her legs and forced her up the stairs into an open area. Now they were taking a different route, down a set of stairs near the back of the building.

"Do you know how many men are in this warehouse?" Buck asked quietly.

"I'm not sure," Zaire replied at a level that matched his. "There were six at the airfield, and there were at least two others here when we arrived, I think. So a total of eight?"

He nodded, as if her guess matched his.

They took the stairs and were almost to the bottom when Cain appeared below them with a gun in his hand. Buck stepped in front of Zaire, his body radiating tension.

Cain grinned, moving onto the bottom step. "Well, well, well, look what we have here. Mr. Swanson, there's no way I'm letting you take her—"

Buck kicked the gun from his hand and dove at Cain. Both men tumbled to the ground and rolled to their feet, squaring off like sumo wrestlers.

Cain swung and Buck dodged. Back and forth they went, circling each other and swinging, neither landing a blow nor getting the upper hand until Buck caught Cain with a solid uppercut. He staggered backward. His brain must have rattled in his skull.

Buck followed with a vicious backhand. "You like to hit women?" he taunted.

Cain swung again, but Buck sidestepped and hit him with a cross jab and another backhand.

Cain's head twisted, and blood spewed from his mouth

and shot a cluster of red dots on the white wall. He recovered quickly and charged Buck. He drove him into the wall with an audible thud.

Zaire watched in helpless distress, gun in hand. She wished she could shoot Cain, but they were moving around too much and she could just as easily hit Buck.

Buck fired two jabs at Cain's midsection and then body-slammed him onto the hard concrete. He stretched out his hand for the knife he'd lost in the fall and stuck it in the middle of Cain's chest. Then he yanked it out. His movements were fluid and graceful, a violent ballet of action that rendered the other man immobile. Blood pumped from the wound as the life ebbed from Cain's body.

Buck pushed to his feet. "Let's go."

Zaire took his extended hand and stepped around the dead man on the floor.

Buck had literally killed two men before her eyes and wasn't even winded. The man was a machine. They ran out of the building.

"Get in the Jeep," he commanded.

Before Zaire could follow his instructions, two men exited the warehouse at a full clip. They didn't see Zaire, so she ducked behind the SUV.

Did Buck have a gun? She couldn't remember. She had to help him.

She shot up from behind the SUV. Arms resting on the hood, she pulled the trigger at the men.

Nothing.

"Shoot. The safety."

She turned off the safety and opened fire. The taller man dove for cover behind a red car. The other was engaged in hand-to-hand combat with Buck. Buck struck the side of his head with a closed fist, and the enemy collapsed to the ground.

He stood over his supine body with a knife in his hand, but the taller one shot forward to stop him. At the same time Buck turned, Zaire fired at the charging assassin. She shot randomly, unloading all the rounds, and watched in shock as a red trail ran from the man's forehead down the middle of his face.

She'd hit him!

Buck looked at her in surprise. Then a smile crossed his lips, and she smiled too.

Holy crap. She had killed someone.

"Get in the Jeep," Buck said again.

This time she hopped in and watched as he stabbed the man on the ground. He sliced holes in the tires of all the vehicles before climbing in behind the wheel of the Jeep. None too soon. Four of men charged through the door with automatic weapons.

Buck floored the accelerator, kicking up dirt and rocks in a mad dash toward the metal gate and freedom. The men chased after them on foot and fired at the vehicle. The back window shattered and shot glass across the back seat.

Zaire's heart pounded in her chest, and adrenaline raced through her veins like a roaring river. Tensing her muscles, she gripped the handle above the window and braced for impact.

Buck drove into the gate, and her body jolted at the same time of the deafening crash, the grille bar at the front ramming the barrier. The metal bowed and twisted as the Jeep plowed through while gunshots peppered the air from the automatic rifles behind them.

The vehicle skidded across the dirt, but Buck kept a steady **hand** on the wheel and wrangled it back under control.

Zaire twisted her head to look at the men. She could barely see them in the cloud of dust, but they weren't following. One of them stared after the retreating Jeep while another kicked the tire of the SUV.

No way could they follow, since Buck had flattened their tires.

They were essentially home free.

Chapter 22

Zaire gripped the seat as Buck raced down the dirt road at breakneck speed. He burst onto the highway, swinging the Jeep into the far-right lane and gunning the engine to put as much distance between them and the terrorists as possible.

"Are you all right?" he asked, shooting a quick glance at her.

Zaire nodded.

"They didn't hurt you, did they?"

She touched her throbbing cheek. "One of the men hit me—the one you killed in the stairwell—but I think you saw that. I'm fine otherwise."

"I did. That guy is—*was*—an ass." His lips tightened with anger.

She relived the kiss he'd given her from that same mouth. Soft, with very little pressure, but enough to make her body come alive despite the desperate, scary circumstances she had found herself in.

Buck was dirty, his shirt torn, and there were scratches on his arms. His face and hair were covered in grime, but despite all that, he was appealing to her.

Maybe because those were signs of him risking his life and doing whatever was necessary to rescue her. He'd risked his life multiple times to save her, keeping his word to protect her. What woman wouldn't appreciate a man doing that? She'd never be able to thank him enough, but she could do the right thing.

She'd been kidnapped and could have been killed. If she had died, no one else would know what exactly was on the recording. Then more people would die. She knew what she had to do.

Buck roared down the highway, easily passing other vehicles and regularly checking the rearview mirror to ensure they weren't being followed. Zaire checked the mirrors, too, holding tension in her belly because she suspected reinforcements could come at any time.

They had been driving for a while when they heard a knocking sound at the front of the vehicle.

"What is that?" she asked.

Surely the Jeep wasn't about to fall apart on them.

"Don't know."

The sound didn't stop. It kept on.

Buck drove for a couple more miles and then veered off the road. He drove deep into a wheat field and finally stopped the car. From there, they couldn't see the highway and couldn't be seen by any of the cars passing by.

He climbed out and Zaire hopped down, too, following him to the front of the Jeep.

They both looked at the reason for the noise. The guard had done what it was designed to do—protect the front of the vehicle—but the left side had been torn from the frame.

"Doesn't look too bad," Buck remarked.

He dropped to his haunches to examine the damage from another vantage point.

"One of the bolts came out." He tested the grille with a tug and then stood. "I don't think it'll fall off, because it's bolted on the other side. We'll keep driving for a little bit until we find a place where we can ditch this Jeep. They'll be looking for it."

He ran his fingers through his hair. Was he tired? He'd trained for work like this, but even men with his training and stamina had to take breaks—didn't they? He wasn't a robot. He was flesh and blood, like she was.

"Buck, I need to tell you something."

Her serious tone caught his attention. "Okay."

Zaire took a deep breath and let it out slowly. "I've been thinking about what you said—that if something were to happen to me, no one would have the recording—and I've decided you should have it."

She reached into her bra and pulled out a small digital recorder.

He arched an eyebrow. "Wait a minute, Randolph said they searched you and didn't find the recording. You had it on you all along?"

She nodded. "Yes, but not in the same place. When I went to the embassy, I had the recording on me, but it was in the heel of my shoe. It's a trick my parents taught me. Whenever we traveled together, we'd keep extra money in secret places—like under the sole of our shoes or in the heel, in a fake tube of toothpaste, that kind of thing. I wore my shoes with the hollowed-out heel and hid the recorder in it."

Realization dawned in his eyes. "That's why you didn't want to give up your shoes at the souvenir shop."

"Yes."

He let out a short laugh. "I gotta admit, I'm impressed."

Zaire's cheeks warmed. "Thanks. I always carry a digital recorder with me. With a client's permission, I sometimes record sessions to review later. It's a way for me to assess my performance and see if there are areas where I can improve. Anyway, since you insisted I change shoes, I had no choice but to switch the location of the recording. I'm glad I did anyway because these tennis shoes *are* more comfortable. At first I moved the recorder to my bag, but then I decided it was better to keep it on me in case I lost the bag or, well— who knows what else could've happened. Or what else will happen. I'm so glad I did, because Cain took my bag. So, here it is. You can listen to what they say." She turned on the recorder and the voices of the men immediately came through.

"The one in Malaysia was nice too. And no one suspects a thing."

"How many more are there? We have to be careful, don't we?"

"One more bombing. Six days from now."

"You're not going to tell me where, are you?"

A soft chuckle. "You know that's top secret. I don't even know. Only the people who need to know, know. Operation Red, White and Blue will soon be over, and the next bombing will be the biggest one yet. She won't—"

"What's wrong?"

"Did you hear something?"

Shuffling sounds.

"Hey! Come back here!"

Zaire turned off the recording. "I ran out of there as fast as I could. That's it, and I'm turning it over to you." She handed Buck the device.

"Thank you," he said, closing his fingers around it.

"Did what he said make sense to you?" Zaire asked.

He studied the device with a frown. "No. Operation Red, White and Blue. It's internal code for the plans they intend to carry out. Could mean anything, but we need to get this in the hands of our analysts. They might be able to figure out what that means—or figure out which embassy is next, based on which ones have been bombed already."

"Could 'Red, White and Blue' mean that the next bombing will take place on US soil?" Zaire suggested.

"Maybe, but if that's the case, it'll be a departure from what they've done before." He tucked the recorder into his pocket and scoured the area, his eyebrows knitted together. "It's going to be dark soon. We can take advantage of the cover of darkness to find somewhere to lay low."

"Which way do we go?" Zaire was completely turned around, and without a phone with GPS, she didn't know how they'd get back to Rome.

"Based on the direction of the sun, we need to head that way, which is north, back toward the city." Buck pointed. "We'll stay off the main roads. It'll take longer, but this way we can avoid running into those men. I'm sure they're pretty pissed."

"They were already upset that you killed some of their men."

"How do you know that?"

"Cain, the head guy with the scar, mentioned it."

"What else did you hear?" Buck asked.

"Nothing really. They didn't do much talking, except to say the other guy— Oh, what was his name? Their leader. He wanted to question me."

"Was he one of the men at the warehouse?"

"I didn't get the impression he was at the warehouse. I think he was in a different location, which is why they took me there. Before they put me in the room you found me in, they said they had to put in a call to him and that he was waiting to find out if they had succeeded. Oh, they said they had to get him out of a morning meeting."

"'A morning meeting,'" Buck repeated in a thoughtful voice. "He's in another time zone."

"I think so."

"So he's Canadian or American, maybe?" Buck murmured.

"I'd guess American since that's the accent I picked up from most of those men, except for the a couple who were European. That fits with your theory, though, right? About the Hammer of Justice being the culprit? They're Europeans and American members working together."

"Yeah, but what do they want? And why haven't they told us yet?"

Zaire couldn't answer that question any more than he could.

"We need to move," Buck said.

They climbed back into the Jeep, and Buck took the back roads heading north. The front of the Jeep rattled as they drove past farmhouses and fields of flowers in the countryside.

As they passed by one of the farmhouses, Buck turned his head and frowned.

Zaire followed his line of sight, craning her neck to see what he was looking at.

"I just saw where we could hide out for a while."

"Back there?"

He nodded. "I saw an empty farmhouse. We'll need to ditch the Jeep. Can you handle walking for a couple of miles?"

"I can." She didn't bother to ask how he knew the farmhouse was empty. She trusted him.

"Good."

Buck drove for a little over three miles, passing by homes scattered across multi-acre properties that boasted rolling hills and ancient olive groves. Finally, he pulled off the road into a field of giant sunflowers, their towering stalks swaying in a gentle breeze. After parking the Jeep, he hopped out and checked the number of bullets in the gun he carried.

"What kind of gun is that?" Zaire asked.

"Glock. I got it off the first guy I killed when I entered the warehouse." His gaze swept the area. "We'll leave the Jeep here. If they find it, they'll think we're headed north, back to Rome."

"But we're going back the way we came," Zaire said.

"Exactly. Are you ready?"

She nodded. With him by her side, she was ready for anything.

They tramped through the fields, the subtle scent of the sunflowers mingling with the aroma of the area's fertile soil.

At least the sun had gone down, making the trip less arduous. The first thing Zaire planned to do when they arrived at the farmhouse was take a shower.

She plowed on, invigorated by the thought that they'd be able to get a bite to eat and sleep for a few hours.

Chapter 23

Crouched low and hidden behind the brush on the low traffic road, Buck watched the farmhouse from across the street.

A truck rumbled by and disappeared into the darkness. Night had fallen, and the closest house was more than a mile away. Very few cars passed along the road in this rural community. He had spotted the house when they were driving and noted the mailbox was filled to overflowing with literature and envelopes, a dead giveaway that the occupants had been gone for a while.

"Let's go," Buck said to Zaire.

They walked through the brush to the edge of the road. He looked both ways before they dashed across the street and crept through the yard to the back of the house. Buck led the way up the steps of the porch to the back door, and a motion light came on. Quickly, he reached up and loosened the bulb, and the light went out.

With darkness around them again, he wiggled the doorknob. Locked.

He checked the window closest to the door, and, as he'd suspected, it lifted open with ease. As someone who had grown up in a small town, he was not surprised they had left a window unlocked. There was a different culture of trust in areas like this.

He pushed the window all the way up. "Stay here," he said to Zaire, and swung a leg over the sill.

Inside, he paused to listen for movement in other parts of the house but heard nothing to indicate he was not alone. No scampering feet of a dog or barking or any other suggestion that another living being was present.

Satisfied, he opened the back door and let Zaire in. She reached for the switch on the wall, but he caught her wrist.

"No lights. We don't want to draw unnecessary attention."

She nodded her understanding.

Buck locked the back door and ambled through the cluttered living room. It seemed as if every corner of the room was filled with possessions.

They were in what he would describe as a den, which contained mismatched overstuffed sofas and armchairs. Almost every flat surface was crowded with knick-knacks, from porcelain figurines to a collection of clocks on a small bookcase. Built-in shelves sagged under the weight of cookbooks, decorative jars and candles. The walls were also cluttered, with a mix of store-bought paintings and family photographs.

"They have a lot of stuff," Zaire said, her eyes sweeping the interior.

Buck nodded. "Reminds me of my grandmother's place," he said with a smile.

Despite its chaotic appearance, this place—like his Nana's—held a certain charm. He imagined there was a story to tell about every figurine, painting and photo.

The kitchen was just as crowded, with all manner of appliances on the counters—a bread machine, stand mixer, large containers labeled *Zucchero*, *Farina*, etc. When he checked the refrigerator, he was happy to see plenty of food—none of which appeared to be expired. Milk, juice, butter, eggs and fixings for sandwiches. Much better than the safe house. The freezer was filled with meat, but he removed a loaf of bread.

"We can make sandwiches," he said, setting it on the counter.

Zaire peered inside an open cabinet. "Lots of canned goods. Vegetables, pâté, anchovies, sardines—the usual." She shut the door.

Buck rested his hands on his hips. "What do you want to do first? Clean up or eat?"

"Clean up. I feel filthy." Zaire wrinkled her nose.

"So do I." He reeked, too, from all the blood, sweat and dirt baked into his clothes.

"So we should check upstairs?" Zaire asked.

Ambient light played over her features, adding a highlight effect to her radiant russet-brown skin. His eyes flickered to her full mouth for a moment, and a heaviness filled his loins as his mind flashed back to their kiss and the sweet taste of her soft lips.

What had possessed him to kiss her? He was lucky she hadn't slapped him, but that kiss was all he could think about now.

"Buck?"

He blinked, heat flaming his skin as he realized he'd been staring at her and hadn't answered her question.

"Yeah, let's go upstairs," he said in a clipped voice, leading the way out of the kitchen.

They climbed the stairs, passing by a portrait of the family. Five of them—two boys, who looked to be in their late teens or early twenties, and a preteen daughter. There were three bedrooms upstairs, one of which the boys seemed to share because of the two beds, and the girl had her own room, decorated in pastels with stuffed animals lined up against the pillows. They found two bathrooms—one in the parents' room and the other in the hall.

"I'll take the hall bath and see if any of the boys' clothes fit me," Zaire said.

"All right. Meet you downstairs in a bit."

Buck tossed his clothes onto the floor of the bathroom and stepped under the cold spray of the shower. The frigid temperature helped keep his mind off getting Zaire naked and horizontal. He washed off the dirt and grime from earlier, watching as the dark water eventually ran clear. He shampooed his hair and gave his scalp a vigorous rub. When he turned off the water, he felt like a new man.

Checking his face in the mirror, he grimaced at the stubble that had grown to an unruly length over the past couple of days. He shaved his face clean and splashed on some of the owner's aftershave, a pleasing blend of spice and citrus.

In the bedroom, he searched for something to wear in the closet and drawers, all bursting with clothes. Luckily, the father was a heavyset man, so Buck donned a purple T-shirt with Italian words splayed across the chest and a pair of jeans he took from the closet, sans boxers. Buck was too muscular for the clothes of the younger men. Even so, the jeans were too big in the waist, so he tightened it with his belt.

He balled up the clothes he'd arrived in and headed for the first floor. Hearing movement in the kitchen, he was surprised to find Zaire had beaten him downstairs.

She grinned when he entered, and his gut tightened at the beauty of her smile.

"What do you think?" She held out her arms for him to inspect her outfit.

"Not bad," he replied, though an odd jealousy crept through him at the sight of her in another male's clothes. The clothes were clearly too big for her, but she looked like a dream—a fantasy come true. What would she look like in *his* T-shirt, her small breasts making a tantalizing print against the fabric the way they did now?

In addition to a gray shirt and jeans, which she'd rolled

up at the ankles, she held her hair back with a pink ribbon that she'd obviously taken from the little girl's stash. She smelled incredible, like rose-scented soap.

"You don't look so bad yourself. You look nice clean-shaven."

"Thanks." Buck stroked his jaw and took the compliment to heart, pleased that she liked his hairless look.

She went back to preparing the sandwiches, stuffing the bread with ham, salami and cheese.

He studied her profile. "Are you okay, Zaire?"

"Yeah, why?"

"I want to make sure, that's all." She was in an oddly good mood, considering what had happened. "You were kidnapped and tied up by very dangerous people. You shot someone, which even for the toughest person could have an adverse effect on their psyche. I'd understand if you felt a little off."

"Nope. I'm good," she said in a chipper voice, flashing another bright smile at him. "That guy deserved what he got. Him or me—or you—right? Hey, do you want to get some plates ready and maybe pour the orange juice? I'm going to put these in the panini press, and then we'll be ready to eat."

Buck opened his mouth to say more but changed his mind. He didn't want to push. At least, not at the moment.

He prepared the plates and poured them each a tall glass of orange juice. When Zaire finished the sandwiches, she placed two on one plate and one on the other. She then opened a jar of artichokes and split them evenly between both plates.

When they took their food and drinks into the den, Buck opened the curtains to let in the light from the moon and stars. Zaire cleared off the coffee table, and they settled on the floor to eat their meal.

Buck wolfed down the first sandwich and then remembered his manners. "These sandwiches are delicious, and I appreciate you adding a vegetable with the artichokes."

"Better than the spaghetti from last night?" Zaire asked.

He smiled at her teasing. "I did my best."

"To be honest, it was pretty good, considering what we had to work with. I guess the CIA doesn't care too much about their agents, huh?"

Pressing his back to the sofa, Buck chuckled. "In their defense, that's an old apartment that probably hasn't been used in a long time. When safe houses go unused for a while, they get run-down until we have an official reason to use them again."

"In that case, we were probably lucky with what we found."

"Very. Could have been much worse, believe me."

She laughed, and the sound rippled through him, and even in the dim light, he caught the sparkle in her eyes. Had it always been there, hidden behind her glasses?

Zaire dabbed her mouth with a napkin and placed it on the table. "What's the plan from here? We still don't know which embassy will be hit next, and the Hammer of Justice—"

"I'm not so sure the Hammer is behind the bombings anymore."

Her brow wrinkled. "Why?"

Buck shook his head. "I'm still figuring it out, but there are some things that aren't adding up. There's no way they could have known we were going to the airfield."

"I was thinking the same thing. That surprised me."

"Surprised the hell out of me too. And that guy, Cain, he knew my name."

"So what does that mean?" Zaire asked.

He didn't want to worry her more than necessary, but they'd become close over the past couple of days, and she deserved to know his thoughts.

"I think there's a leak," Buck replied.

Chapter 24

Buck drained the last of his orange juice and placed the glass on the table with a soft thud.

"Since you fixed dinner, I'll take care of the dishes," he said.

"A modern man. How nice."

He laughed. "Don't you need your glasses?" he asked.

"I can see well enough up close. I'd have to squint if anything was far away, and I probably shouldn't be trusted to drive, but I don't think that'll be an issue anytime soon."

"No, I'll take care of all the driving."

"You probably don't have any flaws, do you?"

Leaning back, Buck stretched one arm across the sofa cushions. "What do you mean?"

"Well, I'm half-blind. Were you born with three toes, for example?"

He laughed. He really liked her sense of humor. He was going to miss her when this was all over. "No, I wasn't. I have all my toes and fingers."

"I'm not surprised. I mean, look at you. You're a living G.I. Joe doll. I literally saw you kill an army of men without flinching."

"Not an 'army,'" Buck said in a self-deprecating voice.

"Army or not, you were unmoved. Meanwhile, I was shaking like a leaf, and all I'd done was run away."

"You did more than run away—and frankly, you seem unmoved too."

Now was his opportunity to probe a little deeper into her mindset, to make sure she was okay.

"I'm not unmoved," Zaire admitted. She picked up the last piece of artichoke and popped it into her mouth.

"What happened to you?" Buck asked quietly.

Her eyes met his and she laughed uneasily. "What do you mean? We're on the run in Italy, trying to stay alive. I might be a tad bit off, but I'm fine. I promise I won't break down in tears again."

"You know what I mean. I'm not talking about the last few days. I'm talking about what happened before all this."

"What makes you think something happened to me?"

"I've learned to read people in my line of work—and besides, I told you my deep dark secret about what my ex did, so now it's your turn to tell a deep dark secret. Did someone hurt you?"

She let out a humorless laugh, but the short, punctuated sound was filled with pain. He felt it in his bones.

When he didn't go along with her fake laughter, she sobered.

"It's not what you think," Zaire said quietly.

"Tell me anyway, and I'll listen without judgment," Buck promised in a gentle voice.

She swallowed, as if reliving the event that had wounded her in the past.

"When I was twelve years old, I was almost kidnapped."

Her words ricocheted through him like gunfire, and guilt seized his throat. He swore softly. "And I let you get taken today."

"No, don't. Don't feel guilty. You did what you had to do to save me, but I admit that I… I was terrified at first."

"Anyone would've been." Buck reminded himself to shut up and let her talk.

"I was dumb. I thought I was invincible. I missed the bus and decided to walk home instead of having my parents come down to the school to pick me up, which they would have done. Anyway, as I was walking home, this guy, he drove by in a truck. I didn't pay him much mind, even when he came back down the street. Except the second time, he stopped, and the next thing I knew…"

Her voice faltered, and she closed her eyes. The pulse at the base of her neck beat faster, and her fingers curled into her palm on top of the table.

"You don't have to go on if you don't want to," Buck said.

He wasn't sure if she heard him, because she continued talking, her voice now a monotone.

"He grabbed me. I hollered for help, but there was no one around on the street. He pulled me into the truck. We struggled. He had a knife. I couldn't let him take me. That's all I kept thinking. A self-defense instructor had given a workshop at our church a few weeks before, and she beat that into our heads—*'Never let them take you to the next location.'* Her advice saved me that day. I was determined that he would *not* take me."

She breathed slowly, as if trying to calm down.

"We fought inside the truck, and he hit a parked car. He stabbed me in the shoulder with the knife. I was bleeding but somehow pushed the door open. It's still a blur how I managed to do that," she said with a little laugh. "I fell out onto the street, and he drove off. An older couple passing by stopped to help me and took me to the hospital."

"Did they ever catch him?" Buck asked.

Zaire nodded. "Not off my description. We found out later that he got rid of the truck but continued to attack young girls.

They caught him when they found a body at his house. She was only thirteen. That could have been me." She shivered.

"I'm sorry that happened to you."

The overwhelming urge to protect her came over him again, but he couldn't go back in time and keep her from the trauma of almost being taken.

"I escaped, but I have a permanent reminder of what happened." She peeled the T-shirt off her shoulder and revealed a keloid scar.

Buck ran his finger over the raised skin. He hadn't noticed it in the dim light at the safe house, when she was wrapped in the towel. "That's why your parents are so protective," he said in a low voice.

Zaire nodded, shifting the shirt back into place. "And look what happened now that I'm traveling alone—something they warned me against."

"What happened isn't your fault," Buck said.

"I know, but I'm sure you can see the irony. Nothing like this ever happened when I traveled with my parents." She sighed.

"You survived the first time, and you'll survive this time."

"Yeah, and at least this time I don't have a scar. I hate this stupid scar."

"Hey, consider it a battle scar. Lots of people have them, including me. Reminds us to be appreciative of life in a way other people aren't."

She shot him a skeptical look. "I'm not a warrior like you, Buck."

"I disagree, and you're even more impressive *because* you don't have the training I do." Surely she saw her own strength. If not, he'd make sure she did.

"How many scars do you have?" Zaire asked.

"Quite a few, unfortunately. I've been punched, kicked,

stabbed once." He showed her the white scar on his palm near the thumb.

Zaire leaned across the table to get a better look. "I never noticed that before."

"I've also been shot. It's the most excruciating pain you can imagine. It's blinding and intense, like being set on fire from the inside out. I've made it my lifelong goal to never be shot again," he said with an attempt at humor.

She smiled at him. "And still you do what you do."

"Can't let the bad guys win."

She angled her head to the side. "Can I see your gunshot scar?"

"Sure." He lifted up the back of his shirt to show the entry wound on his left side.

She came around the table.

"The bullet went in there. I was lucky because it missed all my vital organs."

"You were *so* lucky. Your kidney is right there."

"The bullet came out here." He showed her the exit wound on his waist. His torso was sprinkled with hair, but scar tissue kept hair from growing in that spot.

Her forefinger traced the marred skin. "What you do is so…dangerous. You could have died."

They were close together, face-to-face. When she lifted her eyes to his, their gazes locked. Buck's breathing became labored, and so did hers. Tension sparked between them in the low-lit room, tightening in his stomach like the turn of a screw.

He lifted a hand and cradled her delicate jawline, and her lips immediately parted. He didn't know if she was about to speak or was trying to breathe, but he pulled her onto his lap and kissed her.

He had intended to be soft and gentle, but as soon as their lips touched, he was lost. He kissed her hard, with everything inside him. She straddled his lap, and her breasts smashed against his chest. The kiss was hungry and deep and probing, practically ripping his soul from his body.

He smoothed his hands down the curve of her spine and filled his hands with her bottom. He squeezed gently and she whimpered, her arms tightening around his neck as she resettled on his lap so his hardness pressed directly against her core.

Buck used the heel of his foot to shove the table out of the way and rolled Zaire onto her back. He helped her wriggle out of her T-shirt and also removed her bra. Tossing both articles of clothing aside, he sat back on his heels and gazed down at her lovely body, his tongue going dry with anticipation.

Her small breasts were perfection, their taut chocolate peaks standing at attention as if pleading with him to take them into his mouth. He leaned forward and kissed her again, filling his hands with her, massaging their softness and giving them the attention they deserved.

She arched her back and made mewling sounds of contentment. Buck worked his way down her rose-scented skin, sucking her nipples and licking the soft underside of her breasts. He'd never tasted anything so good.

He tugged off the oversize jeans and almost swallowed his tongue when he discovered she wasn't wearing any panties. She was completely naked, with a triangle of trimmed hair between her round hips.

Damn, she was beautiful. Buck flicked his tongue in her navel, sucked the curve of her abdomen and went lower to slide the tip of his tongue along her wet, slick core.

Zaire gasped and grabbed the back of his head. "Buck…"

He quickly dispensed with his clothes and settled between her thighs, leaning over her on his elbows and gazing down into her lovely brown eyes.

Her hands smoothed over his flat nipples and hair-sprinkled chest, her touch lighting a fire inside him that could only be quenched by possessing her body.

Unable to resist the softness of her lips, he pressed his mouth to hers again. He devoured her. Drowning in the flavor of her mouth, he dropped kisses in a line across her cheek to her ear.

"Are you sure?" Buck whispered.

He wanted to take everything she offered with her soft whimpers and her arched back, but he also understood how an emotional experience like the one she had gone through could alter decision-making. He didn't want her to regret what happened between them if she acted while in an emotional state.

"Yes, I'm sure."

He longed to make her feel good. He longed to hear her cry out her pleasure.

Gripping her hips, Buck thrust into her and shut his eyes, pressing his head to her shoulder. Goddamn, she felt incredible. Tight and wet. Like heaven.

Holding his breath, he lifted his head and looked into her eyes. He saw trust and desire. The same desire eating him up from the inside out.

Her fingers sank into his shoulders, and his fingers clenched her round hips as he pumped his. They kissed again, their breaths and tongues tangling in a passionate embrace.

Zaire's fingers climbed into his hair and added another layer to the complexity of sensations.

"Feel good?" he whispered huskily.

"Yes," she said, then bit her lip, her face contorting into a grimace of utmost enjoyment.

Buck kissed her neck and lifted her higher, diving deeper between her thighs, losing himself in the pleasure of her body.

He kissed her shoulder, and her arms clenched around

the back of his neck, legs wound around his hips. He felt the moment she came, and her cries confirmed she'd tipped over the plane into ecstasy—eyes closed, mouth open, body thrashing beneath him.

Buck ached to erupt inside her. He was on fire, and every one of his muscles strained as he resisted the urge to complete the most natural act between a man and woman. But right before he came, he pulled out and spilled into his hands with a belly deep groan.

Rolling onto his back, he shuddered through a climax that tightened his abdomen and forced a gasp of satisfaction from his lips.

Then he lay there on the carpet, staring up at the ceiling, willing his heart rate to return to normal.

An out-of-place sound reached Buck in the throes of sleep and caused him to open his eyes. He and Zaire had crawled up onto the sofa to sleep. He had pulled on his jeans, and she lay tucked into his side in only a T-shirt, with his hand cupping her bare bottom.

He'd left the burner in the Fiat back at the airfield, and the farmhouse didn't have a landline. The plan was to leave early in the morning and try to find a phone, but he'd been awakened a couple hours earlier than planned.

A light swept across the window beside the fireplace, and he distinctly heard a car engine.

Shit.

Someone was in the yard.

He shook Zaire. "Wake up, love."

"Hmm…? What is it?" Her brown eyes fluttered open, cloudy with sleep.

"We have company."

Chapter 25

Buck pulled on his shirt, and Zaire tugged the jeans up her legs. They dressed in seconds, the entire time Buck whispering how they would proceed. Armed with the Glock, he motioned for Zaire to go upstairs.

She was about to, but then she heard talking—a woman's voice, then a man's. They didn't sound like the men who had captured her.

"They're back. The family," Buck whispered, confirming her suspicions.

"What do we do?" she asked.

Any minute now, they would walk through the door, so he changed the plan, laying out a new strategy for how to proceed.

Zaire heard laughter as she and Buck hid in the shadows of the living room. She stood on one side of the open doorway while he pressed his back to the wall on the other side, his weapon in one hand.

The front door opened, and her heart raced at what they were about to do. This poor family. They were going to freak out when they saw two strangers in their home.

Footsteps shuffled inside. More laughter. Giggling.

They had to pass through the living room first, with the

kitchen in between that room and the den where they were hiding.

"I am so tired," a man's voice said in Italian.

"Not too tired, I hope," a teasing female voice returned.

"Never too tired for you, my love."

They both laughed, and then Zaire heard loud kissing.

Across the room, Buck frowned at her. Zaire was just as confused as he was. She didn't hear any other voices, and if she had to bet, this woman wasn't the man's wife. She sounded younger than the woman in the photos on the wall appeared to be.

They shuffled closer, with the woman's loud moans filling the house. She sounded like a porn star with all that noise. Either he was the best damn kisser or she was a terrible actress.

Buck gave her the signal, and Zaire flicked on the light. The couple jumped apart. At the same time, Buck slid out of hiding. The woman screamed and the man gasped.

"Don't be afraid," Zaire said in Italian, holding up her hands in a disarming way. "We're not going to hurt you."

This woman was definitely *not* the wife. Probably a mistress, about half his age and with black hair, compared to his wife's graying brown hair. He must have left his family and come back early to spend time with her.

"Who are you?" the man demanded, eyes wide.

"He has a gun," the woman whispered, pointing a shaky finger at Buck.

"He has a gun, but he's not going to hurt you, I promise." Zaire spoke to Buck in English. "Lower the gun. They're scared."

"Did you tell them we aren't going to hurt them?" he asked.

"Yes."

"What do you want? Do you want money?" the man asked in English.

Good. He spoke English. That would make this easier.

"No. In here." Buck used the gun to wave them into the den.

The woman clung to her lover's side as they moved to sit on the sofa, thighs pressed together.

Standing before them in front of the fireplace, Buck finally lowered the gun. "What's your name?" he asked the man.

"I am Enzo, and this is…" His voice faltered.

"We know she's not your wife," Buck said, casting a pointed glance at the photos of his family on the mantel.

Enzo's face reddened. "Her name is Lucia."

"Enzo, Lucia, we don't want to harm you. I'm sorry we invaded your house, but we needed a place to hide for the night and saw your house was empty."

"Are you criminals?" Lucia asked in a hushed whisper.

Buck shook his head. "No. We're *running from* criminals."

Enzo looked doubtful, and Zaire couldn't blame him. If she arrived home and found strangers with a gun in her house, she wouldn't believe a word they said either.

"Enzo, we ate your food, and as you can see, we're wearing some of your clothes. When we get to our final destination, I promise we'll pay you back."

"You do not have to pay me. I give you anything you want. Please. Do not hurt us."

"We won't hurt you," Zaire assured him, uncertain if her words provided any comfort.

"Do you have a cell phone? I need to make a call," Buck said.

"Yes. I do."

Buck pointed the gun at the man. "Slowly. Give it to her."

At a snail's pace, Enzo removed the phone from his pants pocket and handed it to Zaire. She gave it to Buck.

With one eye on the couple, he dialed a number. When the person on the other end of the line answered, he said, "Samson, this is Buck." Pause. "Long story. Listen, I'm stuck in Italy, outside of Rome, and I need transportation back to the US. Did you finish your mission?"

He listened as the other man talked.

"Yes, I can do that."

The one-sided conversation continued for a few minutes, some of it coded, so Zaire didn't understand the entirety of their plans. She imagined Buck did that on purpose because of the couple.

Finally, he hung up the call. "Do you have duct tape?" he asked Enzo.

"Duck tape?" the Italian repeated, eyes filled with confusion.

Zaire translated the words for him.

"Ah, yes, I have this tape." He looked a little fearful.

"Where?" Buck asked.

"In the kitchen. In, er…" Enzo motioned with his hand because he couldn't think of the English word.

"The drawer?" Zaire supplied in Italian.

He nodded. "Yes."

"He has tape in a drawer in the kitchen," she told Buck.

"Get it, please," he said.

Zaire went into the kitchen while he continued to hold the couple at gunpoint. She found the duct tape in the second drawer she opened. Almost a full roll.

When Buck saw it, he nodded with satisfaction. "Good. Lucia, place your cell phone on the table."

She removed the device from her purse and placed it on the table with a trembling hand.

"Car keys on the table too. And on second thought, we will need some money."

Enzo reluctantly placed his wallet and the keys to the car on the table.

"Go ahead and take those and remove his cash from the wallet," Buck said to Zaire.

Having no idea where he was going with this, she swooped up everything.

"Let me explain what's going to happen," Buck continued. "We're going to tape your hands together."

"No, please, no," Lucia begged.

Buck lifted a hand. "The only reason we're doing that is to buy ourselves some time. As soon as we're at a safe distance, we'll call the police and tell them to come get you."

Lucia shook her head. She obviously didn't believe them.

"You promise?" Enzo asked. *He* clearly wanted to believe.

"You have my word," Buck said. "We need a head start, that's all. We're also taking your car, but we'll leave it by the side of the road. By the time you or the police find it, we'll be long gone."

Enzo placed an arm around Lucia, and she pressed her body into his.

"Can you tape their hands behind their backs?" Buck asked Zaire.

She didn't want to, but first she taped Enzo's hands, apologizing because less than twenty-four hours ago, she had been in a similar situation. She hated doing to them what had been done to her, but she understood why Buck didn't want them to call the police before they'd put distance between themselves and the house.

She taped their ankles together, too, but didn't tape their mouths.

"You will not forget us?" Enzo said.

"You have my word. I promise we won't," Buck said.

He and Zaire packed supplies in a tote bag—bread and sandwich fixings, bottled water, canned sardines, and crackers.

Before they left the house, they checked on the couple again. They were whispering to each other and immediately stopped when Zaire and Buck appeared in the doorway.

"We'll call the police in about an hour," Buck promised.

He and Zaire then left them alone and raced down the stairs. Outside was dark because the sun hadn't risen yet.

Inside the car, Zaire placed the tote on the back seat. "What's the plan?" she asked.

"We're on our way to Austria," Buck replied.

"Austria?" Zaire repeated in shock. "That's almost a ten-hour drive from here."

He nodded and started backing out of the yard. "I have good friends in Austria—Samson and Travis. They wrapped up a mission and can meet us in Innsbruck. Samson's a pilot and has a cargo plane and can fly us out if we get there. A mutual friend is working a job in Italy and can smuggle us across the border."

Austria and Italy were members of the Schengen Area, a zone comprised of twenty-nine European countries that had abolished border control at their borders, allowing for free and unrestricted movement. However, officials could stop vehicles and ask the occupants for documents.

Since neither Zaire nor Buck had their passports or any identification at the moment, they couldn't risk trying to cross and possibly getting detained. Someone else would have to get them into the country.

"We have a long drive ahead of us if we're going to Austria," Zaire said.

Buck nodded. "Good thing we got some sleep, but we

don't have a lot of time. Pretty soon, another US embassy will be bombed, and we still don't know which one will be hit."

"Why didn't you contact your commander in DC?" Zaire asked.

There was a pause.

"Twice he's said he could get us out of the country, and twice we've been ambushed. I can't depend on him anymore. We'll have to figure this out on our own. We'll ditch this car and then head to the border." Buck glanced at her, his expression becoming hard and determined. "Settle in for a long day."

Chapter 26

Despite falling asleep, Zaire knew the moment they arrived at their destination because the car slowed to a crawl. Her eyes fluttered open, and a building with an attached gas station came into view.

Buck made a U-turn in the parking lot and backed into one of the spaces. He turned off the engine. "We're here."

Zaire checked the clock on the dashboard. The drive should have lasted ten hours, but they'd made good time and arrived early for the meetup, even with having to stop to steal another car and put in the call to the police as promised. She had slept for at least four of those hours.

They climbed out of the car, and Zaire took stock of their surroundings. They had traveled to South Tyrol, the northernmost province in Italy. The area had been on Zaire's bucket list to visit before she left the country because of the breathtaking Dolomite Mountains, the natural beauty of the valleys, vineyards and lakes, and the linguistic diversity of the region—with residents speaking a mix of German, Italian, and Ladin—spoken by many as their native language.

Maybe she'd have a proper visit another time. Right now, they had a meeting with one of Buck's friends, a man he said should get them across the Austrian border with no problem.

The sleek white design of the store stood out against the

natural backdrop of the rolling hills behind it. The number of cars in the lot suggested the location was a welcome stop for travelers seeking a break on their way to Austria. There was no van, though, which indicated Buck's friend had not yet arrived.

While Buck wiped down the inside of their vehicle to get rid of fingerprints, Zaire stretched her arms above her head, loosening the muscles that had tightened after spending hours in the car.

When he'd finished, they walked into the building. The extra-clean interior practically sparkled, and the aroma of coffee and breakfast pastries teased her senses. All types of snacks lined the shelves, from savory to sweet, enticing visitors with their colorful packaging.

People in the café barely looked up when they entered, too preoccupied with their meals, conversations and views of the countryside.

"I need to use the restroom," Zaire said in a low voice to Buck.

"So do I," he said.

After a short conversation in Italian between Zaire and the clerk, the young woman handed over the keys to the bathrooms, and they split up.

Zaire closed and locked the door, releasing a sigh of relief. Only a little ways to go, and they'd soon be home free.

She stared at her reflection. She wasn't the same woman who had entered the embassy a few days ago. She had killed someone. She had made love with Buck, a very sexy man she already knew she wouldn't be able to forget once they went their separate ways in the States. The thought of never seeing him again tightened her chest. That day was coming, and she dreaded it.

After using the bathroom, Zaire washed her hands and faced the mirror. She brushed stray strands of hair from her forehead and then splashed her face with cool water. The cool temperature fully awakened her and cleared away the remaining fog from sleeping in the car.

"Not too much longer," she whispered to herself before exiting the bathroom.

Buck was waiting for her near the counter.

He checked his watch. "Are you hungry?"

He was much more thoughtful than the gruff killing machine she'd met at the beginning of their time together. Sex on the floor of a stranger's farmhouse could do that to you, she supposed.

"No, I'm full from the food we ate in the car," Zaire answered with a shake of her head.

She wanted to get the final leg of their trip over with right away, and none of the snacks she'd normally be excited to try were enough to entice her. She didn't feel completely safe, and probably wouldn't until they were back in the United States and the men trying to kill them had been apprehended.

"I could use a drink, though. Water," she told Buck.

"Me too."

They walked over to the refrigerated section and removed two bottles of water.

"How confident are you that your friend will show up?" Zaire asked as they made their way back to the counter.

"Very confident. He's not the kind of person who fails."

If he had such confidence in the other man, he must really be good at his job.

"Is he also in the CIA?"

"No, he's part of another organization. The CIA isn't allowed to perform domestic security. His group can take security measures both domestically and internationally."

Buck purchased the water, and they slid across from each other into a booth that offered a view of the front door.

Zaire twisted off the cap of her water bottle and took a sip. The cool liquid slid down her throat, and she smothered a moan. The depth of her thirst became apparent only as she savored the drink.

"There he is," Buck said.

Zaire shifted her attention to the man who had just walked through the door.

Holy crap.

This guy was bigger than Buck. At least six-five, in dark jeans and a black T-shirt exposing arms the size of tree trunks.

Buck stood as his friend approached, and so did Zaire. She edged closer to Buck, a little intimidated by the stranger.

Dark-haired with tawny skin, danger was stamped into his face, amplified by a crooked nose that appeared to have been broken at least once and never healed properly.

As he came within a few feet of them, his expression transformed from one hinting at his lethal ability to a smile suggesting a gentler side. Zaire guessed he might be Hispanic, which was confirmed when he extended his hand to Buck and spoke in accented English.

"Someone told me that you need a ride."

"You heard right." Buck clutched his hand and they thumped each other on the back.

The stranger chuckled. "How the hell are you, *hombre*?"

"Excellent and ready to get out of this country."

"That's what I'm here for." His eyes shifted to Zaire, and he extended a hand to her. "Cruz Cordoba."

"Zaire Nichols. Nice to meet you."

His grip was firm but not tight.

"Are you Cuban?" she asked.

His eyebrows shot up higher. *"Sí. ¿Habla español?"*

"Sí, con fluidez. I recognized the accent."

"She's an interpreter and picks up on that kind of thing," Buck explained.

There was no condescension or amusement in his voice. She heard admiration.

"How many languages do you speak?" Cruz asked Zaire.

"Five."

He raised his eyebrows again, clearly impressed. "Let's take a walk," he said.

The three of them went out to the parking lot, where a white van with windows only at the front was parked several cars down from the blue vehicle they had stolen. A sign in Italian on the side advertised the Hernandez Flower Shop.

Cruz tapped the side of the van. "This is how I'm getting you across the border. Do you have a lot of bags?"

Resting his hands on his hips, Buck shook his head. "No, we're traveling light. What you see is what we have."

The other man nodded. "That makes the trip easier. I'll take you to the hotel in Innsbruck as planned. Travis and Samson will probably be there when we arrive. If not, I have the key to the room they reserved for you."

"Good. We should probably get moving. We don't have a lot of time."

"I'm ready when you are." Cruz opened one of the back doors.

Flowers filled the interior, some bound together in bundles. Several large arrangements looked worthy of display at a high-end shop or spa. Roses, geraniums and other flowers filled a shelving system attached to the right wall of the van.

Cruz extended a hand to Zaire. She took it and let him help her into the back.

The interior smelled sweet and inviting.

"You'll get on the floor behind those flowers and pull the black sheet over your head. Once you're lying down, I'll put some of the arrangements on top of you. Lay as flat as you can until we pass through the border. I will let you know when we're safely in Austria."

Cruz spoke to both of them, but his dark eyes remained on Zaire. She was the novice of the three.

"Got it," she said, to make sure he understood he didn't have to be concerned about her following directions. She'd do whatever was necessary to safely enter Austria. She was not going to screw up their chance to get out of the country.

Cruz shot a quick glance at Buck and nodded.

Buck climbed in and shuffled into the middle of the van. So did Zaire.

When he lifted the black sheet, she crawled under with him, and they both lay down on the blankets Cruz had placed on the floor.

"All set?" Cruz asked.

"Yes," they both answered.

He placed flowers on top of them and then shut the door.

"If we get stopped at the border, don't sneeze or cough," Buck said quietly to Zaire.

She giggled. "I'll try not to. I don't want us to get caught."

She figured he made the joke to ease her fears and help her relax, and it worked. Beneath the sheet was so dark, she couldn't see even a sliver of light from the front windows of the van. That gave her confidence that they couldn't be spotted by the border officials should they be stopped.

Cruz backed out of the parking space and pulled onto the highway.

"All right back there?" he asked.

"Yes," Zaire answered.

"We're good," Buck replied.

"We'll be at the border in about ten minutes. Hang tight."

Zaire closed her eyes and relaxed for the ride.

Chapter 27

Buck had his eyes closed under the blanket and remained silent as the van cruised along the road. Lying so close to Zaire, with the sweet scent of her skin surrounding him, was a reminder of their lovemaking the night before.

He never got involved with women while on a mission because of the problems it could cause. Yet he didn't regret making love to her. In fact, he wanted her again and hated that they didn't have time to fully explore what was happening between them.

What was he thinking?

Zaire was sweet-natured, funny and smart. A woman like that wouldn't want to be involved with a man who killed people. Though the sex had been earth-shatteringly good, he didn't expect anything more to happen between them after this situation was resolved. She deserved someone different, anyway. The cerebral type, like her.

Buck jolted out of his thoughts as the speed of the van decreased.

"Border officials up ahead waving for me to slow down," Cruz explained.

Buck heard Zaire's indrawn breath and reached for her in the darkness.

"I'm relaxed," she promised, but he detected the nervousness in her voice.

She'd been through a lot in a short period of time, and to be honest, she was holding up very well. He couldn't imagine being in her shoes, completely green to the type of tumultuous ordeal they'd experienced the past few days. Having to run from assassins and now getting smuggled into another country. He'd had the training to deal with it. She had not.

The van eased to a stop, and Cruz rolled down the window.

"Hello," he said in a friendly voice.

"Good evening. What is your business in Austria?" a man with a thick German accent asked.

"Delivering flowers to the Lelia Hotel, a few miles from here," Cruz answered.

There was a moment of silence, and Buck imagined them examining the exterior of the vehicle, checking for anything suspicious.

"Do you have your documents?" the official asked.

"I do. I have my passport and the order right here. One sec." Shuffling and then the sound of a zippered pouch being opened. "Here you go."

A few minutes later, the official tapped the side of the van. "Step out of the vehicle, please, Mr. Hernandez."

"Is something wrong?"

"We need to inspect the back of the van."

"Come on, I cross through here all the time, and this is an emergency order for the hotel. Are you really going to make me deliver these flowers late?" Cruz said in a disarming way, ending the sentence with a chuckle.

"Please step out of the vehicle. We would like to inspect the inside of your van."

Apparently, the border official didn't find him humorous.

Cruz rightly read the situation and opened his door. Had he continued to argue, the border patrolman might have become suspicious and more aggressive.

"You're wasting your time," Cruz said, hopping out.

Zaire's fingers tightened around Buck's, but she remained silent. He was actually proud of the way she was handling the situation. In a short period, she had learned to control her fear.

The doors at the back of the van opened.

"Like I told you, just flowers," Cruz said.

"What is that?" A new voice contained the same accent and authoritative tone but belonged to a woman.

"Those are geraniums. They—"

"No, that."

The back of the van sank lower when the woman climbed in, and Buck tensed. If need be, disarming the border patrol would be light work. He and Cruz could easily handle them and be on their way, but he hoped the situation didn't escalate to hand-to-hand combat.

The woman shifted a bundle of flowers.

"Be careful with those," Cruz scolded. "They are very delicate and not cheap. The hotel won't want them if they're bruised or damaged in any way, and I'll lose money."

More shuffling as the woman moved deeper into the van. Her foot bumped Buck's.

"Only flowers," she told her partner.

"That's what I told you," Cruz said, sounding like a disgruntled business owner who had been unjustly inconvenienced.

The woman hopped out.

"Thank you for your patience, Mr. Hernandez," the male agent said.

"I know you're just doing your job, which isn't easy. Tell

you what…" The van shifted down again as Cruz climbed in. "The hotel won't notice if a few of these are missing. You can take this, ma'am, and you can take these for your wife or girlfriend."

"We cannot accept gifts," the woman said in a stiff voice.

Cruz climbed out. "It's not a gift. These fell out," he said in a conspiratorial tone.

The doors closed and Buck relaxed when he and Zaire were alone again. She released a soft sigh.

The muffled conversation between Cruz and the officials continued outside the van.

"We're almost out of here," Buck whispered.

"I hope it's soon. My nerves are shot."

They both quietly laughed.

She had a great sense of humor. Another check in the column of positive traits.

Cruz climbed back in and shut the door. "Thank you. Enjoy the rest of your day," he called out as he pulled away.

A minute passed before he spoke again.

"You can come out now. We're safely past them."

Buck threw off the blanket, and he and Zaire sat up.

"You two okay back there?"

"We're good," Buck replied.

"We'll be in Innsbruck in less than thirty minutes."

"You're quite the sweet-talker when you want to be," Buck said.

"It was either that or bash their heads in. I figured they'd prefer to go home to their families."

"Don't we all." Buck shifted flowers out of the way and leaned his back against the wall of the van.

The minutes went by quickly. Before long, they pulled up to the hotel.

They all exited the van, and Buck examined their surroundings, noting parked cars, landmarks and the general activity around them. He knew Cruz was doing the same. They did it instinctively.

They filed into the hotel, Cruz first and Zaire walking between them. The man at the reception desk was preoccupied with other guests and barely gave them a second glance on their way to the elevator. They squeezed into the cabin, Buck and Cruz taking up most of the small space. On the third floor, Cruz maintained the lead and stopped at room 301, knocking first before using the key he pulled from his pocket.

As soon as they entered, Buck saw Travis Carter and Samson Marks, his fellow Omega Team agents.

"Look what the cat done dragged in," Samson drawled in his Southern twang. Currently wearing his dark hair in a buzz cut, he rose from an armchair by the bed and walked over to Buck. "Good to see you, buddy."

He had been recruited from the Air Force Combat Control Team. If it had wings, he could fly it, and damn well.

"Good to see you." Buck clapped his friend on the arm.

Travis walked over from his perch on the windowsill. His copper-brown skin was a shade darker than usual. He had recently spent lots of time in the sun, coming back from a visit to his family in the Caribbean.

"Glad to see you're in one piece." His curious eyes shifted to the only woman in the room.

Buck placed a hand at the base of her spine. "This is Zaire Nichols."

After the introductions were made, Cruz handed the key to Buck. "Time for me to go," he announced.

"Thanks for your help, man. I owe you. Where are you headed now?" Buck asked.

"To complete the job I came to Europe to do," Cruz said, an enigmatic expression on his face.

Buck knew better than to press him. His missions were top secret. While the Omega Team was a known entity of the CIA, his organization didn't officially exist.

"Good luck, though I know you don't need it," Buck said.

They all said their goodbyes, and Cruz left them alone.

"Are y'all hungry? We could get something for you to eat from the hotel restaurant or one of the restaurants nearby," Samson said.

"I'd much rather wash up and get ready for the flight home. What time do we leave?" Zaire asked.

"Ten o'clock. It'll take us twelve hours to get back to DC. With the time change, that means we'll arrive before dawn. We brought you and Buck some toiletries. Figured you'd want soap and toothpaste and whatnot." Samson tapped a bag on top of the dresser.

"See how thoughtful we are?" Travis said.

"Thank you," Zaire said gratefully.

"You're welcome, sugar." Samson folded his arms and looked at Buck. "Before we leave you two alone, Buck, you care to get us up to speed on what the heck is going on? Last we talked, you were planning a trip to the Virgin Islands. How'd you end up in Italy?"

Chapter 28

"Where do we begin?" Buck settled on the edge of the bed and ran a hand down his face. "Commander Ray came by my place in DC and told me that Zaire—Ms. Nichols—had information about a future embassy bombing."

He explained what he'd read in the file and told Travis and Samson what had happened since his arrival in Rome—minus when he and Zaire made love—right up until he called Samson about needing a flight out of Italy.

"Sounds like you two have had a rocking good time." Travis turned his attention to Zaire.

"It's been interesting," she murmured. She sat at the desk near the window.

"The bad news is, we haven't figured out where the next bombing will take place," Buck said.

"I want to hear the recording," Samson said.

Buck took out the recorder and played the audio for the other two men.

"I don't know what any of that means," Travis said. "Have you reached out to Commander Ray?"

"No." Buck kept his answer short and succinct.

"I know what you're thinking, and you're wrong," Samson said.

"Am I?"

Zaire looked between the men, a bemused expression on her face.

"We have no choice but to assume that the organization we work for—the Omega Team—has been compromised."

"What you're suggesting…" As though he couldn't finish the thought, Samson let the words trail off.

Buck challenged him with a stare. "Tell me what else makes sense. First there was the attack at her apartment and the murder of the crew that was supposed to fly us out. Then we got ambushed at the airstrip where we should have caught a second flight out of the country. Doesn't make sense. Both times, only a few people could have known about our plans. We have a leak, or a traitor in our midst."

Zaire cleared her throat. "Excuse me, but if you don't trust your own organization, we're screwed," she said in a small voice.

Travis shook his head in disbelief, and Samson ran his palm back and forth over his short hair. Their silence conveyed more than words could say.

"Do you think your commander is involved? And what does that mean for us stopping these people? More lives will be lost." Worry enveloped Zaire's face.

She shouldn't have to concern herself with this problem, but they needed to address next steps.

"We have to keep our return to the States quiet until we figure out what's going on. I'm not saying Commander Ray is involved, but telling him our moves is not a good idea."

Buck didn't want to believe the commander could have betrayed them. The man had sworn to uphold the Constitution, and his job was to use the intelligence the agency gathered to further the interests of the United States and protect her against threats.

"Which means we'll have to figure out who's been bombing the embassies and where the next bombing will take place—on our own," Samson said.

"Doesn't make sense that no one has claimed responsibility yet," Travis said, stroking his jaw. "Terrorists claim their activity and often have a list of demands. That's the way the world works. It fires up their base and helps with fundraising and recruiting. Each time they're successful— even when they're not—it sends a message that they mean business. Why take the risk and go through all the trouble of planting a bomb if you don't want to claim when it goes off?"

Samson nodded. "Bombing an embassy is not an easy feat, that's for sure. Matter of fact, the actual bombing isn't the hardest part. Not getting caught is the hardest part. The investigation after an act of terror against an embassy is intense. Both countries—the embassy country and the host country—send in the best to figure out what happened. Someone has to pay."

Buck rested his elbows on his knees and linked his fingers together. "We know they're Americans and Europeans, which is why none of the usual suspects have claimed the bombings. At least, I think that's why. They have military training."

"Homegrown terrorists?" Samson asked.

"That's what I'm thinking. They're responsible for most terrorist attacks—more than the international terrorist organizations. These guys just happen to be hitting our embassies instead of attacking inside our borders," Buck said.

"If we don't trust the Omega Team communications— for now—we need to speak to someone higher up the chain than Commander Ray. The director himself or the secretary of state."

Buck mulled the suggestion. "We can turn over everything we have, but tomorrow is Saturday. If the next bombing goes through as scheduled, it takes place on Sunday. We have two names—Cain and Luca. One of those computer jocks can do the research and see if those names come up in any terrorist chatter."

"I like that idea," Travis said.

"Too bad we don't know the name of the head guy—the one they answered to," Samson said.

"Maybe we do," Zaire said.

Three sets of eyes turned toward her.

"I just remembered something. When those men grabbed me at the airstrip, they said a name. I was so scared I barely paid attention, but it started with a *B*. Ben or..." Brow puckered, she shook her head in frustration.

Buck sat up. This was new information. "Take your time," he said softly, willing her to remember.

"No, it wasn't *B*. It was a *P*. Pl—Pen?"

Buck's heart jolted, and he sat up straighter. "Payne?"

Her eyes brightened. "That's it! They called him Payne."

"What am I missing? Who's Payne?" Travis asked.

Buck shook his head and wanted to roar with anger. The answer had been there all along, right in front of his face. All the missing pieces suddenly slid into place. "Rick Payne. He's the CEO of Javelin Security."

"Wait, what?" Zaire said.

Samson chuckled. Then the laughter slowly died on his face when he saw Buck wasn't laughing.

"Hold up, you're serious?" Travis asked.

"Who benefits from the increase in security at the embassies?" Buck asked.

"You know what I always say. Follow the money," Samson said in a dry voice.

He was a cynic. Having grown up wealthy, he had seen how his parents used money to control the world around them. He'd walked away from his family's wealth to forge his own path—a decision they had not been pleased with. To this day, they hadn't given up on convincing him to change his mind.

Buck continued explaining his theory in detail for Zaire's benefit. "After every bombing, the government launches a full investigation. Agents are sent over to the country where the bombing took place to assist the local government with the investigation. Then there are security upgrades—lots of security upgrades—among other things. The Marine Corps is the only branch of the military that provides security to the embassies, but contractors are also used. If there's an ongoing threat to the embassies around the world, we'd need more contractors. And who has been the go-to contractor the past few years?" He waited.

"Javelin," Travis answered.

"Yes. Payne himself comes from a military family and is a former Marine. His firm has become indispensable since the first attack. Right now, they're providing additional resources to protect our men and women overseas."

"There's currently a bill in Congress that's been fast-tracked ever since the second bombing. The secretary of state is hesitant about turning over security to a contractor, but it's worth billions to the company that wins it," Zaire said.

"How do you know about that?" Travis asked.

"After I overheard the conversation at Zigna, I started doing my own research about embassy bombings. When was the last one, what happens after a bombing, security measures that are taken. That's when I found out about the bill."

Buck nodded slowly. "A contract worth billions, and they already have favored status because of the work they've done for the State Department over the years. Tell me that's not enough incentive."

Zaire laughed uneasily. "Okay, wait, let's think about this for a moment. The company that is contracted to protect the embassies could actually be the bomber. That's *insane*."

"Greed is a helluva drug, darlin'," Samson said.

Zaire covered her mouth with her hand, as though the thought was too horrible to contemplate, but right now it was the only thing that made sense. "Innocent people died," she whispered.

Her words had a sobering effect on the room. It was never easy to think about innocent lives being lost, and it was even worse to think about the people charged with protecting those lives being the ones to take them.

"There's a hole in our theory," Travis said to Buck. "Didn't you say that Javelin Security members were killed when you were ambushed at her apartment?"

"Collateral damage. Probably low-level guys who were expendable. This is the only thing that makes sense right now, and we don't have any other leads. If it's not them, then who? No one is claiming credit, which you pointed out is highly unusual. At one point I thought the culprits could be the Hammer of Justice, but these guys are more tactical than the Hammer and have a lot more resources."

Samson pushed to his feet and paced the floor. "We land in DC tomorrow, which means we'll have less than twenty-four hours to figure out where the next bombing takes place. The embassies are on high alert, but if it's an inside job, we might not be able to stop them."

"We'll stop them," Buck said with confidence. "We need to get to Rick. He's the head of the company and he's the reason we were ambushed twice. When I met with Commander Ray, the guy was *in the limo with us*. He offered his men as escorts, to help get Zaire back into the country. The commander's phones could be tapped, which means if we contact him, we have to be careful what we say because the calls could be intercepted."

"Then we talk to him in person," Travis said.

"Any chance we can get out of here before 2200 hours?" Buck asked Samson.

"I can try, but I doubt I'll get clearance from air traffic control. We weren't supposed to fly out until Sunday, so they've already given us an earlier slot."

"We need to fly out earlier if we can. If not, then the current departure time will have to do."

"I'll work on that when I get back to my room," Samson said.

Travis rose from the bed. "If Javelin Security is behind this like we think, I can't wait to crush some heads." He punched his fist into his palm.

"Get in line," Buck said grimly.

"I'll let you know if we can leave earlier." Samson headed for the door with Travis right behind him.

Chapter 29

Zaire checked her appearance in the bathroom mirror. She had removed the pink ribbon and smoothed her hair away from her washed face. She finger-combed the strands, letting them fall against her cheeks. This was the best she could do since she didn't have a comb. She didn't even have lip gloss anymore—something to brighten her appearance. Oh well, at least she was alive and had taken a shower and smelled good, thanks to the toiletries Travis and Samson had bought for them.

Buck was hanging up the phone when she exited the bathroom. He didn't look pleased.

"Bad news?"

"That was Samson. We won't be able to leave any earlier than planned." He sank onto the bed. Disappointment seeped out of his pores.

He was a beautiful specimen of a man, and she wished to touch him again—not only to smooth the frown lines from his brow but also to revel in the contact.

She sat on the bed across from him. "I can't believe we're finally going home. It'll happen this time, right?"

"Oh yeah. Nothing will keep us from flying out, and I'm ready to go. I want to stop these bastards from hurting anyone else."

"I hope your plan to trap Rick Payne works."

"It has to," he said.

Then they'd go their separate ways. How could she possibly say goodbye to him without feeling as if she'd lost a piece of herself? It felt as if a lifetime had been packed into less than a week.

"Can I ask you something?" Zaire asked.

"Since when have you ever been afraid to ask questions?"

She laughed. "True." Nonetheless, she hesitated again.

"What's wrong, love?"

Love. That was the second time he had used the endearment. The first time had been after they'd made love in the farmhouse.

Buck had shown her what she was missing and made her believe that an exciting life could be hers and survivable. She didn't always have to play it safe—with her life or her heart.

"I want to ask you something, but I feel silly."

"Go ahead and ask. I'm an open book."

She licked her suddenly dry lips and folded her hands together. "Do you ever get scared?"

"Sure."

"Not like a little scared. I mean really, really scared. Terrified."

"It doesn't happen too often, but I've been scared in my life. I've been scared the past couple of days because I was worried that I wouldn't be able to keep you safe."

Happiness twisted through her. "You were worried about me and not yourself?"

She wasn't surprised by his answer. She'd come to understand that Buck was a man of honor and the work he did was because he wanted to protect others.

"I'm not afraid of dying."

"Is there anything you're afraid of?"

Knees apart, he leaned back on his hands. "Probably, but I can't think of it right now."

"That's a cop-out."

He laughed softly. "It's the truth."

Zaire took a deep breath. "I'm afraid."

"You're safe now, and once we get back to the States and get Payne, you won't ever have to worry again."

"I don't mean I'm afraid of this particular situation, although it has been scary. But this—adventure, I guess you could call it—has made me rethink my life. I've been missing out. I want to be brave. I'm afraid that if I'm not brave and don't take the leap to do things that I'm afraid to do, life will pass me by."

"It's understandable why you would hesitate. You had a traumatic experience when you were younger, and your parents have been very protective. But you're strong, Zaire. I told you that before. You came to Rome on your own, and you've impressed me during the time we've spent together. You have a lot of fight in you."

"Thank you." His words gave her the courage to take the next steps.

She stood up and started undoing her jeans.

Buck sat up straight, eyes locking on the movement of her fingers. "What are you doing?" he asked throatily.

Zaire's heart banged her rib cage. "Being brave."

She'd never seduced a man before, and she hoped he didn't reject her. She let the pants drop and stepped out of them.

His nostrils flared. "Zaire, last night was incredible, but you were in an emotional state, and we probably shouldn't have made love. I think what you're feeling is a little bit of hero worship."

"Do you really think I don't know my own mind?"

"I'm not saying that."

"Then let me do this. We'll be back in the States tomorrow and will eventually go our separate ways. I want to have sex with you one more time. It's just sex, Buck. It doesn't have to be any more complicated than that."

He looked taken aback by her words. They had been wrung from the back of her throat, a denial necessary to convince him she could handle more time in his arms. She was strong enough emotionally, and there was no need to try to protect her.

She pulled the shirt over her head and let it flutter to the floor. Reaching back, she unhooked her bra and let it fall to the carpet. Now she was completely naked.

Buck swallowed hard, then he extended his hand and she took it. He pulled her between his legs and smoothed his large hands up the curve of her waist.

He pressed a kiss to the space below her navel. "You smell so good," he said in a hoarse whisper against her flesh.

Rising to his feet, he stripped out of his clothes and then pulled Zaire onto the bed on top of him.

They kissed. Deep and long. She enjoyed his kisses. They were the best kind of foreplay—teasing and passionate at the same time—and made her feel desired, as if he couldn't get enough of her.

She opened her mouth and allowed his tongue to delve deep. This kiss was different from when they had kissed before. It had more intensity and intention.

Buck ran his hands along her sides, tracing the bends and dips of her torso and bottom and then sliding higher over her shoulder blades. All the while, they continued to kiss, tongues sliding and diving into each other's mouths.

He shifted his fingers through her loose, dark hair and cupped the back of her head to hold her securely against him. Lifting his hips, he ground his pelvis into hers, and she experienced the fullness of his solid erection, hot against her belly once again. The sensation of that heavy weight made her even hornier.

She took her time exploring his body. Licking his pecs and hard nipples, listening to his throaty groans as she cupped his length and massaged him with firm strokes.

Buck flipped her onto her back and sent the blood in her veins pumping hot with desire. His mouth moved to her throat, and she arched her head back to allow him greater access, a soft moan floating across her lips at the unprecedented pleasure.

Grazing fingers smoothed over her belly, and he lowered his head to her breast. Sucking hard on the nipple, he brought the peak to diamond-hard stiffness. Zaire gasped and shivered. His warm mouth was driving her crazy. He moved to the other breast and replaced his mouth with his hand on the first one, his touch sensual and possessive all at the same time.

Buck slipped two fingers inside her, and her core tightened around the digits. She worked her hips against his hand, in a desperate quest to grind herself to ecstasy.

"Buck." She moaned his name as a needy plea.

"The way you say my name…" he groaned.

He swore softly.

Zaire caressed his body everywhere, moving over his muscular back and down to his tight buttocks.

What a fine man he was.

Buck placed his hands on her hips and shifted their bodies so he lay between her thighs. He kissed her again, his mouth hot and demanding now. Arms wrapped around his neck, Zaire trailed the fingers of one hand through his hair.

"I need you. Now," he whispered, right before he thrust into her.

Zaire's body jerked, and she cried out as a storm of pleasure raced through her. She felt full and completely overtaken by him.

"So good. You feel so good," she said in a shaky voice.

He kissed her neck, while using slow movements to guide his hard length in and out of her wet body. He whispered sweet nothings in her ear, and the combination of his hot, sexy words and the constant rhythmic thrusting of his hips was almost too much to bear. He was killing her—killing her with pleasure.

His lips moved across her skin, dropping kisses to the side of her neck and then the raised scar on her shoulder. Pushing her right knee to her chest, Buck used one hand to clamp her wrists together against the pillows above her head. He had complete control of her now. She was at his mercy and relished every moment of his domination.

She experienced pleasure like she had never experienced as he slipped his tongue inside her mouth again. This time the kiss was sloppy and feverish, and Zaire loved the out-of-control way they both enjoyed each other.

Buck was incredible. He tasted so good—like heaven. Complete and utter bliss. She sucked his lower lip, gasping in shock as he went even deeper.

"You feel incredible," he whispered in a pained voice. "I'm trying so damn hard not to lose control."

The steady rhythm of his pistoning hips increased. Zaire knew he was almost to the brink of climax, and she was almost there too.

Then she came, her body jerking spasmodically, her soft cry turning into a wail of pleasure as she clawed his back.

Buck jerked between her thighs and, with a guttural groan, pulled out and ejaculated into his boxers. He buried his face in the pillow beside her and shuddered as deep pleasure rocked his body.

Zaire breathed heavily for a minute with her eyes closed. Then she turned onto her side and slipped one leg across the backs of his thighs. She couldn't help herself. She wanted to keep touching him. Kissing his shoulder, she sighed.

They lay there for a while until Buck shifted. "I need to clean up in the bathroom."

He slipped from the bed, and seconds later Zaire heard water running in the sink. She crawled under the covers, thinking of when Buck had kissed the scar on her shoulder.

His tenderness had touched her. *A battle scar*, he had called it. She closed her eyes with a contented smile on her lips.

Chapter 30

Who would have thought that Zaire Nichols would be having afternoon sex with a hunk she'd met less than a week ago? Tickled by the idea, she smiled to herself, as satisfied as a cat with a belly full of cream.

She lay in Buck's arms as he gently stroked her hair, the rhythmic motion—along with the great sex they'd just had—was the icing on the cake the day had become.

She appreciated how he'd made sure not to release inside her without protection, but she wished he didn't have to do that. She wished a lot of things.

She wished the monsters blowing up the embassies had never taken innocent lives and struck fear across the world for money. She wished Josie was alive. She wished that when she returned to Atlanta, she and Buck could continue seeing each other, but she was smart enough to know that wouldn't happen.

They'd go their separate ways. Perhaps he'd take on another mission somewhere else around the globe, and she'd continue translating conversations at Worldwide Language Solutions.

Slipping her thigh between his, Zaire edged closer to Buck and swung her arm across his waist. One more wish: she wished she could stay in his arms forever.

"Is Buck your real name?" she asked.

"Where did that come from?"

"I'm curious, that's all."

"My real name is Atticus. Atticus Swanson the Third, to be exact. The nickname Buck came from one of my cousins. He said I was hardheaded and always bucking the system—as if he was any different. The name stuck, and I liked it better too."

"So when you have kids, I guess you're not naming your son Atticus?" Zaire asked.

"Sadly, I'm considering it," he replied.

Zaire laughed. "It's a perfectly fine name."

She spread her fingers across his broad hair-dusted chest and encountered the scar on his waist.

"You never told me how you got this scar. Where were you when you were shot?" Her fingertip traced the mangled tissue. It was tougher and darker than his surrounding flesh.

"I can't give you the details, but it's from a mission in South Africa. Rescue operation that went south. We did eventually retrieve the asset we were sent to rescue, but our team endured some injuries, and we lost one of our brothers."

Hearing the heaviness in his voice, Zaire pushed up onto her elbow. "Have you seen a lot of death?"

"More than the average person, but not necessarily a lot. I guess it's all relative." He spoke in a normal voice, but his eyes contained shadows she hadn't seen before.

"But I bet you couldn't imagine doing anything else, could you?"

"No, I couldn't," he admitted.

He and his ex had probably been mismatched from the beginning. He hadn't known how she felt about the violent part of his job, and she hadn't understood how much his job meant to him.

Buck wound a strand of her hair around his finger. "What about you? Do you ever think about being anything other than an interpreter?"

"Sometimes I fantasize about being an educator like my parents. I'd like to get my PhD in something like intercultural communication and teach at a university." She had never told anyone about her aspirations.

"You should do it. What's holding you back?"

She shrugged. "Time. I'd probably have to drop back to working part-time so I could concentrate on my studies. Or I'd have to go to school part-time. School or work would suffer because I don't foresee doing both of them full-time."

"You would make a great teacher, but you know, the CIA is always looking for recruits with foreign language experience."

Zaire belted out a laugh. "Oh, no, I am absolutely not interested in being a part of the CIA."

He smiled. "Why did you say it like that, as if being an agent is the very last thing you'd ever want to do?"

"After what we've been through? *No*, thank you." She shook her head to emphasize her decision.

Buck laughed, his entire body shaking with amusement. "You wouldn't have to do anything too crazy. You could train other agents or interpret, like you're doing now. There are safe desk jobs that you might like, especially after you earn your PhD."

"It's not for me," Zaire said, wrinkling her nose. "I'll stick to teaching and expanding young minds through language and learning about other cultures. I have to do something with all this information in my head."

"Whatever you decide, I'm sure you'll be great at it."

"Thank you," Zaire said, resting her head on his shoulder. Every compliment she received from him made her feel special and spread warmth in her chest. "Do you think you'll be able to stop the next embassy bombing?"

Buck didn't answer for a while, and the seconds ticked by. Finally, he replied, "I hope so."

Since they couldn't leave earlier than planned, Zaire and Buck took advantage of the hours they had to spare and napped.

When they woke up, they met up with Travis and Samson and they all ate a late dinner in the hotel dining room. Zaire enjoyed a plate of authentic Wiener schnitzel while Buck played it safe with a couple of sausage dogs and a salad.

Listening to the men talk, it was clear they were more than colleagues. They were family and knew quite a bit about each other. It was obvious in the way they teased each other.

"Where are you from?" Travis asked, lifting his water to his lips.

"Dallas, Texas," Zaire replied.

"Oh, another Texan like my boy, Buck. You two have something in common." He flashed a smile and Zaire smiled back.

"You still live in Texas?" Travis asked.

Zaire shook her head. "I live in Atlanta now. I've been there for years, since high school."

"Sam and I live in Atlanta," Travis said.

"You do?" What a coincidence.

He nodded. "Yeah. Sometimes we can even coax Buck into leaving the craziness of DC and coming to see us. It's only a two-hour flight."

He shot a look at Buck, and despite Buck's inscrutable expression, Zaire sensed a message passed between them without words. Had Travis guessed they had slept together and was suggesting Buck might have another reason to come to Atlanta now? Had Buck told them?

She dared not get her hopes up, but her heart skipped a beat nonetheless.

When they finished their meal, they all climbed into Samson's rented car and took off for the airport. She and Buck didn't have bags like the other two. The trip home was vastly different from her arrival, which had included two bags and a carry-on for her three-month stay in Italy.

At the airport, Zaire stepped cautiously behind Buck into the belly of the cargo plane, a huge open space much different from the cramped quarters of commercial airlines.

The magnitude of what was happening hit her. She was finally going home. She might kiss the ground when they landed in DC.

Mostly empty, the interior of the plane held a few boxes and one massive cargo container strapped to the floor.

"Welcome aboard. You get to choose where you sit," Buck announced, pointing at the only two seats.

Bolted to the wall, they were located behind the cockpit, where Samson currently sat, going through his preflight check.

"I guess I'll take that one." Zaire pointed to the seat at the interior of the plane.

She sat down, and Buck crouched in front of her to secure her harness. While he worked, his fingers brushed her hip. His proximity and the care he took made her heart beat faster.

Buck gave the belt a final tug to ensure it was fastened tightly. "There, all set," he said.

Their eyes met for a moment, and memories of mere hours ago shot through her brain. His hands between her thighs, his body slicing into hers as his warm breath feathered along her jawline. The way they'd lain together, wrapped in each other's arms afterward.

Would she ever know that feeling again, of utter and complete euphoria in a man's arms?

Zaire swallowed. "Thanks," she said, her voice husky and low with emotion.

Buck opened his mouth as if he wanted to say something, then shook his head. He sat in the seat beside her and started fastening his own harness.

"Samson is an excellent pilot. He'll get us there safely and in one piece."

"I'll be happy when the doors close and we're in the air. We haven't managed to do that yet."

Travis entered, carrying a knapsack over his shoulder. He handed it to Buck. "Food for the trip. Fruits, snacks and bottled water."

Buck thanked him and placed the bag on the floor.

Travis clapped his hand and walked toward the cockpit. "Let's rock and roll!" He sat in the copilot seat.

The back of the plane closed and the engines hummed to life. Zaire took a deep breath, closed her eyes and said a quick prayer for safe passage.

The plane vibrated on the taxi down the runway, and she felt each tremor in her bones. A few minutes later, they lifted off the tarmac and started their ascent into the sky.

Zaire blew out a breath of relief.

Buck squeezed her hand and smiled. She smiled back.

No ambush this time. They were really in the air.

Twelve hours to go.

Chapter 31

The flight landed after four. As planned, Travis called Commander Ray on the way to Buck's town house.

"Commander, this is Travis. Samson and I are back in the country, and we need to discuss a development with you."

Buck heard the commander's deep voice but couldn't parse the words he was saying.

Travis spoke again. "No, sir. It's very important and can't wait until morning. We're stopping by within the hour."

Benjamin spoke again, and then Travis hung up. "All set," he said.

The rest of the ride continued in silence. Zaire stared out the window, watching the cars and buildings go by. Buck wondered what she was thinking about. They were back on US soil, but he still had to keep her safe until Rick and the rest of his mercenaries were apprehended.

At Buck's town house, Samson parked next to his blue Blazer, and they all climbed out of the vehicle. When they entered, a sense of calm came over Buck. No matter where he was or what he did, whenever he came home he experienced a sense of peace.

"Where's your bathroom?" Zaire asked.

"Down the hall, to the left."

"Thanks."

She was oddly subdued, but perhaps it was because she recognized, like they did, that the next bombing would take place very soon. Depending on what part of the world it took place in, they had less than twenty-four hours to stop it.

"I'll be right back," Buck said to Travis and Samson.

He raced up the stairs and retrieved another weapon from his safe. He tucked it into the side waistband of his jeans, against his hip, and pulled his shirt over it.

When he returned to the first floor, he found Travis and Samson in the kitchen.

"We should go."

"Right behind you." Samson drained the glass of juice in his hand and placed the glass in the sink.

"Keep her safe," Buck said to Travis.

He was leaving Zaire in his care while he and Samson went to Commander Ray's house.

"Do you really think you need to tell me that?" Travis asked.

"No, I don't."

There was no imminent danger, and if there was, Travis was more than capable of keeping Zaire safe. Despite this, Buck felt anxious about leaving her with him. Deep down, he believed he was the best person to ensure her safety.

Zaire entered the kitchen, arms folded over her midsection.

"I'll meet you outside," Samson said, excusing himself.

Travis also left them alone.

Buck and Zaire looked at each other. Their arrival in the United States created a finality to their relationship that he hadn't expected. She was slipping away from him. He'd lose her and what they'd had in Italy.

"You're safe here. No one is getting through Travis. Hopefully, by the end of the day, I'll have good news—that we stopped Payne and his men."

"I'm sure one of the analysts will be able to figure out their plans," Zaire said.

"Let's hope."

Buck stepped close to Zaire and placed his hands on her upper arms. Without a word, he pulled her in and kissed her, giving himself permission to enjoy her soft lips one more time.

His fingers smoothed across the line of her shoulders and slid to the small of her back, pulling her closer. She melted against him, her body softening against his chest. Her hands found the nape of his neck, and her fingers tangled in his hair.

Buck angled his head to deepen the kiss, and a soft moan left her throat. Everything he couldn't say was in the kiss. His regret that they couldn't have met under different circumstances. His longing to get to know her better and have the kind of relationship that men in his position often couldn't find.

When they finally separated, she hugged his torso and rested her forehead against his chest. They were both breathing heavily.

Buck looked into her eyes, his thumb gently caressing her cheek. "I have to go," he said, his voice rough with emotion.

Zaire nodded, her smile bittersweet. "Get those bastards."

He smirked. "We will. I promise."

He reluctantly let her go and walked toward the front of the house, his mouth still tingling from their passionate kiss.

When he exited, he saw Samson waiting beside his blue Blazer. They both climbed into the car, and his friend shot him a look from the passenger seat.

"You all right?"

"I'm fine," Buck said in a gruff voice, starting his car.

"Sure you are," Samson said with a smirk. "If I didn't know better, I'd say you have feelings for Ms. Nichols."

"If I didn't know better, I'd say you need a punch in the nose."

Flinging back his head, Samson belted out a hearty laugh.

Unable to help himself, Buck let out a low chuckle, shaking his head. "I like her," he admitted.

"And she likes you."

"Yeah, I guess."

"What do you mean, 'Yeah, I guess'? What's the problem?"

Buck punched the accelerator. "We live in different cities."

"And? That's why airplanes exist. She seems smart as hell too. You need someone like that to ground you."

"Maybe." He let the dark DC streets draw his attention.

He couldn't admit his real concerns to his friend, that he worried her feelings for him—whatever they might be—were influenced by a healthy dose of hero worship of him. When all of this was over, would she still want *him*?

Commander Ray's home was in an affluent suburb of DC, where long-term politicians who had become millionaires while in office as "public servants" resided. An iron gate and high wall kept out intruders. Buck pulled up to the gate. Before he could punch the call button, it swung inward.

Three Dobermans trotted out from the back of the house. The dogs were trained not to bark until they had snuck up on unsuspecting trespassers. Buck and Samson knew better than to get out, and soon Benjamin was standing in the doorway. He'd taken the hour to dress in a blue-striped shirt and dark slacks.

He made a motion to the dogs and said something Buck didn't hear, and immediately the dogs disappeared behind the house again.

Buck and Samson descended from the Blazer, and when the commander saw Buck, his mouth fell open.

He was about to say Buck's name, when Buck put a finger to his lips. He stepped forward and showed a piece of paper with a note written on it to Benjamin: *Has Rick Payne ever been in your home?*

The older man read the message with a frown and shook his head.

"We had to make sure. We have a theory about the bombings," Buck explained, holding up the recorder. "I have the audio."

Benjamin's frown deepened. "All right, come in. I need to get caught up on what's going on. I thought you were dead, or at the very least missing."

They entered the spacious entryway with black-and-white tile and followed Benjamin into the kitchen.

At the big island in the middle, he turned to face them. "Travis said he and Samson were coming. Where is Ms. Nichols?"

Buck and Samson gave him a summary of their thoughts and the fact that they believed Rick Payne was tapping his phone or otherwise able to access information he had shared.

"You don't seem surprised by what we told you," Samson said.

Benjamin's face settled into a grim line. "I had my suspicions. When I discussed the second extraction at the abandoned airfield, the director was in my office, and I also called the secretary. She gave permission to fly you out, using people she already had over there in Spain. They never made it. Their bodies were found inside the plane, and when I never heard from you, I assumed the worst."

"I had to go radio silent. I knew there was a leak somewhere, and I couldn't risk reaching out to you and having our location compromised again."

"My phone wasn't tapped, but I had my office swept, and a listening device was found." Benjamin let out a short laugh. "I'm surprised you didn't think I was involved."

Samson and Buck shot a quick glance at each other.

"You thought I was involved?" Benjamin exclaimed.

"For a very short period, but we quickly realized you couldn't have betrayed us."

"I'm only your team commander. Thank you," Benjamin said sarcastically.

"I'm sure if you were in our position, you would have thought the same about us for a bit too," Buck said.

Benjamin let out a begrudging grunt of agreement. "Back to Rick. You're confident it's him?"

"I'm 99.9 percent sure."

"I am too. It's him," Samson said.

"Then we need him to confess and tell us where his group will strike next. I'll have intelligence listen to the recording and see if they get any ideas, but after listening to that, it's a long shot.

"We have to do something. In a very short time, another bomb is going off."

Benjamin shook his head. "The secretary was right all along. She didn't like the idea of an outside contractor having so much control over security at our embassies. She's almost single-handedly been holding up that bill in Congress."

"Yet another reason for Rick to terrorize the embassies. It makes her look bad, and her holding up the bill means more lives will be lost. Blood on her hands."

"Son of a—" Benjamin shook his head.

"We want you to set up a meeting with Rick," Buck said. "Get him to meet you alone instead of with his men around him. He knows that Zaire and I escaped his warehouse in the Italian countryside, but he won't know yet that we're back in the country. I want to surprise him and get him to tell us where the next bombing will take place."

"I'll make the call. Let's hope this works," Benjamin said.

Chapter 32

Zaire sat in the den, listening to Travis recount his exploits overseas. While he didn't give her details, she hung on his every word. With their experiences, these men had lived dozens of lives compared to her single lifetime. She marveled at all they'd seen and experienced.

In the middle of a story about a bar fight in Tanzania, the phone rang.

"It's Buck." He hit the speaker button on his cell phone. "Hey, Buck, we're both here. What's the word?"

"We talked to Commander Ray, and we're on the same page," Buck said.

Hearing his voice was as comforting and energizing as receiving a hit of dopamine.

"He agrees with the theory that the embassy bombers are Javelin Security. He called Rick and told him he wants to discuss what happened to us in Italy in a private location, away from prying eyes and ears."

"Does he know you'll be there?"

"No, and the commander told him he's bringing him in on his plans since he was already an integral part of our security and had a vested interest because he had lost some men at the hands of the terrorists. We're meeting him in a couple of hours to discuss it. We've already sent the audio to the analysts for review and given them the names of the men on the recording. We're hoping there's something in the audio that will tell us where they plan to strike next so we don't even need Rick."

"We've seen how dangerous this man and his people can be. Please be careful," Zaire said.

"We will be," Buck answered. "We'll be in touch soon with any updates."

Travis hung up. "He'll be all right. He knows what he's doing."

Zaire rubbed her hands together. "I know, I've seen him in action. I don't know why I said that."

His lips took on a rueful twist. "I know why."

She ventured a glance at him.

"You have feelings for him, don't you?"

The question took her by surprise, and she let out a short laugh. She didn't want to lie, so she chose not to answer instead of admitting her feelings for Buck to his friend.

"I noticed you didn't answer," Travis said.

"I don't know what you want me to say."

"The truth. Listen, I know what it's like to be on the run with someone of the opposite sex. You get close, you become scared, you depend on each other. It's perfectly natural to develop feelings for someone in those circumstances."

"Are you saying Buck has done this before?" Zaire asked quietly. Maybe she wasn't as special as she'd thought she was.

Travis shook his head. "No, that would be me. Buck usually has better control of those romantic inclinations, to be honest. Matter of fact, he doesn't usually get involved with women he's charged with protecting."

"Oh." Zaire played with her fingers. "What I feel is…silly."

"Nah, it's not. I know Buck has feelings for you, too."

That caught her attention. "What makes you say that?"

Travis smiled knowingly. "Because he told me to make

sure that I kept you safe, as if I'm a novice. This man has known me for six years. He knows what I'm capable of, yet it was obvious that he didn't think anyone else could take care of you as well as he could."

His words made her feel better.

"He told me about Lana," she said quietly.

Travis's eyebrows rose higher. "The two of you *did* get close. He doesn't like to talk about her."

"We opened up to each other about painful events from our past. Personally, I think she was a fool."

Travis chuckled. "I agree. Hey, give him time. When all of this is over, he'll be in a better headspace. Right now, he's focused on bringing down Payne and his murderous thugs." He pushed up from the sofa. "Are you hungry? I could make breakfast while we wait."

"I could eat," Zaire replied.

"Let me see what my boy has in the fridge. Knowing him, there's bacon and eggs and sliced bread in there."

"His standard breakfast, if you add oatmeal," Zaire said.

Travis paused on his way out the room. "The two of you really did get close, huh?"

As he walked into the kitchen, Zaire stood up and stretched. She needed to keep her mind off what was happening, so she strolled through Buck's town house, moving restlessly from room to room, examining his furniture and checking out his trophies and awards.

His home was simply furnished, with traditional pieces, which didn't surprise her. Being a Southern man from rural Texas, and based on what she had gleaned about him when in Rome, it came as no surprise that he had gone the traditional route in his decor.

She paused when she stumbled upon several photo albums tucked into a bookcase in the den. Taking them to the sofa, she began perusing the photos. The first album wasn't very thick and contained pictures of Buck and his Navy SEAL buddies. Flipping through the pages, she wondered in which parts of the world they had taken the pictures.

One photo showed the men around a fire, dressed in fatigues with their weapons in hand. Buck had a buzz cut and looked much younger, but he still looked very fit, showing off his muscular arms in a sleeveless white tank top.

Her favorite photo album was the one featuring him when he was younger with three other boys, whom she assumed were the cousins he had told her about. In every photo where they were all together, they definitely looked mischievous.

"You ready to eat?" Travis called from the kitchen.

She'd been so preoccupied with the albums, the scent of bacon and eggs hadn't registered.

"Yes," she said enthusiastically.

They sat at Buck's small table and ate the food. "Do you mind if I use your phone after? I need to call my parents."

"Go right ahead. It's all yours."

Zaire had been hungrier than expected and cleaned her plate. After the meal, she picked up the phone from the coffee table and called her mother's number because she was more likely to answer than her father. On too many occasions, he couldn't even find his phone. She remained at the table while Travis settled in front of the TV and watched a martial arts film.

"Hello?" her mother said.

"Mom, it's me."

Elisa Nichols gasped. "Oh my goodness, Zaire! Where are you? Your father and I have been trying to reach you since yesterday. We couldn't get in touch with you, we couldn't get in touch with Josie. We were so worried."

Knowing her mother, if today had been a weekday, she would have called Worldwide Language Solutions too.

"Mom, I have a lot to tell you, but I can't go into details right now. I'm in DC."

"DC! What are you doing there?"

"It's a long story, and I'll explain later, but I wanted you to know where I am and that I'm safe."

"Honey, when you talk like that, you scare me. You know that kind of answer is not good enough for me, because now I'm worried anyway. Did something go wrong in Rome?"

Boy, did it ever. "Like I said, I—"

The sentence broke off as Zaire watched the scene on the television. What caught her attention was a flag that flashed across the screen.

"Mom, I have to go."

"Honey, are you sure everything is okay? Do you need us?"

"No, I'm fine. I promise. I'll call you later, okay? Love you. Tell Daddy I love him too."

"Okay, dear, make sure you do call me later. You know how I get. Love you."

"I promise I'll call you back." Zaire hung up without saying goodbye. "Travis, what movie is this?"

He looked over the back of the sofa at her. "I don't remember the name, but it's on Netflix."

"Do you mind if I rewind it? Something caught my eye."

"No, go ahead."

Zaire went over to the sofa and took the remote from him. She rewound the film and froze the frame on the flag flying over the government building in the movie. A Malaysian flag. It was very similar to the US flag—red, white and blue— though their flag also included a yellow crescent and sun.

Seeing it reminded her of another flag. The flag of Liberia was similar, including the color blue and red and white stripes. Except where the US had the fifty stars, Liberia only had one star.

Using Travis's phone, she pulled up the image of the flags of both countries. Sure enough, all three flags looked very much alike.

Operation Red, White and Blue, she thought. That was the common thread between the embassies that had been attacked. Malaysia and Liberia's flags bore a striking resemblance to the flag of the United States.

What had Cain actually said in the recording?

Zaire closed her eyes to recall his exact words.

One more bombing.

Operation Red, White and Blue will soon be over, and the next bombing will be the biggest one yet.

"Thanks." Heart racing, she handed back the remote.

"Everything okay?"

"Um, I'm not sure."

Had they been looking at the clues all wrong? Cain said there would be another bombing. He never said there would be another *embassy* bombing.

There was a pattern, but they hadn't known what it was. The pattern was in the flags. The last bombing was going to take place on US soil. She was certain of it. But where?

New York? LA?

"Travis, I think I've figured out where the next bombing will take place."

"What?" He hopped to his feet.

She turned the phone screen toward him. "The flags are the common thread. Malaysia, Liberia, the United States. They all look alike. All red, white and blue. He started with Malaysia and Liberia, but now he's going to set off the third bomb here, on US soil—not at one of our embassies overseas."

"Holy…"

"We have to tell Buck and the others."

Chapter 33

Hiding in the stairwell, Buck kept his eyes on Commander Ray, who was standing next to his personal vehicle, a white sedan parked on the top floor of an old parking deck outside the DC area.

Benjamin wore one of his three-piece suits. He also wore a wire in case he could get incriminating evidence from Rick. Two members of the comms team were in an unmarked van several blocks away, listening in.

They had chosen this spot for its seclusion and the ability to determine if Rick brought anyone else with him. They didn't think he would, but they couldn't be certain.

Samson was at the other side of the deck, near the elevator, keeping an eye on the entrance with binoculars. They all had earpieces so they could communicate, especially if things went south.

The time dragged by. Rick was late.

"I don't see anything. He's not coming," Samson said.

"He's coming. He wants to know what's going on, and he has to continue to play the role of hero and helper," Benjamin said.

"I agree. He'll be here," Buck said.

A few minutes later, Samson was saying something entirely different. "He's here. At least, I think it's him. He's driving a black SUV. Looks like he's alone."

Excellent.

Shortly afterward, the SUV slowly approached Benjamin and came to a stop some feet away. Rick jumped out of the driver's seat in a pullover and jeans. Straightening the spectacles on his nose, he approached.

Benjamin extended a hand. "Rick, it's good to see you. I appreciate you dropping everything and coming on such short notice."

"Of course. As soon as you told me what happened, I was concerned. You still haven't heard from Buck or Ms. Nichols?"

"Not a word. We had tried to get them out using contacts in Spain, but those people were killed, and we haven't heard from Buck."

Rick shook his head, broadcasting concern. "Tell me what you need. How can I help?"

"You have people in Italy, and I'm hoping you could deploy them to help us do a ground search for Buck and Zaire. I should warn you that it might turn into a full-fledged rescue operation, and last time you helped us, you lost men. I wish I didn't have to ask for your help, but this is an off the books operation, and I don't have the resources available to me that I normally would."

"I understand, and I'm willing and able to help. But why are we meeting here?"

Benjamin shook his head. "I think there's a leak in our office."

"What?" He was good. He actually sounded surprised.

Buck's phone buzzed on his hip. With a quick glance, he saw Travis was calling.

Was everything okay? Could something be wrong with Zaire?

He put his comms on Mute and answered.

"Buck, it's me."

Immediately on alert, he held the phone hard to his ear. "Zaire, what's going on?"

"I think I know where the next bomb will go off. It's not an embassy. Payne is going to blow up a building here in the US."

"How did you come to that conclusion?" Buck asked.

He listened to her explain about the similarity of the flags, and what she said made sense. He understood Rick's plans for the embassies, but what was the end game with an attack on US soil? They had to find out and figure out where the attack was going to take place.

"I'll get the message to Commander Ray. Have I ever told you that you're smart?"

Zaire laughed. "I guess all that information in my head turned out to be useful after all."

They hung up, and Buck turned his comms back on.

"...they're good at covering their tracks," Rick was saying.

Buck dialed Commander Ray's number.

"Excuse me," the commander said, taking his phone out of his breast pocket. "Hello."

"Act normal," Buck warned. "I just got a call from Zaire. She's figured out that the next bomb is set to go off in this country. Rick is planning something beyond the embassy bombings."

"I see. I'll be in the office shortly, and I can pass on the information to the secretary."

"I think we should apprehend him now."

"Do that."

Now that he'd been given the go-ahead, Buck walked toward his commander and Rick. As soon as Rick saw him, he took a step back in shock.

"What's going on here? You told me that he was missing."

"I lied," Commander Ray said.

Buck pulled his weapon from his waistband and pointed it at Rick. "It's over. We know what you've done."

"What are you talking about?" He was still pretending. Still lying.

"We know that you're the one who set off the bombs at the embassies in Malaysia and Liberia. We also know that you were the one who tried to eliminate me and Zaire in Italy."

"Why would I do that? I was trying to help. I lost *men* because I was trying to help," Rick snarled.

"You pretended to try to help, but instead you were only helping yourself," Benjamin countered.

"We know where the last target is. It's time to end this," Buck said.

"Do you, now?" Rick was practically laughing in Buck's face.

"Your next target is a building in the United States. Where are you planning to hit? New York? DC?"

Rick shook his head. "Ridiculous, and I don't have to stand here and have my reputation destroyed. I'm a former Marine. I love my country. The real terrorists are out there, and I'll gladly help you find them, but that's not what you want. You want to point fingers and find someone to blame for your own inadequacies."

"The only inadequacy in security was allowing you and your men access to information you shouldn't have had access to and allowing you in spaces where you could take advantage and plot to terrorize our diplomatic staff."

Rick's lip curled up. "Like I said, I won't stand here and

be insulted." He moved to turn away, but Buck lifted the weapon higher and aimed for his head.

"Hands in the air. Now."

"You really want to do this? You really think that I tried to kill you?" Rick demanded.

"If this is all a big mistake, you have no problem coming in for questioning," Buck said calmly.

Rick let out a humorless laugh. "Questioning? Is that what you call it when you spooks torture people into confessing to crimes they didn't commit? What proof do you have that I was involved in those bombings?"

"We'll get proof."

"So a fishing expedition. Exactly as I thought. You have nothing." Rick spat out the last word with disgust.

"Because you covered your tracks so well?" Benjamin interjected.

"No, because there is no proof."

"Put your hands in the air," Buck repeated.

"Just ugly allegations." Rick lifted his hands in the air and pointed his right forefinger toward the east. Buck immediately recognized it as a signal and barely had time to react.

He flung his body at his commander, and they hit the ground a split second after a silent round whizzed through the air and shattered the window of the white car.

"Sniper in the building to the east!" Samson yelled in Buck's ear. "I'm on my way!"

Buck and the commander scrambled on their hands and knees as two more rounds hit the vehicle. One sliced through the front door and the other went through the front tire, barely missing Buck's leg.

They hid behind the vehicle. Frustrated, Buck didn't know where Rick had gone. He had disappeared behind the SUV.

"Rick, what the hell are you doing?" Buck yelled. "You don't have to do this. Let's talk."

He took comfort in the fact that Rick didn't know they were communicating via comms and likely didn't know Samson was on the way to disable his sniper.

Rick laughed darkly. "Oh, you want to talk? A minute ago you accused me of setting off those bombs at the embassies and planning to do the same here. As far as I'm concerned, you can all go to hell. You'll never find the bomb, and you'll never find me. You and that bitch interpreter can spend the rest of your lives looking over your shoulders until the day I put you both in the ground."

Buck gritted his teeth when he heard Rick threaten Zaire.

Then he heard a door slam.

No. He was in the SUV.

The engine started.

He looked at the commander.

"I'm fine," Benjamin said. "Go get him."

Rick drove away with a squeal of tires, and Buck shot up from behind the car and raced toward the staircase. He dodged bullets that splintered the concrete beneath his feet and raced down the stairs, two at a time. He pushed his way out the steel door and into the third floor of the parking deck as Rick came careening around the corner.

When he saw Buck, he stopped, and they had a temporary standoff.

"It's over, Rick!" Buck yelled at him.

"No, it's not!"

Rick drove straight at him, but Buck was ready. Feet shoulder width apart, he pointed his weapon, aimed and fired. Three rounds pierced the windshield of the vehicle and then he dove to the side, rolling out of the path of Rick's SUV.

Rick lost control of the car, and it crashed into a wall with a loud crunch of metal.

Buck shot to his feet and rushed over. He smashed the window and yanked open the door to find Rick slumped over the deployed airbag, blood leaking from wounds in his shoulder and arm. He made a half-hearted move to block Buck, but Buck punched him in the face and knocked his head sideways.

Rick grunted at the force of the blow. "This isn't over, Buck," he moaned.

Buck dragged him from the vehicle and placed him on the ground, face down. "It is for you."

"I'm not telling you bastards anything."

"We'll see about that."

Chapter 34

"Any word yet?" Buck paced the floor of his den, phone to his ear.

"Nothing yet," Travis said, sounding disgusted.

After receiving medical attention, Rick was placed in FBI custody, and at Benjamin's insistence, Buck and Travis had swapped places. He wanted Buck to get some rest, but the last thing Buck wanted to do was rest.

He had returned home, and Travis had gone to an FBI off-the-record holding site, which is where he wished he could be. The FBI used the secure facility to interrogate particularly dangerous or high-profile suspects.

With Rick apprehended domestically, they had taken the lead, reducing the Omega Team to observers, and it was frustrating. Rick was refusing to talk and insisted he knew nothing about the bombings.

"They should let *us* talk to him," Buck said in a grim tone.

Travis grunted. "I wish. At least agents have already raided Javelin Security headquarters, and they're coordinating with law enforcement in Italy to search the offices there. Based on the information you provided, they were able to locate the warehouse in the Italian countryside and are questioning the men there. They're searching through the electronics in both locations. They're bound to find something."

Buck stopped pacing and ran a hand over his hair. "We're running out of time."

"I know. Tomorrow's Sunday."

"What about the sniper at the parking deck?" Buck asked.

"He says he doesn't know anything, and we're inclined to be believe him. He seems low level. I'll continue observing Rick's interrogation. In the meantime, get something to eat. Get some rest. I'll let you know if anything changes."

That wasn't what he wanted to hear, but nothing else could be done. "Thanks, Travis." Buck hung up the phone.

Zaire looked at him expectantly from the sofa. "Any luck?"

He shook his head. "Nothing. There has to be a way to figure this out."

"What about the analysts?" she asked.

"They don't know, either. We're at a dead end." He sank onto the sofa and looked over at her. "Travis told me to get some rest. You should get some too."

"I can't, and I doubt I'll be able to sleep tonight. I'm too worried about what will happen tomorrow—and when."

He had the same concerns and doubted sleep would come. To get so close to finding out about the bombings and not being able to put the final puzzle piece together was frustrating.

"Come here." He lifted his arm, and Zaire snuggled up next to him. "Let's hope the FBI can get that bastard to talk, or they'll find out his plans from someone on his staff or through sifting through his electronics. If not, at least we know we did all we could."

That was the best spin Buck could put on the disappointing outcome.

His stomach growled, and he realized with a start that he hadn't eaten since morning.

Zaire lifted her head from his shoulder. "Are you hungry?"

"Apparently. What about you?"

"I haven't eaten since breakfast," she said.

Buck checked the time. "We might as well get something to eat. There isn't much we can do while we wait. What are you in the mood for?"

"Do you know any good Mexican places?" Zaire asked.

"There's one not too far from here." He stood and helped her to her feet.

After locking up the town house, they climbed in the Blazer and took off.

"How can you stand this?" Zaire asked.

"What?" Buck shot a glance at her.

"The waiting. The not knowing. My stomach is in knots."

"I've learned over time that I can only do what I can do, and I have to let other people handle the parts that I can't."

She folded her arms across her chest and stared out the windshield. "More people are going to die, and it doesn't seem right that I'm going to have Mexican food."

"Not eating isn't going to change anything," Buck pointed out. When she didn't respond, he continued. "Not every operation goes according to plan. Remember the extraction I told you about in South Africa? Our team suffered injuries, including me, and we lost one of our brothers. These things happen. All we can do is our best."

"I still hate it," Zaire whispered.

"I understand. I hate it too."

"I want the good guys to win."

"We haven't lost yet."

They were silent for a while, and then she asked, "What made you decide to become a Navy SEAL?"

Buck made a left turn. "It wasn't exactly my first choice. I disappointed my parents by not going to college, which shouldn't have been a surprise to them, based on the kind of kid I was growing up."

"College isn't for everyone," Zaire said.

"True, but that's a bitter pill to swallow for educators."

She nodded, indicating she understood.

"I'd seen enough people who didn't know what to do with themselves when they didn't go to college or find a job right away. Bo, my cousin, didn't want to go to college, either. We both decided that rather than floundering around doing nothing, we'd join the Navy. We were two adventurous kids from Dripping Springs trying to figure out life. During basic training, my commanding officer asked if I'd ever considered becoming a SEAL and said I'd be the perfect candidate for training."

He still remembered the conversation with his CO. He had talked to a SEAL recruiter about Buck, emphasizing his physical endurance and mental toughness.

"And then you were recruited from the SEALs to work for the Omega Team?"

"That's right."

"Are Travis and Samson SEALs too?" Zaire asked.

Buck shook his head as he pulled into the parking lot of the restaurant, where a flashing sign with a man wearing a sombrero hovered above the doorway.

"The Omega Team is made up of special ops agents from the various armed forces. Travis was Delta Force, and Samson was recruited from the Air Force's Combat Control Team."

He hopped out of the Blazer and held the door of the restaurant open for Zaire. Inside, Mexican music blasted through hidden speakers, and the scent of onions, garlic, and spices hit his nostrils.

"*Hola*. Two for dinner?" a young woman asked, holding up two fingers.

"Yes," Buck replied.

She led them to a booth where they had a view of the parking lot. They sat across from each other and perused the menu. When the waitress arrived, they placed their orders.

He ordered the steak fajitas, which arrived sizzling on a hot plate to the table. Zaire had a chicken burrito with a side of refried beans and rice.

They drank non-alcoholic sangrias and kept the conversation light while they ate their meal, both of them making a conscious effort to keep their minds off the pending disaster. Twice during the dinner, Buck took a surreptitious look at his phone to make sure he hadn't missed an update.

He wished the FBI would let him get his hands on Rick. He'd beat the answer out of the bastard.

They were almost finished with dinner when his phone rang, and the caller ID showed *Unknown*. His heart rate quickened, and he immediately answered.

"Hello?"

Zaire stared across the table at him. *Who is it?* she mouthed.

Benjamin, he mouthed back.

"Buck?"

"Good news?"

"Not yet. Payne won't budge, but the tech guys are combing through his electronics as we speak as an alternative to getting the answers we need. That's not why I called. I was talking to one of Secretary Hilton's assistants, giving her an update on Rick's apprehension and the questioning of him and his people. There were questions I couldn't answer, and the secretary wants as much detail as possible, with the hope that she can use her resources and influence to see if we can crack the location of the next bombing. She wants to speak to you and Ms. Nichols in person. Is Ms. Nichols still at your house?"

"She's right here with me. We're having dinner."

"Good. The secretary is flying out on an important diplomatic trip to Mexico tonight. She's been making final preparations, meeting with her staff and advisor to ensure everything goes well before her departure. Time is short. She wants you to meet her on the tarmac before she flies out. Both of you."

"When?"

"*Now.* She's on her way to the airfield."

"We'll be there."

"You know the drill. Give her every bit of information you can, and encourage Zaire to do the same. We're going to hit this thing from all sides."

"Understood, sir."

Buck hung up the phone, reinvigorated by the conversation. "That was Commander Ray. Secretary Hilton wants to talk to us in person."

Zaire's eyebrows raised higher. "The secretary of state?"

"The one and only. She wants us to meet her before she flies out on a diplomatic trip."

"When do we leave?"

"Right away. She's on her way to the plane."

Buck stood, and Zaire hopped up from the booth too. He stopped at the register to pay for their meal before exiting the restaurant and climbing back into the Blazer.

"She'll want as much detail as possible. Mention everything you can think of that might be able to help stop these terrorists."

Zaire nodded her understanding as Buck backed out of the parking lot and pulled into traffic.

Chapter 35

Benjamin must have provided photos of them ahead of time because when they arrived at Joint Base Andrews, a member of the secretary's staff greeted them in the terminal—a woman who looked to be in her thirties, with her short dark hair tucked behind her ears.

"Mr. Swanson, Ms. Nichols?" she inquired.

"Yes," Buck and Zaire said at the same time.

"I'm Jennifer Alcott, assistant to Secretary Hilton," the woman said, extending her hand. "Unfortunately, we're short on time, and there's a storm brewing that the pilots would like to get ahead of so the secretary doesn't miss her meeting tomorrow. She asked if you could join us on the five-hour flight to Mexico. As she'll be there for several days, we'll arrange to have you flown back to DC upon landing. We understand this is a huge inconvenience, but she would very much like to hear everything you have to say about what happened in Italy to figure out how we can protect our diplomatic staff moving forward. Can you join us on the trip?"

"Yes, absolutely," Buck said and then looked at Zaire, who also agreed.

"Excellent. Please follow me. As a precaution, security personnel will need to conduct a thorough search of your person before you board the plane."

She led them through an unmarked door where two uniformed personnel were waiting—one woman and one man.

"This way, Ms. Nichols," the woman said.

Zaire looked back at Buck before she was led into a room. He caught a quick glance of the interior, which included a metal table and plain white walls. The male officer led him into a similar room, where he was asked to disrobe down to his underwear.

After the search for weapons was completed, he was taken back into the hallway, where he and Zaire reunited with Jennifer.

"Follow me," the assistant said.

She escorted them across the tarmac to the waiting plane. The modified Boeing C-32 was white on top and blue on the bottom with United States of America written in block letters above the windows.

Jennifer led them up the staircase and through the door, nodding at the male flight attendant as they passed.

They walked through the plane past staff members. Some barely glanced at them, others outright stared at the newcomers.

Jennifer led them through a door into an open area. "This is the senior staff area," she explained, where two men and a woman sat in front of computers with wireless printers.

Their final destination was a small room with a black leather chair and a blue and red sofa across the table from it.

Jennifer clasped her hands together. "The secretary will be with you shortly. Would either of you like something to drink—water or juice?"

"I'm fine," Buck said.

"Me too," Zaire replied.

After she left them alone, Zaire glanced at him. "This is wild."

"You'll have some stories to tell your kids some day," he teased. He looked out the window at the well-lit terminal.

"Definitely," Zaire agreed.

Buck sent a text to Benjamin to let him know that he and Zaire were on the flight with the secretary, and she'd be conducting the interview on the way to Mexico.

Moments later, the plane's engines roared to life, and it began to taxi down the runway.

Not long after, Secretary Hilton entered the room with a man carrying a laptop. He was dark-haired and wore a suit. The secretary was also well-dressed in a navy-blue pants suit, her gray hair cut in a pixie style. She wore very little makeup, and her only jewelry was her wedding and engagement rings.

Buck came to his feet and so did Zaire. "Madame Secretary," he said, extending his hand.

She shook his hand. "Mr. Swanson. Ms. Nichols." She shook Zaire's hand too. "Please, both of you, have a seat."

The secretary and the man sat in the leather chair across from them.

Buck noticed the deep concern on the secretary's face. He suspected she'd spent a lot of sleepless nights wondering how to resolve this issue.

Crossing one leg over the other, she rested her elbow on the chair's armrests and steepled her fingers. "Thank you for accommodating me. I know this is highly unusual, but the past eight months have been extremely stressful as we try to determine who attacked our embassies. As if that's not enough, it's an election year, and the opposition is using these heinous acts to launch attacks against our party." Her lips flattened into a thin line. "Commander Ray has given me a summary of what he believes is Javelin Security's role, but as I understand it, we haven't figured out *where* the next bombing will take place."

"That's correct, Madame Secretary, but there are people working on it," Buck assured her.

"Well, I can't sit idly by and do nothing. I want to do everything within my power to make sure that we get the answers we need. This is David. He'll be taking notes. Tell me everything you know."

They gave her a full rundown of what they knew and events that had taken place in Italy from the time Zaire overheard the men talking in the break room at Zinga. The conversation lasted almost two hours. The secretary asked a multitude of questions, and it was obvious her main concern was the safety of her people.

As the meeting came to a close, she smiled at Buck and Zaire. "Thank you very much. Based on what you've told me, I agree that the next time they strike, it will be on US soil—but again, the question is where exactly? I'm going to make some calls now and see what I can do to get answers." Her mouth set in a determined line, and she stood. "If either of you need anything, simply step outside this room. A member of my staff will be happy to help you."

"Thank you," Buck said.

After the secretary and David left, Zaire turned to Buck. "What do you think?"

"I think she's about to put her foot on someone's neck. At least I hope so."

"Me too. Man, I need a drink." She laughed lightly. "But I'll settle for water. Do you want anything?"

"Water for me too, please."

"Be right back."

He watched her leave, and immediately his thoughts went to what would happen after this ordeal was over. Zaire would go back to her life in Atlanta, and he'd go back to DC and his missions.

He took another look out the window at the darkness. He felt like that's what his life would become without Zaire. Dark. Void. Empty. Without light.

"Damn, Buck, what the hell is wrong with you?" he muttered, scrubbing his fingers through his hair.

Zaire returned and handed him a bottle of water. He opened it and took a sip.

"How did you end up becoming an interpreter?" he asked.

Zaire drank some of her water too and then carefully placed the bottle on the table. "It wasn't because I was a bad kid, like someone I know."

He chuckled. "Define bad."

"You know what you did," she said. "No, seriously, the idea to become an interpreter came to me a long time ago, in middle school. Like you, someone else noticed my skills and steered me in the right direction. That person was my French teacher, Mrs. Brixton. Mrs. Brixton was impressed with how quickly I learned French and said I had an aptitude for languages. She planted the idea of becoming an interpreter, but it didn't take much nudging because I enjoyed languages and learning about other cultures so much. Traveling with my parents reinforced the idea. I took the necessary classes in college—linguistics, cross-cultural communication—that kind of thing. I loved them all.

"In some ways my job makes me feel…powerful, I guess. My clients are dependent on me. They need me. Without me they can't communicate, which makes me take my job very seriously."

"Hmm. Now that you mention it, you do have a lot of power," Buck remarked.

Zaire smiled mischievously. "With great power comes great responsibility."

He let out a laugh. "Okay, Miss Superhero," he teased.

She grinned, and he was glad to see her smiling, which meant she was no longer thinking about where the next explosion would take place. There would be plenty of time for them to worry about that as the hours continued ticking toward Sunday and an unknown deadline.

In fifty-one minutes it would be Sunday. Would the next bomb go off right away or later in the day like the last two?

There was a soft knock on the door, and Jennifer entered, holding a phone. "Buck, there's a call for you."

He frowned. "Me?"

"Yes. Someone named Samson." She handed over the phone and left them alone.

If Samson was calling, maybe they had good news. Maybe the FBI had finally broken Rick Payne or one of his men.

"Hello, Samson?"

"Buck, I need to talk to you. Are you sitting down?"

"Yes. Tell me Rick cracked and told you where the next bombing will take place."

"He did, but you're not going to like it."

"What do you mean?"

There was a minute pause.

"The bomb is on the secretary's plane."

Buck shot to his feet, and Zaire stared up at him in surprise. *"What?"*

"Rick gleefully told us where the bomb is located. He started ranting about how the secretary had destroyed his chance to get the contract because she'd pulled in favors to stall the bill in Congress. His lobbying efforts hit a brick wall because of her. He doesn't care that we know what he's been up to. His actions are all about revenge now."

Buck muttered a curse. "So the plan was to kill her all along?" he asked.

"Yes. The embassy bombings were to force her hand. He

had decided that if they didn't work, he would eliminate her. He had an inside man help him. One of the baggage handlers. Rick wanted the contract to secure the embassies, and she was the one person standing in his way, so he did what he had to do—his words."

"*She* was standing in his way." Buck recalled how the recording had been cut off at the end, right as Cain and Luca caught Zaire listening to their conversation. *She won't*—

He'd assumed Cain had been referring to the country as "she," but it was a person all along. The secretary. With her out of the way, the bill was more likely to pass through Congress, with Javelin Security favored to benefit.

"Where is it?" Buck asked.

"Cargo hold. The FBI has a bomb tech on standby. You're going to have to disarm this thing, and he'll guide you through it. Benjamin is on the phone with the head of the secretary's security detail right now."

The door burst open, and a man with short red hair stood in the doorway. "Buck Swanson?"

Buck lowered the phone from his ear. "Yes."

"Tom Ridgefield. We need you in the cargo hold."

"What's happening?" Zaire asked, rising to her feet.

"Rick finally told them where the last bomb is located," Buck replied. "He wants to kill the secretary, and the bomb is on this plane."

Her eyes opened as wide as quarters.

Buck lifted the phone to his ear again. "I'm on my way to the cargo hold."

Chapter 36

As Buck followed Tom, another member of the security team, a man with dark hair, joined them. As the three men rushed through the plane, the eyes of the other passengers followed them. Some filled with hope. Some filled with fear.

"It's in one of the electrical panels," Samson continued. "We don't know which one. You'll need a screwdriver to open them."

"We'll need tools," Buck said to Tom.

The secretary of state was standing near the front of the plane. When they approached, she gripped one of Buck's biceps with tight fingers.

"Can you do this?" She spoke in a calm voice, but a thread of fear laced the question.

"I can, Madame Secretary." There was no way he was letting Rick Payne win and have him take any more innocent lives.

A female member of the staff approached. "The pilot is searching for a place to land, Madame Secretary," she said.

Secretary Hilton released Buck, and he followed the dark-haired man down the stairs and into the cargo hold.

The spacious area was dimly lit with overhead lights providing minimal lighting. It contained luggage and boxes, some of which were tied down. The walls were made of metal, and the loud hum of the aircraft's engines and systems filled the air.

Buck stepped across the rolling tracks baggage handlers used to load luggage into the bay. He walked over to one of the panels. "How many electrical panels do you think this thing has?" he asked Samson.

"A bird that size? I'd say six, maybe eight panels."

"How much time do we have?"

"Less than an hour, if Rick told us the truth," Samson replied. "It's supposed to go off at 12:01 a.m."

That didn't give them much time at all.

Buck heard movement behind him, and Tom came toward him with a box of tools. Buck took a Phillips head and flathead screwdriver. "The bomb is in the electrical panel, and there may be as many as eight of them down here. I'll work here in the luggage bay, and the two of you can start opening the panels in the back. Take. Your. Time. The last thing we want to do is set off the bomb."

Both men looked at each other.

"Got it." Tom inhaled and let out a deep breath before he and the other member of the security team disappeared toward the back.

"You still there?" Buck asked.

"I'm here, brother. Give me a sec, and I'll patch through the bomb tech."

Wedging the phone between his shoulder and ear, Buck set to work removing the screws of the first panel. He took his time, slowly loosening them with the flathead screwdriver, worried that one wrong move and the entire plane would be blown to bits.

"How's it going?" Samson asked.

"We're not dead yet," Buck answered.

"Glad to see your sense of humor is intact. I have Alex

on the line. He'll guide you through disarming the bomb when you find it."

"Hi, Buck," Alex said.

"Hey, Alex. Wish we'd met under different circumstances, but you get me out of this, and I'll buy you a beer."

"I'm more of a whiskey man."

"Done," Buck said.

He removed the last screw and held the door in place with his hand. Slowly, he removed it, but didn't see any suspicious wires attached. He let out the breath he'd been holding and examined the interior.

"Nothing unusual in this first one. On to the next."

"Buck?" He swung around. Zaire was standing before him.

"What are you doing down here?" he said in a loud voice, to be heard above the noise.

"Can't let you have all the fun," she said with a weak smile. "How can I help?"

"You need to go back upstairs."

"What difference does it make? Upstairs or down here, if the bomb goes off, we're all dead. How can I help?"

He noted the stubborn set to her mouth and decided she was right and he might as well accept the help. He handed her the phone. "Put that on Speaker and hold it for me. The bomb tech is going to walk me through disarming the bomb."

He moved past some luggage and found the next panel. Starting the process again, he slowly loosened the screws until they were all undone. In careful slow motion, he eased back the door, and his heart sank. Deep down, he'd hoped that maybe the baggage handler hadn't done his part and installed the bomb.

Unfortunately, that was not the case. The device was nestled among wires and might otherwise have been overlooked if not for the LED display counting down the seconds from twenty-five minutes.

"I found it."

"What did you say?" Samson asked.

"I found the bomb!" Buck said louder.

Zaire came closer and looked inside the panel.

"Tell me what you see," Alex instructed.

"Red, black, blue, and green wires. They're all mixed up in there with the electrical wiring. It's hard to figure out what is what. Wait, I'll send a picture to Samson, and he can forward you the image."

Right as he took the photo, Tom walked up. "Oh no," he murmured.

"Sending now," Buck said.

The wait seemed to take forever, but the span of time was only a few minutes.

Finally, Alex spoke. "Okay, couple of things I need to make real clear. This is a highly sophisticated device with a couple of tamper-proof mechanisms built in. You can't remove it from that location without risking an immediate explosion."

Zaire, Tom, and Buck all looked at each other.

"I wasn't planning to do that, but good to know," Buck said.

"It also contains a barometric pressure sensor. What that means is, any sudden altitude changes could activate the bomb. The pilot needs to maintain the current altitude."

Buck shot a glance at Tom. "The pilot was trying to find a place to land."

"He can't do that!" Alex practically yelled.

"I'll let them know." Tom ran off.

Buck returned his attention to the panel, head throbbing as

a maelstrom of emotions coursed through him. "Okay, we're taking care of the issue of altitude. Now what?"

"Now I'm going to tell you how to disarm it. You need to follow my instructions exactly as I tell you. Do you understand?"

"I have no desire to be a rebel. If you tell me to tug twice on my ear while cutting the red wire, I'm tugging my ear twice, Alex."

The bomb tech laughed a little. "That's what I like to hear. All right, what I need you to do is cut the blue wire. The one closest to the timer."

Buck studied the interior. "There are a lot of blue wires in here," he said.

It was also hard to see because of the dim lights. Meanwhile, the numbers on the display continued to decrease. They were under twenty minutes now.

"Find the one closest to the timer," Alex said.

"Dark blue or light blue?"

"Dark blue."

The dark-haired member of the secretary's security team approached. When he saw the bomb, he whispered something Buck couldn't hear, but he understood the gist of it from the alarm on his face.

"Where is the toolbox?" Buck asked. "I need a flashlight."

"I left it at the back of the plane." The man went to retrieve it.

"How are we doing?" Alex asked.

"Waiting on a flashlight so I can see better."

"Okay, you have plenty of time, so take your time."

Security returned with the box and handed over the flashlight.

"Are there wire cutters in there?" Buck asked.

The man rummaged through the box. "No, but there's

this." He held up a pair of needle-nose pliers with a wire cutting edge.

"That'll work." Buck took the tool.

He turned on the flashlight and held it aloft. His eyes followed the line of the blue wires, and he made sure he was looking at the one closest to the timer.

"I'm about to cut it," he announced.

He shot a quick glance at Zaire and the man standing beside her. They both looked like they were holding their breaths.

He took a deep breath and edged the pliers to the wire. Closing his eyes, he said a quick prayer.

Then he cut the wire.

The display went dark.

"Buck?" That was Samson.

"It worked." Buck let out a laugh of relief. "The countdown has stopped—"

The display flashed on, and instead of the slow countdown of seconds from before, the numbers decreased at an alarming rate.

What the...?

The smile on Buck's face died, and underneath the noise around him, he heard Zaire's gasp.

"Alex, what the hell! The countdown restarted, and it's going much faster!" he said.

"What's it doing?"

"*Counting down*," Buck grated.

"That's impossible. Wait. Give me a second."

"Hurry!" Buck looked at Zaire and saw nothing but naked fear in her brown eyes.

He hadn't brought her all this way to have her killed in the middle of the air. He had to save her.

The numbers continued their relentless descent. Less than fifteen now.

His eye darted frantically over the mess of wires. Was it his fault? Had he cut the wrong one?

Tension locked his jaw and tightened his belly as he shoved the flashlight closer.

Less than ten.

"Alex."

Zaire sagged against the side of the plane but continued to hold up the phone. The close protection officer seemed to freeze in place, his eyes locked on the rapidly decreasing numbers that raced them toward death.

"It was a decoy!" Alex yelled. "Listen to me. You have to cut the red wire. It's right next to the blue one, near the timer. The red wire, Buck. Cut it."

Buck cast the light over the contraption again, searching for the connection to the timer that was needed. Then he saw it. With a steady hand, he fit the pliers around the wire and clipped it.

His body tensed. Time stood still. The display didn't go dark.

It read 00:02.

Closing his eyes, Buck released a ragged sigh of relief and rested his forehead against the wall.

"You did it." Zaire's face broke out into a grin.

He blew a deep breath from between his lips. "Alex, I owe you a whiskey, my friend. Thank you."

Alex let out a laugh. "I'm holding you to it."

"Good job, Buck," Samson said.

"Thanks, brother."

"Call us when you get to Mexico."

"Will do."

Zaire hung up the phone. "You did it!" She flung her arms around his neck and gave him a kiss.

He squeezed her tight, savoring the softness of her mouth and her body against his.

When they finally separated, the secretary's security shook his hand. "That was close."

"Too close," Buck agreed.

He and Zaire climbed up the stairs after the close protection officer. When they arrived topside, the officer announced to everyone that the bomb had been disarmed.

"Thanks to this man." He gripped Buck's shoulder.

"I had help," Buck said, but hardly anyone heard him for all the whooping and clapping that took place after the announcement.

Secretary Hilton approached and took his hand. "I see you're a man of your word."

"I try to be," Buck replied.

She smiled, relief evident in her expression. "Thank you."

Chapter 37

"Is there anything you'd like to add?"

"No, I don't have anything else to add," Zaire answered.

After the secretary's plane landed safely in Mexico, as promised, her team had arranged for Buck and Zaire to return to the United States while she continued on her diplomatic mission.

At the moment, Zaire sat across the desk from a woman in a gray suit and white blouse. She was an agent in the Department of Justice, and the questioning had gone on for hours. She'd asked the same questions in different ways, and each time Zaire gave the same answer. The entire process was exhausting, but Buck had warned her it was coming.

Early on she had been separated from him, and she wondered how his interrogation was going. He was probably used to this, but for her it was a little nerve-wracking. She knew she was supposed to be honest, but at the same time she was worried about saying the wrong thing. That's how most people behaved around law enforcement, she supposed, because the questioning made you feel like a criminal.

At least they'd fed her during the entire ordeal. But it had been a long day, and her body was crying for sleep.

The full power of the government's law enforcement organizations were coming down on Rick Payne and his people.

She'd overhead a conversation between two of the interviewers that people in Rick's offices were working with local authorities in other countries to apprehend the rest of his men and collect all electronics.

Zaire had been kept away from televisions so she couldn't see the news. She had no idea what was being said about them. The only other information she had was that the secretary had made a brief statement about the incident on her plane and thanked everyone involved for ensuring no lives were lost.

"Then we're done here," the agent said.

Zaire let out a breath of profound relief.

The woman smiled. "Thank you for what you've done. You've been through a lot, and I know that it was traumatic. You helped save a lot of lives, including a high-ranking Cabinet member. That's a pretty big deal."

She escorted Zaire out the door. In the hallway Buck, Travis and Samson huddled together. She approached them.

"They didn't treat you too badly, did they?" Samson asked.

"I survived," Zaire said.

"I'm going to get out of here. It was nice to meet you, Zaire. Looking forward to seeing you again sometime." He looked at Buck.

"Same." Travis gave her hug and took off behind Samson.

Now she and Buck were alone in the hallway.

"You sure you don't want to join the CIA?" he teased.

Zaire laughed. "No, thanks." She rolled her shoulders, feeling both the physical and emotional toll of everything that had happened.

"You look tired," Buck said.

"I'm exhausted," Zaire admitted.

"Well, I have good news. Richard, our driver, is waiting

downstairs for you. He'll escort you to a hotel where you can get some rest. Everything is paid for and on the government's dime, so if you're up to it, treat yourself to a nice breakfast tomorrow. In the morning, a car will pick you up and take you to the airport, where you'll have a first-class flight back to Atlanta."

"I'll be getting the royal treatment."

"It's exactly what you deserve."

"What are you doing tonight?"

"Now the debriefing interviews are completed, I have lots of paperwork to fill out."

"Is it always like this?" Zaire asked.

"Not always, but often."

Zaire stood awkwardly for a moment. She wanted to discuss the possibility of them staying in touch and decided to shoot her shot. "Before I go, did you want to…" She swallowed, unsure of how to ask him to exchange numbers. She didn't want to sound needy and wished he would initiate the topic himself.

"Zaire, you're a special woman."

Pain twisted through her. She knew what was coming. "But?"

"I've thought long and hard, and I can't give you what you want."

She saw pity in his eyes and hated it. "How do you know what I want?" she demanded.

"What you deserve is stability and someone who isn't constantly living in the shadows and risking his life. You're an incredible woman. You deserve an incredible man."

"It's not me, it's you, right?"

He had the grace to blush. "I know you don't believe me, but it's true."

"What if I told you I don't care about what you do?"

"You should."

"Why? It's a job like any other. Does what I feel matter, or do you automatically think you know what's best for me?" Zaire asked.

"Do you think I want to do this? I care about you deeply, but you and I won't work. I can't promise you that my work won't bleed over into our lives. You could have died last night on that plane! And one day I might go off on a mission and never come back, and the government won't tell you what happened to me because it's classified."

She nodded her head. "Got it."

She didn't believe a word he was saying. She was no fool. He didn't want to be with her, but rather than tell her that, he was coming up with excuses.

"Zaire." His voice was pained.

"No, really, I understand. I appreciate you thinking about me and doing what's best for me. Once again, you're protecting me, and I have to say, you're really good at this hero thing."

She swallowed hard and dipped her gaze, blinking rapidly to push back the tears that burned her eyes. She would not fall apart in front of him. She would *not*.

"I'll check in on you in a few weeks," Buck said.

"Don't," she said in a wobbly whisper, lifting her head.

He looked surprised.

"Don't," she repeated in a firmer voice, gaining strength. "It's all or nothing with me. Don't check in on me. Ever."

"Zaire, we don't have to cut each other off as if we don't know each other."

"Actually, we do. I know I've told you before, but thank you for keeping me safe. For saving my life multiple times. For coming to get me after they took me at the airfield."

"Zaire," Buck whispered, stepping closer, reaching for her.

She dodged his touch. "Goodbye, Buck. Stay safe."

Walking away, she kept her chin high and her back straight.

She knew that he was watching her the entire time she walked down the hall because she felt the burn of his gaze in the middle of her back.

She stopped at the elevator and hit the down button. Inside the cabin, she looked down the hall and Buck was still standing there, staring after her. Their gazes connected for an eternity. At one point he moved slightly, and she thought for sure he'd rush toward her and say he'd made a terrible mistake.

That didn't happen.

The doors closed and shut her inside, away from him. The finality of it was debilitating. She slumped against the wall, weak with the devastation of longing and sadness.

I'm not going to cry. I'm not going to cry.

She repeated the words until the doors opened on the first floor. A man in a blue uniform and wearing a black cap was seated on one of the leather couches in the lobby, and he stood when he saw her.

"Ms. Nichols?"

"Yes."

He extended a hand. "I'm Richard. Commander Ray has asked me to take you to your hotel for the night. I'll also pick you up in the morning so you can catch your flight."

"What time is the flight?" Zaire asked, falling into step beside him.

"Twelve o'clock, so you can sleep in a little if you like," he said with a smile. He opened the back door of a black sedan. "The hotel is really nice, by the way. Everyone says the beds are soft and the service is excellent."

"Can't wait."

Richard settled in the driver's seat. "Do you have a preference for music?" he asked.

"Something quiet, maybe?"

"Not a problem."

He played soft jazz on the way to the hotel. Like Atlanta, the streets were busy at night, and they passed by a few restaurants that appeared to be packed at that late hour.

When they arrived at the hotel, he walked inside with her and checked her in using a government credit card.

"I'll see you in the morning at ten?" he asked.

"Sounds good."

The room they'd reserved for her was exquisite—more of a suite with a great view of the city. There was a care package waiting for her with a change of clothes and toiletries. She picked out the toothbrush and toothpaste, thinking she'd brush her teeth and then go to sleep.

Instead, she collapsed on the bed and buried her face in the pillow.

She didn't keep the promise to herself.

She cried.

Deep, heart-rending sobs of hurt and loss.

Chapter 38

"I'll take two pounds of wings and four chicken breasts, please," Zaire said.

Saturdays at the DeKalb Farmers Market were always crazy, but Zaire visited twice a month to stock up on meat and seafood. The produce was also inexpensive, and they had so many choices. Almost too many. But for someone who liked to experiment like she did, it was heaven.

She took the two clear plastic bags filled with chicken and placed them in her cart. Her gaze swung to the deli area.

Had she forgotten anything?

She was pretty certain she hadn't, so she pushed her way through the crowd.

"Excuse me," she said, steering her cart past the seafood section, where she'd already picked up fish and shrimp. She didn't allow her eyes a glimpse of the delectable-looking desserts in the pastry shop display case. They were too tempting.

She pushed the cart toward the cash registers at the front of the store and fell in line behind a woman with a handbasket. She had a sudden recollection of her and Buck at the market in Testaccio buying breakfast.

Her heart constricted. That feeling cropped up every so often—when the painful nostalgia of what they had shared for those wonderful, terrifying days in Italy didn't allow her any peace.

She closed her eyes and Buck's face appeared. The tightness in her chest expanded. She breathed through her mouth to alleviate the next stage—the searing pain of loss and regret.

Everyone says things happen for a reason, but when your heart is breaking, you can't help but wonder what that reason could possibly be. What was she supposed to learn from losing Buck and the happiness she'd experienced in his arms?

A tear slipped from her right eye, and she quickly caught it and wiped it away. Darn it, she'd promised herself she wouldn't cry anymore. Embarrassed, she glanced around to make sure no one had seen her.

Funny how he had become such an integral part of her life though they had only known each other a short time. Her mother thought she had developed an unnatural attachment to him because of the emotionally charged situation they had been in, but Zaire knew that was not the reason why.

She was more than attached to him. She didn't think it was possible, but in that short period, she was fairly certain she had fallen in love with Buck. Tall, brave, and funny, he made her also feel brave and funny, as if she could do anything. She was no longer boring old Zaire with him.

Then, of course, she had the memories from the night at the farmhouse and the night in Innsbruck. She would never forget the way he'd turned her inside out with his kisses and firm caresses.

The line moved, and she edged closer to the front. Then something caught her eye, and she twisted her head to the left. She blinked. Were her eyes playing tricks on her? Was that...?

Tall, broad shouldered, blond.

She couldn't breathe. Riveted, she stared at the man across the store.

"Buck?" She whispered his name in disbelief.

Could he actually be here?

She shook with anticipation, and then the man turned in her direction, and her heart dropped.

That wasn't Buck.

The man carried a baby strapped to his chest and wore glasses. He was handsome, yes, but he was not Atticus "Buck" Swanson the Third.

Disappointment shoved her shoulders lower. She wished she didn't know he had friends in Atlanta. She kept thinking there was a possibility of them running into each other, but there were millions of people in the metro Atlanta area. The chances were slim that they would.

"Next!"

The cashier's sharp cry indicated this wasn't the first time she had called out to Zaire.

"Sorry," she mumbled, pushing her cart forward. She unloaded the groceries onto the counter. When the worker finished ringing up the items, she paid and then carried her goods outside in two totes.

In the car, she sat at the wheel and stared out the windshield. Buck was never going to call, and she didn't have the courage to reach out herself. He could have insisted on having her number that last day, but he didn't. Oh, how she wished he had, though.

The blond man walked across the parking lot with his baby strapped to his chest. A woman Zaire assumed must be his wife walked beside them.

"I'm going to have a family one day," she said in a determined voice.

She needed time to get over Buck, that's all. It wouldn't be easy, but she was determined to do it.

Forget Buck. Start dating. Have the time of her life.

In that order.

She started the car and hit the road to go home. As she pulled to a traffic light, her cell phone rang, and her mother's number popped up on the screen.

Elisa Nichols had been her usual overbearing self ever since Zaire returned from overseas two months ago, but it wasn't all bad. Her helicopter parenting had come in handy after Zaire had gone to Josie's funeral.

Guilt had created a sadness in her that only disappeared after she had spent the weekend with her parents. They had shown her love and compassion and helped her accept that Josie's death was not her fault. Rick Payne's henchmen were the reason for her death. They went by the apartment looking for Zaire but found Josie. According to news reports, law enforcement officials suspected she had been killed simply because they didn't want any witnesses.

Zaire answered the phone.

"Hello, Mom."

The light turned green, and she hit the gas.

"Hello, honey. How are you?"

"Doing fine. I left the DeKalb Farmers Market a few minutes ago, and I'm on my way home."

"Do you have any plans this evening?"

Saying no was on the tip of her tongue, but at the last minute she changed her mind and decided to lie. "Yes, I'm going out with a couple of friends."

"Friends? Anyone I know?" Her mother was not shy about getting into her business.

"No, you don't know them."

"I was going to invite you over for dinner with me and your father, but since you have plans…"

"Only you and Dad?" Zaire asked with a healthy dose of skepticism.

The last time she went to her parents' for dinner, their single neighbor had happened to stop by, and they invited him to eat with them.

She still remembered her mother's disappointment afterward when Zaire had said she wasn't interested.

"But why not, honey?"

"Because I can pick my own dates, thanks."

"Of course it'll only be me and your father."

Zaire decided to give her the benefit of the doubt. "Maybe tomorrow night."

"That sounds good. Are you sure you're okay? You sound a little…odd."

"I'm fine. You probably hear the tiredness in my voice because I've been out all day running errands."

"That must be it." Slight pause. "Have you heard from your friend?"

Immediately, Zaire knew that was the real reason her mother had called. Sure, she would like for her to come and have dinner with them at the house and possibly meet an eligible bachelor, but ultimately she wanted to know if Zaire had heard from her "friend"—Buck.

"No, I haven't heard from him, and I don't expect to. That part of my life is over, Mom."

"I know you say that, but—"

"No, I'm not just saying that. That period of my life is over. The government might call me to testify, but that will be the only thing that pulls me back into what happened in Italy. And I definitely don't want to think about him."

"Well, I'm glad you're safe and sound, and if you need anything, you know your father and I are here for you."

A twinge of guilt twisted inside her. Her mother meant well, and had she not confided in her about her feelings for Buck, she would not be asking these questions.

She'd refrained from telling her they'd had sex, though. They had a good relationship, but it wasn't good enough to withstand a mother's judgment for sleeping with a man who was practically a stranger.

No matter what they had been through, and the fact that he hadn't felt like a stranger at the time they'd made love, her mother wouldn't understand.

"I appreciate you being so supportive," Zaire says.

"I'm your mother, honey. Of course I'll be supportive. I don't know any other way to be."

Zaire smiled. And that was why she could not stay angry at her mother. She had experienced love and acceptance all her life.

"I'm about to pull into the complex now. Can I give you a call later?" she asked.

"Not necessary. Have fun with your friends, and we'll catch up next week."

"Sounds good. Love you, Mom."

"Love you, too, My Gift."

Zaire smiled as she pulled onto the park pad in front of her townhome. She didn't know which book she would dive into tonight, but the choices were between a literary fiction piece and a mystery that had blown up the charts in the past week.

She removed her bags from the back seat of the vehicle and walked to the front door. As she moved, a strange feeling came over her, as if she was being watched.

Could it be someone in one of the apartments near her was peeking out their window?

She popped open the door and turned the knob while looking over her shoulder.

Or was it simply her imagination?

She shook her head and carried her bags inside.

Chapter 39

Buck watched Zaire walk up to the front door of her town house with two totes filled with groceries.

He had been sitting in the car for a while, waiting for her to show up. Now that she was here, he was stricken by a wave of nervousness.

She set down the bags and popped open the front door. Then she paused, looking over her shoulder, as if she sensed someone watching her. After a brief hesitation, she picked up the bags and went inside.

Buck remained in the car, debating what to do next. *Jeez*, what was his problem? Zaire was right.

You're not so brave after all, are you?

He muttered a curse.

He had avoided Rome for years because it had reminded him of his humiliating split with Lana, but he had a different view of the city now. Rome meant freedom from past hurt and disappointment. It was the place where he met a sexy, passionate know-it-all he hadn't been able to forget in the two months since Rick Payne's arrest and the downfall of his business empire.

To make matters worse, he hadn't been himself lately. He never took his planned vacation and instead had thrown himself into another assignment. And another. Yet nothing worked to alleviate the sense of…emptiness that engulfed him. That was the only way to explain this feeling, as if he had a hole in the middle of his soul.

He had flown here because he couldn't count on his friends to help. Sensing that his problem must partially result from the constant swirl of thoughts about Zaire, he asked Travis and Samson to "check" on her. See how she was doing. Find out if she was seeing anyone.

They'd both refused.

"We're not going to spy on her for you. You want to know what she's up to, come down here and find out," Travis had said.

Samson had backed him up. "As usual, you have a place to stay if you do."

"Some friends," he muttered to himself, thinking about the conversation.

Oh well, time to yank off the bandage and do what he'd come here to do. Find out if there was a chance for him and Zaire after he'd pushed her away back in DC. He'd never regretted anything as much as he regretted letting her walk away that day.

He exited the car and walked to the front door of her town house. He knocked on the door, and after a few moments, Zaire appeared in front of him.

The sight of her temporarily overwhelmed him. She was as stunning as he remembered, with pretty dark brown eyes behind her glasses and a lush mouth that was soft and seductive. Her dark hair fell around her face in loose curls and made him yearn to pull her in his arms, kiss her senseless and beg her forgiveness.

"Buck, what are you doing here?" she asked softly.

He'd expected anger, maybe, but she sounded more surprised than anything else.

That's when it hit him. His decision to come here had been completely impulsive. He'd flown on a plane for a couple of hours and driven to her home, and during all that time, he hadn't rehearsed an explanation for standing on her door-step. He had no plan.

A man who always operated with a plan and knew next steps in any situation he found himself—had no plan.

"I'm in town on business and went by to see Travis and Samson. Thought I'd stop by and see how you were doing. I know you told me not to bother but…" He shrugged.

"I did say that, didn't I?"

"Yes, you did. How are you? It's been a while."

"Yes, it has been a while. I'm doing fine. You?"

"Good. I'd be better if you invited me in."

She hesitated, and for one brief, horrifying moment, he expected her to say no. His entire body tightened in antici-pation of the rejection. Then she stepped aside, and relief charged through him.

"Come in. I just got back from the store and was putting away my groceries."

Buck followed her toward the back, passing a room on the right—a small library with every shelf filled with books. It also contained a recliner, table, and window seat. He imag-ined her sitting there with a book, reading to her heart's content. Filling her head with more so-called useless in-formation.

"Can I get you something to drink?" Zaire asked in the kitchen.

"No, I'm fine," Buck replied.

"Have a seat. I haven't seen much in the news about what happened to Payne and Javelin Security. I saw a couple of interviews with the secretary of state where she confirmed for the public that the threat had been eliminated, and they mentioned Javelin, but that's it."

He sat on a stool in front of the bar. "They won't say much because of the sensitive nature of the charges against him, and they don't want anyone to know how close we came to having a member of the Cabinet assassinated. The investigation is ongoing to root out all of his accomplices and crush anyone who might think of retaliation."

He'd done what he could on his end to keep her from having to be involved any further, including having her name redacted from all the reports. Her interviews were used to justify getting search warrants and collecting evidence by law enforcement. After raiding the Javelin Security offices here and overseas, the government had found plenty of proof of Payne's criminal dealings, making it easy to keep her name out of the proceedings.

Sadness filled Zaire's eyes. "So many people died."

One of her many positive qualities was her empathy for others.

"*We* almost died," he reminded her.

"Yes. Multiple times." She put chicken and shrimp in the freezer.

"Did you ever have that big plate of ribs you said you were going to eat?"

She laughed softly, her eyes lighting up in a becoming way. "That was the first thing I did when I came back to Atlanta. I treated it like a last meal and ordered a whole rack and multiple sides. I ate myself into a food coma."

He laughed, too, imagining her with a giant plate of ribs and sides. "How's work?"

"Good. I looked into getting my PhD and discussed my work load with my manager. He thinks it's a great idea and said we can adjust the number of clients I work with so that

I could move forward with my plans. So I guess I'll be getting my PhD." With that bright smile on her face, she was glowing.

"That's great! I'm happy for you."

"Thank you." She pulled vegetables and herbs from her tote. "You said you're here on business. What kind of business?" She opened the refrigerator to put in the vegetables.

Time to stop playing around.

"Personal business."

"Oh. Okay." She acted like she understood, but he could tell she was confused.

"You're not going to ask any more questions?" Buck asked.

"Do you want me to?"

He stood from the stool and walked around the bar. Her eyes followed his movement with bemusement.

"What's going on, Buck?"

"I can't stop thinking about you. For the past two months, my mind keeps going back to Italy and the time we spent there together. The country used to have bad memories for me, but now I barely remember them. They've been replaced by better ones."

"Good grief, how bad were your memories before?"

She laughed at the joke, and he smiled.

"I'm sorry, Zaire. I should have never pushed you away in DC."

"You were right. We don't really have a future."

"I disagree. I know we put the cart before the horse by sleeping together. I'm not sorry it happened, but I want to spend more time with you. Get to know you better. I miss you like crazy."

Her eyes widened. "I don't know what to say." She put distance between them with a step backward. "This is quite a change from what you said in DC."

"I wasn't thinking straight in DC."

"And you are now?" Skepticism clouded her eyes.

"Yes."

"I don't know, Buck. I've had time to think, too. I don't want to be a passing fling until the next woman comes along—probably someone nothing like me."

"You could never be a passing fling. You mean much more to me than that. You opened my eyes to what could be—a fun, teasing relationship filled with trust and mutual respect. If you're okay with being with a guy that sometimes has to kill people, I want to pursue a relationship with you."

She gnawed her lip. "But you live in DC, and I live here."

"There are such things as long distance relationships, but we don't have to do that. A funny thing about the work that I do, I can do it from anywhere. And as you know, two of my Omega Team brothers—Travis and Samson—live in Atlanta. I have three perfectly good reasons to be here—often. Maybe move here. What do you think?"

He held his breath.

"Well… I think that's a great idea," Zaire said carefully. "I have an extra bedroom if you want to crash at my place every now and again when you visit."

"I wouldn't have to sleep on the sofa?"

"Nope." A faint smile tilted up the corners of her lips.

"That's good, though I was kinda hoping I could sleep in your bed." Buck tested the waters by taking two steps forward.

"My bed?"

"Yes. What do you think about that?"

"I think you're being presumptuous."

"Something tells me that you like presumptuous." He removed her glasses and placed them on the bar. Leaning in, he asked, "Am I right?"

"You might be right," she said softly, breathlessly.

Buck ached to kiss her, but before he did, he had to confirm that she really and truly wanted to be with him.

"Do you forgive me?"

Her eyes softened with affection, and she nodded. "I forgive you. After all, you're a man, and men often have to withdraw to process their emotions."

He slid his arms around her waist and pulled her against his body. His loins tightened as memories of their lovemaking came back to him.

"Is that one of those useless facts you like to spout?"

She giggled. "Mm-hmm. Another one is that men usually fall first in relationships."

Buck narrowed his eyes. "You're making that up."

"Am I?" She smiled sweetly at him.

"Hell, it doesn't matter."

He captured her lips and indulged in the lush depths of her mouth. She tasted so good, he groaned, squeezing her tighter and filling his hands with the fullness of her bottom.

When her hand came up to cup the back of his head, he knew he was lost. Zaire was the one for him, and he wanted to give her the proper courting an incredible woman like her deserved.

She pulled back and gazed into his eyes. "I forgot to mention. I missed you like crazy too."

Buck kissed her again.

Epilogue

The sun began its descent in Saint John, USVI, where Buck had purchased a small condo as a gift to himself years before—a place where he could escape from the stress and grind of work.

He had never brought a woman here, and perhaps it was because, in the back of his mind, he was waiting for the right person to come along—and she finally did.

Zaire lounged on the covered patio in a fluorescent green tankini, wearing sunglasses as she read a book on her iPad. They had been together a year now, and this trip was to celebrate one year together.

She needed a break too. She'd been working hard ever since starting the PhD program in International Conflict Management at Kennesaw State. She hadn't specifically mentioned an interest in working for the CIA, but he had a hunch that she might eventually go that route. That type of degree and knowledge would be helpful to the agency.

Two weeks in the tropical sun had darkened her skin to milk chocolate, and his own complexion had deepened to a swarthier color, presenting a striking contrast to his blond hair.

They had spent a lot of time outdoors. They'd gone hiking, and he'd convinced Zaire to go parasailing, which she admitted was not nearly as scary as she'd thought it would be. He was still trying to convince her to go water skiing, but…baby steps.

Beyond the patio, the tranquil blue waters of the Caribbean Sea glimmered in the waning sunlight. Gentle waves lapped at the shore and created a symphony of soothing sounds to accompany the display of crimson and orange splashed across the landscape from the setting sun.

Buck turned on the blender, crushing ice and fruit together to create piña colada cocktails, which Zaire had requested as a before-dinner drink.

He walked out to the patio. "Here you go, love."

Zaire looked up, smiling at him. "Ooh, thank you, babe," she cooed, taking one of the cold glasses.

She took a sip and hummed her approval.

"Good?" Buck asked.

"Mm-hmm. You know it is."

He placed his glass on the table beside her. "What do you think about going out to dinner tonight instead of staying in? It's our last night on the island, and I have a taste for lobster and that mango salsa we had at Edy's Inn the first night we arrived. I was thinking we should go back there. The food was so damn good."

"And it's right near the water. Yes, please. The grilled fish I had was, *ugh*, so good." She sighed dramatically.

Buck chuckled, completely understanding her reaction. In truth, they hadn't had a bad meal the entire time they'd been on the island.

"That's where we'll go, then."

Zaire sighed. "Do we have to go back to the States? Can't we stay here forever and pretend this is our new home?"

"Sorry, love, we have to go back. Unfortunately. But since

the islands are only a three-hour flight away, we can come back sooner rather than later."

Her eyes brightened. "I would love that."

He took pleasure in giving her anything she wanted, and her happiness was contagious.

"That's what we'll do, then. By the way, I should have all my stuff packed up by the end of the month."

He was finally moving to Atlanta. It only made sense, since he'd spent most of the past year there anyway. He flew from DC and spent weeks at a time and used Atlanta as his base when he had to fly out on assignment.

He and Zaire had spent a lot of time with Travis and Samson, who often brought dates along on their get-togethers.

"I guess I need to do my part and make room for you, huh?"

"That would be nice, yes," he teased.

Her place was smaller than his, but he could make it work. He was selling some of his stuff, most of what he wasn't attached to. The rest he'd keep at her place or in storage.

"Be right back."

Buck left Zaire outside and went into the bedroom, doing a quick check over his shoulder to make sure Zaire didn't follow. He unzipped the backpack he brought as a carry-on and removed a black velvet box. An emerald-cut diamond sparkled inside.

After dinner tonight, he planned to invite Zaire for a stroll on the beach. When the right moment came, he'd drop to one knee and ask her to be his wife.

He was excited and couldn't help but smile. He was anxious to pop the question and anxious to see her reaction. He already knew she'd say yes. They were that in tune with each other and spoke often about their future together.

She wanted three kids like he did, and eventually they

wanted to move farther outside the city of Atlanta to raise their family. He wanted his kids to enjoy the outdoors the way he did—fishing, hiking, tubing—and go on all the same fun adventures he did as a youth. Well, maybe not *all*. But he wanted them to have an enjoyable upbringing, and it was nice to be with someone on the same page.

He'd already talked to Zaire's father and asked for her hand in marriage. He never thought much about the tradition before, but knowing how protective her parents were, he had wanted to assure them that he would take good care of their daughter.

Fortunately, he'd already met them and developed a good relationship. Zaire had also met his parents at his grandmother's eightieth birthday celebration several months ago. Surprisingly, the Swanson clan hadn't scared her off with their antics.

He snapped the box closed and slipped it into the pocket of the pants he would wear to dinner. Then he returned to the patio.

"What time do you want to leave?" Zaire asked.

"We can start getting ready in an hour. I want to enjoy the rest of this sunset."

He sat on the lounge chair and stretched out his legs.

Zaire placed her sunglasses and iPad on the table and squeezed onto his chair. He tucked her under his arm.

"No rush, huh?" she said, snuggling closer and looping an arm across his chest.

"No rush," Buck agreed.

They had their whole life ahead of them.

* * * * *

Harlequin® Reader Service

Enjoyed your book?

Try the perfect subscription for Romance readers and get more great books like this delivered right to your door.

See why over 10+ million readers have tried Harlequin Reader Service.

Start with a Free Welcome Collection with free books and a gift—valued over $20.

Choose any series in print or ebook. See website for details and order today:

TryReaderService.com/subscriptions